MY CHRISTMAS FIANCÉ

by

SERENITY WOODS

Copyright © 2017 Serenity Woods
All rights reserved.
ISBN: 1542602475
ISBN-13: 978-1542602471

DEDICATION

To Tony & Chris, my Kiwi boys.

CONTENTS

Chapter One...1
Chapter Two...7
Chapter Three...14
Chapter Four...20
Chapter Five..27
Chapter Six..34
Chapter Seven..43
Chapter Eight..50
Chapter Nine...56
Chapter Ten...63
Chapter Eleven...71
Chapter Twelve...78
Chapter Thirteen..85
Chapter Fourteen...92
Chapter Fifteen...98
Chapter Sixteen..104
Chapter Seventeen..111
Chapter Eighteen...118
Chapter Nineteen...124
Chapter Twenty..131
Chapter Twenty-One...138
Chapter Twenty-Two...145
Chapter Twenty-Three..152
Chapter Twenty-Four..160
Chapter Twenty-Five...166
Chapter Twenty-Six...172
Chapter Twenty-Seven...180
Chapter Twenty-Eight...187
Chapter Twenty-Nine..194
Chapter Thirty...201
Chapter Thirty-One..207
Chapter Thirty-Two..214
Chapter Thirty-Three...222
Chapter Thirty-Four...232
Epilogue...240
More from Serenity Woods...247
About the Author..248

Chapter One

Stratton

I put on the tie Meg's bought me for my birthday, take a sip from my coffee cup, and promptly spill the rest down my front.

Meg looks at me over the top of her reading glasses. "If you didn't like it, you could have just said." Her soft, amused voice, and the warmth in her baby-blue eyes, sends shivers down my spine.

"I do like it," I protest truthfully, flapping it around in the air to dry. It's pure silk and dark blue with a thin lilac stripe—exactly the kind of tie I would have chosen myself. I'm impressed that even though my birthday's only ten days before Christmas, she's resisted buying me something festive. It might be early summer and seventy-five degrees here in Auckland, New Zealand, but we still like to pretend it's winter during the festive season, and since I was a child my birthday presents have either borne reindeer or snowflakes or they've been wrapped in festive paper.

Meg sighs and pulls a tissue from her handbag. I take it from her and attempt to soak up the drips. Women's handbags never fail to amaze me. They're like small boys' pockets without the snails, containing everything a man could ever need in an emergency. Most women—like my mother, and Natalie, my ex—distribute the items with a look of exasperation as if they're thinking *For God's sake, you're such an idiot*, but Meg's lips curve up whenever she helps me out. I like to pretend she's thinking *Aw, you're so sweet*. As our PA, she's used to being our knight in shining armor, and I think she kind of likes the role.

So do I. Whenever Meg smiles at me, even my goose bumps get goose bumps.

"So… now Stratton's not-so-subtly tried to tell me he doesn't like my gift, does anyone have any other business?" She pauses from taking the minutes of the meeting, slides off her glasses, and gets up to refill my coffee cup. I hold it out for her, liking that she's bothering to help when I've just been a dork, and enjoying the brush of her hand on mine as she tips up the jug. I study her face while she pours, noting her long dark eyelashes and the touch of color that appears in the apples of her cheeks as she obviously feels my gaze on her. She likes me. In spite of everything, I've known that for some time.

Then someone clears their throat, and I scowl and lower the cup.

Two others are seated around the table—Rich, my best mate since high school, and Teddi, my younger sister. Rich, Teddi, and I are the directors of Katoa—a technology company that makes computer games and equipment, much of it focused on visually impaired people.

The reason for the focus of our company glances across at me, and even though she can't see me—Teddi lost her sight after contracting retinoblastoma when she was two—I know it's a glare of warning. How does she always know when I'm trying to flirt, even when I'm not saying anything? I'm tempted to tell her to mind her own business, but unfortunately she's right to warn me off. I remind myself that Meg's not available, and that I'm not a marriage breaker. I happen to think marriage is a precious thing that should be honored and revered.

Even when it's fake.

*

I first met Meg nearly five months ago when she arrived at our offices for an interview.

We'd already seen four other candidates, and I was distinctly unimpressed.

"Jeez." Rich rolled his eyes when I crossed out the fourth candidate's name as soon as she left the room. "You're setting the bar too high. Our PA doesn't have to keep the launch codes for nuclear missiles."

"New Zealand doesn't have nuclear power," I reminded him. "And I'd like my secretary to be able to say 'Good morning' to customers on the phone without stuttering."

"You made her nervous," Teddi said. "I bet you were ogling her legs while you were talking to her."

"I was not! I did it while she wasn't looking. And she had thick ankles."

"Strat…"

"Come on, give me some credit. We're not looking for any old secretary here. We don't just need someone for the typing pool. A personal assistant is like a work wife. We've gotta click." I meant it, too. Contrary to what my sister thought, I wasn't looking for a model, and even though Number Four had possessed thick ankles, that wouldn't have stopped me from hiring her if she'd had that zing I was looking for. But I did want someone hardworking, efficient, smart, and… I don't know… sassy, I suppose. Witty and yet nice. A girl who'd stand up to me and boss me around and then blush when I complimented her on her shoes. Someone I could have fun with—not sexually, because sleeping with your PA is like shitting on your own doorstep, as my dad would so tactfully put it—but a person who was able to take a joke and give as good as she got, who wasn't easily offended and understood my English sense of humor, a woman who would brighten my day.

Then Meg Brown walked into the room, and I lost the power of speech.

She's tall—not as tall as me, obviously, because that would be weird—but around five nine, slim without being skinny, and that day she wore a smart dark-gray business suit with a skirt that reached an inch above her knees and a white shirt that only had the top two buttons undone, the epitome of sophistication. It was winter, and she wore sheer black tights and black heels that were sexy without being too high. She had shiny blonde hair she'd pinned up in a classic, elegant roll, and pearls in her ears and around her throat.

I took one look at them and thought about the other kind of pearl necklace a man can give a woman, and then I knew I was in trouble, and she'd only just walked through the door.

"I'm sorry I'm late," she said as she shook our hands and then sat at the other side of the table. "I somehow broke the bolt on the loo door and locked myself in." We all stared at her, and she pulled an *eek* face. "And now I'm realizing that's probably not the best admission to make at the beginning of an interview."

"How did you get out?" Rich asked, amused.

"I keep a Swiss army knife tucked in my stocking top and I managed to lever the bolt off." She looked at me and laughed at my raised eyebrows. "Not really. Sorry. I yelled the place down until someone came in."

It started right there, at that moment, with images in my head of the pearl necklace and the stocking tops. I felt a tingle between my shoulder blades, and a warm prickle ran down my spine.

I knew from the start that it wouldn't come to anything. She wore a wedding ring, for one thing, and as I began asking her the questions on our sheet, I discovered that she'd recently moved up from Christchurch, that her husband was in the army, and that she had a thirteen-year-old son. But it soon became clear that she was everything I was looking for in a personal assistant. She'd worked as PA to the CEO of a large company, and her secretarial skills were exemplary. But, more importantly, she was warm, witty, as sassy as I could have hoped for, and more than able to hold her own with the three of us.

The best bit came at the end. When we rounded off the interview, Teddi asked the question she always did to new people she met, because it gave her an insight as to how the person was going to react to her condition.

"You may have noticed that I'm blind," she began.

"I wondered why there was a dog under the table," Meg replied with a smile. Teddi's guide dog, a Labrador called Bella, sat by her feet.

"Is there any question you'd like to ask me?" Teddi tipped her head to the side, fixing Meg with a stare. If you didn't know, you'd never be able to tell just by looking at her that she has two artificial eyes, apart from the fact that the pupils don't react to light. And the fact that she can pop them out at will, much to the horror of her teacher when she was at primary school. "Anything at all," Teddi continued.

Meg surveyed her for a long moment, and I wondered what she was going to say. In the past, questions had ranged from "Do you see in your dreams?" to "How do you view color?" and even to "How do you know when you've finished wiping your butt when you can't see the paper?" That one had been from a dude who'd been trying to chat Teddi up. Needless to say, that relationship hadn't worked out.

"Can you tell me where you have your hair done?" Meg asked. "I just love the cut."

And that was the moment the tingle turned to a warmth that spread right through me.

Teddi laughed and told her, and that concluded the interview. We all shook hands and promised to let her know as soon as we'd made a decision. I watched Meg walk out, then turned my gaze to the others.

"Ankles?" Teddi asked.

"Superb," I said. "Let's hire her."

"Strat…" My sister warned. "You heard her. She's married and has a kid."

I waved a hand. "Yeah I know. Don't worry. I've never had an affair with a married woman, and I'm not going to start now."

Rich raised an eyebrow. "It's not that we don't trust you, but since you broke up with Natalie, you've been…"

"What?"

"Odd," Teddi said.

I doodled on my notepad. "Yeah, well… Having to enter the dating game again at thirty-three tends to have that effect on a man." It was true that I'd been moody and withdrawn, but that didn't mean I'd go all out to ruin someone's marriage.

"I like her," I said. "Meg, I mean."

"Of course you like her," Rich said. "She's gorgeous, and she thought you were funny."

"She'll worship the ground you walk on," Teddi added, "and that's only going to lead to trouble."

I dismissed the notion with a wave of my hand. "Come on, tell me you don't think she's perfect for the job."

They couldn't, and therefore that was it—Meg was hired, and she started work the next day.

*

They were right, of course. She's both the best and the worst thing that could have happened to me after breaking up with Natalie. The best because Meg's everything I want in a PA—okay, in a woman—and the worst because, well, she's everything I want and I can't have her. And it's torturous seeing her every day knowing that.

I haven't met her husband yet. Meg insists he's away in Afghanistan, and that he might come home for Christmas, but Teddi—who has a sixth sense about this sort of thing—tells me something doesn't ring true about it.

I haven't said anything to Meg yet, because she's a very private person and I can sense she doesn't want to talk about it. I have tried talking to Oscar—her son—about his dad. I get on well with Oscar, and when I discovered that he enjoys gaming I hired him as a tester for our new games. For twenty bucks an hour he comes into the labs twice a week after school to try out Rich's latest projects while he waits for Meg to finish work. One day I asked him if he missed his dad. He hesitated, looked at me as if he was about to confess something, then replied flatly, "No." I didn't push it, but it's clear there's more to it than meets the eye.

But anyway, I've got more important things on my mind now than Shakespearean-style unrequited love. Meg's asked if we have any other business, and it's time to make my announcement.

"Yeah, I have." I stop trying to blot the coffee from my tie and lean back in my chair, linking my hands. I watch Meg as I speak. "I'm getting married."

Chapter Two

Meg

I stare at Stratton as my heart begins to pound. To my surprise, his lips curve up a little at the corners and he tilts his head to the side, and I can see immediately that he's interested in my reaction. Hmm. His mismatched eyes—one blue, one green—are twinkling. Something tells me he's fibbing.

He's exactly the sort of man my mother warned me about when I was a teenager. I don't mean to imply that he's dangerous or would take advantage of me—and Lord knows I'm the expert on men like that—more that he's gorgeous, sexy, and charismatic, and he's perfectly aware of the effect he has on women. If I had to describe him in one word, I'd choose naughty.

I know he's thirty-four today—a year older than me—but there's something boyish about him that adds to the aura of mischievousness he exudes at all times. Maybe it's because he's always clean shaven and I've never seen him with even a hint of stubble; perhaps it's because he's made his living from making video games and equipment, which a secret part of me will always associate with teens, even though he and Rich are both grown men, and even though I also play. Oscar tells me he's never met a guy with such a high score on *Dark Robot*—their bestselling game—apart from Rich, who apparently once beat Stratton by two points and has never let him forget it.

Or maybe it's just because he's still single and likely to remain so—his words, not mine. Teddi's told me all about his ex, Natalie the Nympho Nutter, as she's named her, and I've had to answer her crank calls most days, so I know what a psycho she is, and how wary Stratton is of committing himself to anyone again because of what she's done to him. I can understand that. I'm in no hurry to stroll down Lovers' Lane hand-in-hand with a man anytime soon either.

Still, it makes me sad to see him so cautious and hurt. Teddi told me he used to be really sociable, but he hardly ever goes out now, that he tells me about, anyway. In fact, I revise my opinion—the one word I'd choose to describe him would be sad. Part of that's down to Natalie, I know. The other part is because there used to be four people running Katoa, and one of them died.

Rich is half-Maori—his middle name is Tamati and his mother was from the Ngapuhi *iwi* or Maori tribe from the Northland. He also had a twin brother, Will. Rich and Will met Stratton at school when he came over from England, and they all grew up together, and then when Will was twenty-two he started dating Teddi. From what I understand, the two of them were crazy about each other, and they were planning to get married. All four of them were into gaming, and between them they developed *Dark Robot*, which went on to be the number one bestselling New Zealand game, and soon spread to the rest of the world.

After the success of *Dark Robot*, they turned to developing equipment and games designed for the visually impaired, driven of course by their love for Teddi and the fact that she couldn't always join in, and the company grew in both prestige and influence. The four of them must have seemed as if they had everything.

And then, on Boxing Day—the day after Christmas and the day before his and Rich's thirtieth birthday—Will died.

It was a pulmonary embolism that killed him, and nobody really knows why it happened, because apparently even though he was a gamer and spent a lot of time sitting down, he didn't smoke or drink much, he went to the gym, and was young and fit, just like his brother. But it happened, and it had a profound effect on all three of the other members of Katoa. Teddi, of course, because she lost the love of her life. Rich, because he lost his twin brother. And Stratton, because he loves them all.

It wouldn't surprise me if Will's passing announced the death knell of Stratton's relationship with Natalie. The death of someone close often makes people reassess their own lives, and whereas up until then it sounded as if Stratton was your average playboy who didn't take anything or anyone seriously, I think perhaps he decided it was time he grew up and admitted that he didn't love her, and it wasn't fair of him to stay with her if he wasn't going to commit in the long term.

They broke up a month or two before I started at Katoa. I'm guessing that Stratton has dated several girls since, although he's never mentioned anyone so I suppose none of them has been serious.

He likes me—I know he does. At least, I think he does—it's not easy to tell. He's polite and gentlemanly, and not overt with his admiration, plus I know he likes women in general, and he's what my mother would call a ladies' man. But even so, I've watched him with others—customers, colleagues, friends—and he doesn't look at them the way he looks at me, with that small, intimate smile on his lips as if he's mentally removed all my clothing, and he's picturing me in black lacy lingerie and sexy high heels.

He'd never make a move on me, though. If I've learned anything about him over the last four months, it's that he's honest and has principles, and he'd never consider dating a girl unless she was single.

I've made my rather-uncomfortable bed, and I'm afraid it's too late to unmake it, and I have to lie in it alone. But it takes every ounce of willpower I possess not to slide the wedding band off my finger, throw it across the room, leap on him, and crush my lips to his.

"Married?" Teddi says, clearly puzzled. "To whom?"

The mischievous look returns to Stratton's eyes. "I don't know yet."

*

I commented on his eyes during my interview. "They're different colors," I stated, not realizing I'd said it out loud until his eyebrows rose.

"It's called heterochromia. Is it a problem?" he asked in a tone that suggested it wouldn't be the first time he'd freaked someone out just by looking at them.

I shrugged. "If it's good enough for David Bowie, I don't see why it would bother me."

His resulting smile warmed me to the core.

A month later, when I joined the others and a couple of potential American customers for a formal dinner at his house, I saw all his original Bowie albums on the walls and realized why he'd smiled. As I stood there admiring them, he admitted that comment of mine had landed me the job. I have my suspicions it was probably rather more to do with my legs as he often admires them when he thinks I'm not looking, but I like that he pretended it was something deeper.

I wonder whether his heterochromia is in some way connected to Teddi's blindness. It seems odd that even though he has his sight, his eyes are so unusual. I haven't yet plucked up the courage to ask him. He and Teddi are very open about her condition, but I know his need to give her as rich a life as possible was behind the creation of their company—Katoa does mean whole or inclusive, after all. I'm convinced it remains a topic that's very close to a heart that's cotton-wool soft behind the steel wall he's erected around it.

*

"So let's get this straight," Rich says. "You're getting married, but you don't have anyone in mind?"

"Kind of." Stratton stretches out his long legs and plays with his pen, which tells me he's thinking about how to phrase what's on his mind.

He wears a suit every day—tailor-made and high quality, no off-the-rack ill-fitting clothing for either of these guys—and he always looks smart in the morning. But by eleven o'clock, especially in summer, he usually loses the jacket and rolls up his shirt sleeves. He does it now, popping out his cufflinks and turning over the cuffs of the shirt in that sexy way men do. His forearms are tanned and scattered with brown hairs a shade lighter than the dark hair on his head, which also sports a touch of gray at the sides, as if he's rested his temple against a freshly painted post. I want to reach across the table and slip my fingers into that gray streak, to see if his hair is as soft as it looks. I don't, of course. Any touching of Stratton Parker is done strictly in my dreams.

Rich is just as well-dressed as his business partner, although his hair is as curly as Stratton's is straight, and his skin is naturally a few shades darker than Stratton's healthy tan. He's just as gorgeous, too, but in a different way. Although he's also boyish and playful, he doesn't have Stratton's practical air. Stratton's the engineer—the one who designs the innovative controllers with Braille for blind people and special grips for one-handed players. Rich is the game designer, and his head is always in the clouds, daydreaming about his next creation.

Teddi's the one who keeps them both rooted to the ground. She has shiny brown hair cut in a long bob, and she's the one with the business head, the driving machine behind the company's success. I adore her. I can only imagine how difficult her life is—it must be a hundred times harder for her to do even the simplest tasks than it is for me. And of course she lost her partner—I'm amazed she can even get out of bed in the morning after a terrible tragedy like that. But she's always funny and cheerful, with a touch of the Parker naughty gene, and she's an amazing business woman.

I love them all, and I adore working here. I know I fell on my feet when I got this job, and that's another reason I'm determined not to screw it up by making a play for my boss, even though it's murder having to see him every day and knowing he can never be mine.

I wait for him to reveal his new scheme. He wants a reaction from me, and I'm determined not to give him one. The thought that he's met someone secretly who he loves enough to want to marry is potentially shocking, but I don't think that's what's going on here.

He doodles on his notepad, and suddenly something catches deep inside me as vulnerability flickers on his face. He's still hurting. This is about Natalie.

"Are you trying to get regular sex?" Teddi's light tone tells me she's also picked up on his mood. "Because you don't have to get married to get laid, sweetie. You need to finish developing that groin attachment for the porn game on the console."

"I keep trying, but Rich wears out all the prototypes."

Rich snorts. Teddi and I chuckle. Stratton gives a wry smile, but the impish light has been replaced by something else. Sadness again. And... surprisingly... a touch of irritation, or even anger.

"What's Natalie done?" I ask.

Teddi's told me a bit about her. She said that, from the start, the Nympho Nutter wouldn't let him out of bed. Well what man wouldn't be captivated by a woman like that? Teddi said that initially he seemed crazy about her, but of course eventually you have to get up, and that's where the problems started.

They must have had something special, though, because a man doesn't stay with a woman for five years just because she's good in the sack. Does he? Not even Stratton's that shallow, surely. I think that probably he was just so caught up in his work that the time went by without him realizing. He works long hours—he's usually in before me in the morning and he's often here until seven or eight in the evening—so he wouldn't have seen much of her. Like what happened with me and Bruce, if you spend lots of time apart, it doesn't matter so much if you aren't soul mates providing that when you are together neither of you wants more.

But Natalie did want more. She kept on dropping hints that turned less and less subtle that he should propose, and Teddi said he never had any intention of going down that road. True guy style, he only ever thought of what he wanted that day and that week. Natalie wanted forever, and she pressured him to commit. And in the end—possibly as a result of what happened with Will—Stratton walked away.

Since then, she's begged him every day to come back to her. I don't know whether she loves him and is truly sorry, or she just misses his money. Maybe both.

"I'm tired of it, that's all." He presses his pen down as he doodles, and I suspect he'll leave a mark on the gorgeous mahogany table, but I don't say anything. "She won't leave me alone. It's fucking constant—emails, texts, phoning me at work—that's not something you should have to deal with." He glares at me.

Surprised, I shrug. "I don't mind."

"Meg's very good at it," Rich says. "I don't know how she does it, but she speaks so nicely and yet somehow manages to make it sound as if Natalie's escaped from the local asylum."

Stratton doesn't even smile. "That's not the point. It's impinging on other people now, and I want it to stop."

"You could go to the police," Teddi says, but the flick of his fingers tells me he's already discounted this.

"That's a last resort. She's hurting too, and I don't want to make things worse."

I wonder how much worse it can get unless she literally turns into a bunny boiler, but again, I don't say anything. I'm surprised at his leniency, but I remind myself that he must have felt something more than physical attraction considering he was with her so long.

I'm surprised by the jealousy that stabs me in my gut. Not just for Stratton, although the thought of him in the arms of another woman makes me want to stamp my feet like a toddler. But I'm also jealous of what they shared and how he obviously still feels something for her. I can only imagine what it must be like to be the focus of a man's affection and desire. Will I ever experience that? I'm beginning to think I won't.

"No," Stratton says, "I've come up with a better idea. I'm going to get myself a fake fiancée." He points his pen in my direction. "And you're going to help me."

Chapter Three

Stratton

"Am I now?" Meg looks distinctly unimpressed. In fact, all three of them are looking at me as if I've said I'm going to move to Venus in the New Year.

I expected this, though, and I'm not going to be deterred. "Yep. I want you to get in contact with a modelling agency and ask them to supply candidates who would be prepared to act as my fiancée for the festive season."

"I see." Meg taps something on her keyboard, which could be my directions but could equally be *Jesus, he's finally gone off his rocker.* "And what would the requirements be for the successful candidate?"

"Pretty," I say, more to wind them all up than anything else. "Nice legs. Big tits."

Meg's fingers pause, and her gaze meets mine. Out of the corner of my eye I see Rich chuckle. He knows I'm winding the girls up.

"I'm joking," I say. "Sort of. Look, she has to be beautiful because I want her to make Natalie jealous."

"Why?" Teddi asks. "Is this some kind of screwed up plan to get her back?"

"No!" I bang my fist on the table, which makes much more noise than I meant it to. Meg jumps a foot out of her chair, and Bella shoots out from under the table. "Sorry." I run a hand through my hair. "But it's quite the opposite. The only way Natalie's going to understand it's over is if she thinks I've proposed to someone else. Seeing me engaged to another woman will be the final straw—I know it."

"How is that kinder than reporting her to the police?" Teddi wants to know. She looks genuinely puzzled.

"Reporting her to the police won't get to her heart." I know Natalie well enough to understand that. She truly believes she knows what I want better than I do. She thinks we're perfect for each other, and that I'm refusing to give in because I want to punish her. She's right, but she also thinks I've decided on a cool-off period, and that when it's over and she's done her penance, I'll welcome her back with open arms.

I need to make her understand that we're finished. And this is the only way I can think of.

"You're serious about this," Meg says softly.

I tear my gaze away from her big blue eyes and investigate my tie to see whether the coffee stain is still visible. It is, and I sigh. "I am. I want to hire a model—or an actress, or preferably she'll be both—for Christmas. I'll make it worth her while." I name a sum that makes Rich laugh and Meg's eyes nearly fall out of her head. "I'll also give her a clothes and jewelry budget. I'll need her to accompany me to the Solstice Ball on the twenty-first."

The Solstice Ball is a charity event being held in our capital city, Wellington. Everyone who's anyone is going to be there, including Natalie, because she's president of the New Zealand Association for the Blind, which was how I met her. She's not all bad. Her father's blind, and she works hard for the charity. She's also gorgeous and fantastic in bed. If she was a nicer person, and she didn't have a screw loose, she'd be the perfect girlfriend.

"So…" Rich says, "Natalie's supposed to accept that even though nobody's seen this woman before, you've fallen so madly in love that you've popped the question. You, who's made it quite clear that you're anti-marriage."

"I'm not anti-marriage," I clarify. "I'm anti-marriage with Natalie."

"Why?" It's Meg who queries, the first time she's ever asked me anything personal. "You obviously had feelings for her. Why didn't you ask her to marry you?"

"She wants kids." I finish off my coffee. "I don't." I meet Meg's gaze. She wants to ask why but she's very adept at not overstepping the line of professionalism. I'm from English stock and the English sense of humor tends to be a little more vulgar than the Kiwi one—in spite of our reputation of having a stiff upper lip and being very reserved, it's accepted that sexual references and flirting is all part of conversation and people rarely take offence at it. Rich is well used to me by now, but I think I shocked Meg when she first came to work here, although she's relaxed a lot since then and I think she enjoys our teasing. I have to remember that line, though, because I don't want to be sued for sexual harassment, and as a result we rarely talk about our personal lives. However, she puts herself between me and my crazy ex several times a day like a bodyguard, and now I'm asking her to find me a fake wife, so I think she deserves an explanation.

But in the end, it's Teddi who answers. "The bilateral retinoblastoma I had as a child is a heritable genetic form. There's a mutation in the RB1 gene on chromosome thirteen, inherited from my mother. I have a one in two chance of passing it on to a child. There's no evidence that heterochromia is linked in any way to the defective gene, but Strat's afraid because of his eyes that he might be a carrier and could pass it on to his children, if he had any."

Yeah, that about sums it up.

Meg studies me with her calm gaze, her eyes moving from my blue eye to my green eye. "And Natalie knew this?"

I nod. "Yes. She thought it was worth the risk. I didn't."

"So it's a risk, not a certainty? Even if you were a carrier—and you're not sure you are—it doesn't mean your children would automatically inherit the gene and develop the cancer?"

"No," I say. "A fetus could be tested for the mutation, and it could be delivered early to allow treatment of any eye tumors. But I don't want to risk it. I couldn't put a kid through what Teddi's been through. I'd rather put my own eyes out."

Meg's gaze softens. "Okay," is all she says.

I slide my gaze over to Teddi. She hates the fact that I don't want kids for this reason. She's gone pale, and, as I watch, she rises, clicks her fingers at Bella, and heads for the door. She slips out, closing the door quietly behind her.

Rich rises. "I'll check on her," he says, and follows her out.

I wait until the door shuts and then look across at Meg. It's the first time in the four months she's been here that anything like this has happened. We're all very open about Teddi's blindness, and Teddi's the first of us to come up with jokes about it. One of her favorites is *How do you make a Venetian blind? Poke him in the eye!* She's not hypersensitive about it, and she doesn't expect people to remove the words "look" or "see" from their vocabulary.

Equally, she never developed the feisty, prickly sort of character that blind people have in books and movies, where they get angry and resentful if you try to help them and mistakenly imply they can't manage. She understands people and is skilled at making them feel comfortable when they're with her, even if they've never met a blind person before. She's not defined by her blindness. If you were to ask her to describe herself, she'd say "short with a dark bob". Will helped with that—her blindness never seemed to be an issue for him at all.

But the vulnerability is there in her, just as it is in me. It's the chink in our armor—our Achilles' heel. I hate her disability. I wish it were a thing I could kill like one of the demons in Rich's games. If a child of mine inherited the gene and I gave it cancer, I'd never forgive myself. I'll never risk it because I know what she went through. I'd blame myself, and Teddi blames herself because I won't have kids. What a fucked up family we are.

"So…" Meg says softly. "I have—what—five days to find you a beautiful fiancée."

My lips curve up of their own accord. I love her for recognizing how I feel and changing the subject. "*Easy as,*" I say, leaning back in my chair again. "Should be a simple task for such an outstanding PA."

She laughs. "Rich is right, though. Won't Natalie twig when this woman appears who nobody's seen before? Won't it seem odd that you've produced a stranger who's not only a date but a fiancée?"

"I've practically been a recluse since we broke up. It's not like I've been seen everywhere alone. As far as anyone knows, I could have met this girl the week after we broke up and have been dating her since."

She tips her head from side to side. "I suppose. It still seems a stretch to say you're engaged, though. Natalie will ask around, won't she? She'll want to know if the woman's been into your office or been seen at your house."

"Yeah. So part of the deal will be that this woman will need to stay at my house and in my hotel room when we're in Wellington."

Now Meg looks exasperated. "No woman in her right mind is going to agree to that."

"Well, thanks."

"I don't mean…" She thinks about it and rolls her eyes. "What am I saying? You're offering money and the chance to share your bed. They're going to fall over themselves to be first in the queue."

Her compliment warms me, but I pick up on her choice of word. "Room," I correct. "Not bed."

"Yeah, right," she scoffs. "You're going to share your room with a gorgeous model and not come on to her?"

"Absolutely not. I am a gentleman."

She laughs. "Yeah. You're also a man. And Teddi told me what happened when you met Natalie." Her gaze is amused but also challenging. If I was prone to blushing, I'd be scarlet by now. It's true that Natalie had a high sex drive, and I was happy to take advantage of it. I like sex as much as the next guy, and it's not every woman who's in the mood every night—and sometimes more than once. I think she wore my dick down by an inch over the five years we were together.

But the one thing she has taught me is that energetic sex isn't enough, not by far. Maybe when you're twenty-five it is. But I'm thirty-four now, older, wiser… well, older anyway, and aware that a couple have to have more than a love of sex in common for their relationship to succeed.

I hold Meg's gaze and raise an eyebrow, and it's her cheeks that redden, forcing her to look down. I hide a smile. It's fairly easy to make her blush, and I try to do it at least once a day.

"Sex isn't on the table," I state.

"What about on the carpet?"

That makes me laugh. Her nose wrinkles as she smiles. Not for the first time, I wonder what she's like in bed. Not as experienced as Natalie, I think, but she'd be gentle and eager to please. I like the thought of that. I wonder what kind of lingerie she wears. I decide it's white, virginal and innocent. And beneath it, her skin will be warm and tanned, her nipples a light pink, or maybe a dark rose color because she's had a child. Her body will be rounded and soft, pliable beneath my fingers…

I blink. I'm getting a hard-on, and I don't want Meg to notice. I lean forward in my chair, wince and shift, and clear my throat. "This is a strictly platonic arrangement," I clarify.

"And what if she's gorgeous and into you, and you fancy her?" Meg's unusually persistent.

"Then after the arrangement's over, maybe I'll ask her out." I'm determined not to admit that I could have a lapse of my strong self-control. I wasn't joking when I said I consider myself a gentleman. I'd never make a move on a woman with whom I had a business deal.

"What are you going to do after Christmas?" she asks, puzzled. "As soon as Natalie knows your relationship's over, won't she think she's in with a chance again?"

"Well I won't announce it's over, and hopefully by the time she discovers that's the case, she'll have finally moved on. She will," I say at her doubtful look. "She's an intelligent woman, and she's not weak. She won't wait around forever. I just need to convince her I'm not holding out on her—that I'm definitely over her. Once she realizes that, she'll get over me. I'm not that special." I mean it. I have many, many faults, and I'm just amazed that women don't spot them more often.

Meg's gaze caresses my face. "You shouldn't do yourself down. You're good looking, young-ish, and have money coming out of your ears. Any woman would be mad not to fancy you."

"Including you?"

The words are out before I can stop them. *Shit*. It's the first time I've ever alluded to the fact that I fancy her. *Fuck. Bollocks.*

I watch the pulse in her neck accelerate, her eyes widen. She moistens her lips, and oh Jesus Christ I want to lean forward and kiss her.

"I'm married," she whispers.

Oh. Yeah. I forgot.

Chapter Four

Meg

I return to my desk and sit there for a moment, covering my face with my hands. Stratton's words ring in my head, *Including you?* Holy fuck, I was right—he does like me. Oh Jesus. How am I going to carry on working for him when I have that little piece of information branded on the inside of my skull?

"Mum?" Oscar's voice appears out of nowhere. "You okay?"

I lower my hands and lift my head, staring at him in puzzlement for a moment before I remember that it's Thursday, one of the days he comes in for an hour to playtest Rich's games.

"Hi love, yes I'm fine, just a bit of a headache." I rise as he comes into my office and hold my arms out for a hug, and he crosses to me and envelops me in his arms. At thirteen, he's the same height as me. In a year or two he's going to be taller than me. That'll be weird. Where did my little boy go?

He squeezes me and then drops into a chair. "Got anything to eat?"

"What kind of mother would I be if I didn't?" I open my top drawer and retrieve the ham and cheese roll and the oatmeal bar I'd prepared for this very moment. "Here."

"Ah, thanks." He tucks into it as if he hasn't eaten for a fortnight, even though I know he would have visited the tuck shop at school at lunchtime and probably morning tea too.

"How's your day been?" I ask, leaning on my desk and watching him fondly.

He shrugs. "Usual."

"Learnt a lot?"

"Nah." He grins and unscrews the top on the bottle of water I bought him, then drinks half of it in one go. "What about you? What's going on here today?"

"I'm about to organize a wife for Stratton." I look at the notes I've typed on my laptop, which are interspersed with abbreviations like WTF? And OMG!

Oscar lowers his bottle. "What? Sorry, I thought you said wife."

"I did." I explain Stratton's plan. Oscar and I have no secrets. We made a pact when we left Christchurch that if we were going to do this, we would have to be completely open with each other. So far, I think we've both been true to that.

Oscar laughs. "I think he's lost the plot."

"Well, duh."

"He must really hate Natalie."

I think about it. "No, I don't think he hates her. I think he loved her, but she doesn't seem to have understood him at all. She wanted children, but Stratton doesn't."

"Why?"

I tell him the reason.

"That's sad," Oscar says. "He'd make a good dad." His eyes harden, and I know what he's thinking. *Better than mine.*

I sigh. "Oscar…"

"You should do it," he says.

"Do what?"

"Pretend to be his fiancée."

I glance at the open door to make sure nobody's standing there and then look down again and adjust the position of my laptop. "I'm married."

"No, you're not."

"Yeah, but he doesn't know that," I point out.

"Don't you think you should tell him?"

"No," I say sharply. "We're not telling anyone. We agreed on this."

"I know." Oscar looks suddenly upset. "I don't like lying to him and Rich, though. Don't you trust them?"

"Yes. But we can't tell them. We can't risk it. You know that."

"They wouldn't mind," he protested. "They'd understand."

"Maybe they would, maybe they wouldn't." I think about what Stratton's been through with Natalie and think that he probably would. "But we can't risk it. What if they felt the need to tell someone—the IRD, or the police? At the moment, if he rings and asks for Maggie Walters, nobody's going to have to lie and say they've never heard of her." I don't have to explain who 'he' is.

"I guess."

"Aren't you happy here?" I whisper. "I thought you liked your new school."

"I do."

"And our apartment."

"I do, Mum. We did the right thing, I know. But I like Stratton, and Rich, and Teddi. They've been good to us, and lying to them just feels... wrong."

My eyes fill with tears. He's right. I never thought this might happen when we first made the decision to come here. I thought I'd always be on the outside looking in, struggling to make new friends, and I certainly didn't expect to land such a great job. I love all three of my bosses, and Oscar's right, they've been good to us.

For a moment I imagine telling Stratton the truth. Would he be shocked? Sometimes I think he's half-guessed. There have been occasions, mainly in the early days, when he's called for me and I haven't responded, not yet used to my new name. And once I referred to myself as a brunette and had to hurriedly correct it to blonde. He just laughed and must have put it down to my general ditziness, but he's a smart guy, and it wouldn't surprise me if he suspected something. After all, even army soldiers come home once in a blue moon.

"I think he'd enjoy it if you pretended to be his fiancée," Oscar says. "He likes you. And you like him."

"I do not. Not in that way."

Oscar just looks at me. I stick my tongue out at him, feeling myself sink to his age.

"He'd be better off with you than some dumb model."

"Models aren't dumb," I correct. "We all use the talents God gives us to make a living."

"Even so. He'd hate being with someone stupid, and you're really clever."

"And you're really biased."

"No, I'm not. You're *smart as*."

I chuckle. "Thank you, sweetie."

"I mean it." He's delightfully earnest. Then his expression turns curious. "What's his ex like?"

"Natalie? I don't know. I've never met her." There's a photo of her, though, on the wall in Stratton's office. It's of a group of people at some charity function. She's leaning against him, one hand on his chest as if making sure that everyone knows he belongs to her. She's small, slim, and stunning, and I know that Stratton likes that she works for his favorite charity.

Once again, I can't believe she was dumb enough to lose him. If I had a man like Stratton, I'd never, ever let him go.

"I bet she's fat," Oscar says.

"Who's fat?"

I look up to see Stratton standing in the doorway. I don't miss the fact that my heart skips a beat. He leans against the doorpost, his hands in his trouser pockets. I can smell his aftershave from here. He's so delectable that he makes my mouth water.

Oscar has the grace to look embarrassed. "Ah..."

Naughtiness surges through me. It must be catching. "We were talking about Natalie."

Oscar's eyes widen, but—as I knew he would—Stratton just laughs.

"Mum said you're looking for a wife," Oscar says.

"A fake wife." Stratton smiles.

"It won't work." I pull my laptop toward me.

"Yes it will. I'll make it work through sheer determination."

I bet he will, as well. He's pretty single-minded when he wants to be.

"Why don't you just date someone and propose early?" Oscar suggests.

"I'm off dating," Stratton says. "Girls suck."

Only the good ones, I'm tempted to add, but Oscar's nodding in agreement, enjoying sharing the older guy's attitude to the dreaded girl situation.

"I just want to pretend for a few weeks." Stratton makes it sound perfectly normal.

"Makes sense," Oscar says. "Mum could do it."

I inhale sharply and glare at him. He glares back.

"I don't think your dad would be too happy about that," Stratton says, amused.

"He's away a lot," Oscar points out. "He'd never know."

"Oscar," I snap irritably. "That's enough."

Stratton chuckles. "Your mum has to put up with me day in, day out. The last thing she'd want is to pretend we're a couple." He meets my gaze, and his eyes hold humor and a hint of something else. Yeah, that naughty glint is back.

"Too right," I said. "Now will you two go away and stop making a nuisance of yourselves?"

"That's what we're here for, eh, Oscar?" Stratton curls up his fingers and holds out his hand, and Oscar fist-bumps him. I roll my eyes, but can't stop my lips curving up as Oscar rises and they walk to the door.

"What am I testing today?" Oscar asks, grabbing his schoolbag.

"A new horror game," Stratton says. "R18. Lots of blood and guts, swearing, and sex."

"Cool," Oscar says as they disappear through the door.

I don't react, knowing they're winding me up. Stratton and Rich don't let him play anything over an R13. As far as I know. Maybe they do and I just don't know about it. That makes me think about the groin attachment, and I laugh as I open my browser. I don't think this plan is going to work, but Stratton's in trouble and I want to help, so I put my misgivings to one side and start looking for his fake fiancée.

*

"I've found four possible candidates," I tell Stratton the next morning.

"Already?" His eyebrows rise, and he leans back in his chair and links his fingers as he surveys me. "Okay, give me the rundown."

I take a seat in front of his desk, the printout on my knees. Katoa Limited rents prime office space at the northern end of Auckland's central business district with views across the harbor of the City of Sails. Today it's hot and bright outside, and the sun streams through the windows and falls like melted butter across the gorgeous old mahogany desk Stratton bought at an auction a few years ago. He insists the wood is from Captain Cook's ship, the Endeavour. I know that ship was scuttled outside the city of Newport, Rhode Island, to stop a French fleet entering the harbor back in 1778, but I always nod politely whenever he says it and let him think he's got the better of me. The sun bounces off the tinsel I've pinned along the edge of his desk. Because Will died on Boxing Day, none of them are into the festive season that much, but I insisted the office had to have some

MY CHRISTMAS FIANCÉ

Christmas spirit in it that wasn't whisky, if only for the sake of the rest of the staff.

Teddi's office is all chrome and glass and white walls; Rich's has kauri wood furniture and cream leather and is pristine because he's hardly ever in it, as he's always down in the computer pod with the other programmers. But Stratton practically lives in his office, and it shows. It speaks of his English heritage—his father is from Oxford, which always makes me think of Inspector Morse—and the office reminds me of a don's room at Balliol or Christ Church College. The whole of one wall is filled with shelves of books—an eclectic mix, from engineering text books to history books to fiction. The cream carpet bears a gorgeous, plush brown rug around which a dark red leather sofa and chairs are placed for more relaxed meetings. The whole of the north wall consists of windows, while the other two walls bear elegant paintings from Kiwi artists, as well as a variety of photos. Including the one with Natalie the Nympho Nutter.

My gaze rests on it for a moment before coming back to him. He's watching me, and a shiver runs down my spine.

"You don't like that photo," he says.

"What photo?"

His lips curve up. "The one taken at the conference two years ago." He gestures at it.

I shrug. "I have no feelings about it one way or the other."

He studies me for a moment, then stands and walks over to it. He examines it for a moment before lifting it off the wall. He carries it back to the desk and places it on the floor, leaning it against the table leg, with the photo facing away from us. "Can you please make a note to ask Philip at the gallery to find me something nice to replace it?"

I swallow hard and write it down. "Of course."

His smile is gentle and genuine. "I appreciate you looking out for me, Meg."

I like how he says my new name. I can imagine him whispering it in my ear as he kisses down my neck. In my secret fantasies, alone at night, I often wonder what he's like in bed. Playful, I think. Skilled, no doubt. Perhaps a tad dominant, the way a girl likes a man to be. A tiny bit kinky. I moisten my lips with the tip of my tongue. Maybe he's a big bit kinky. I'm not even sure what that means, but it makes me clench inside as I picture various alternatives.

25

He's watching me with amusement as I stare at him. I clear my throat. "You're welcome," I squeak.

"You are an excellent PA. Just what I was looking for."

My face warms. "Well, that's nice to know."

He plays with his pen. "When we were interviewing, I told the others that a PA is like a work wife. Do you agree?"

I frown, suspicious that this has something to do with my current task. "There's more typing and less sex," I say before I can stop myself.

He laughs. "Yeah."

I wait for him to say "It doesn't have to be that way," or something similar, but he doesn't. Even though he can be flirty, and he and Rich can be near the knuckle with their banter sometimes, he's never overstepped that line to being over-familiar with me. Apart from when he said *Including you?* I can still remember the look on his face when he said that—he shocked himself. I admit that I pushed him a bit by telling him that any woman would be mad not to fancy him, but when he said *I'm not that special* he'd looked so sad that I'd melted a little inside.

Don't you think you should tell him? Oscar's words ring in my head, and suddenly, more than anything, I want to confide in Stratton, and have him comfort me and tell me everything's going to be all right. That we can stop running, and that he'll protect me from Bruce if he should ever find us again.

But there's no guarantee he'd say that. He might get cross with me for lying and sack me on the spot. Or he might side with Bruce and assume the fault had to be mine—he might even try to contact him. I don't know Stratton well enough to gauge what his response would be, and although my gut is screaming that I should trust him, my gut's been seriously wrong in the past, and I don't have faith in it anymore.

"All right," he says softly, and I wonder for a moment whether he had given me the opportunity to open up, and realized I wasn't ready yet. "Come on. Tell me about the list."

Chapter Five

Stratton

Meg's lashes lower as she consults her notepad, giving me the opportunity to study her without her noticing. I make the most of it, as I always do.

Natalie is beautiful in a classic, almost ethereal way, with high cheekbones, sculpted lips, and pale, blemish-free skin that looks as if it's been Photoshopped. Everything about her reflects her Eastern European heritage—she's like a porcelain doll, elegantly painted to perfection. If she had kids, she'd be one of those 'yummy mummies'—she's a vegetarian who prefers organic food, she'd have her figure back in a week, and she's against immunization.

Meg is beautiful too, but in a completely different way. For a start, she's beautiful on the inside as well as the outside. Natalie can be witty and she's smart, but she has a sharp tongue, and she thinks nothing of pointing out other people's faults, especially other women's. But I can't imagine Meg ever being nasty about anyone.

I'm not trying to find ways to make up for a lack of physical beauty, though, because she has that too. She's a Kiwi girl through and through. She's tall and generously proportioned but well-toned, suggesting she works out often, and she's mentioned to me that she enjoys swimming, which makes me smile because Natalie hates getting her hair wet. Meg's skin bears a warm tan, and she sparkles with health. I know she eats burgers because Oscar told me, and she's also declared that people who don't immunize their children are nuts, presumably without knowing Natalie's views. She's like the polar opposite of Natalie.

I like that.

As she scans her list, I wonder whether her tan extends all over her body. Or does she have white triangles where her bikini goes?

She looks up at that point, catching me mid-ogle. Her eyes return to her list, but I think I see a smile play on her lips.

"So I've arranged for four young, beautiful ladies to come in for an interview this afternoon," she says.

"Excellent. What else do I need to know?"

"I don't think there's any point in giving you their CVs," she says. "I think choosing a fiancée is about gut feeling, and whether you click."

"*Fake* fiancée," I remind her.

"Yes, but even so, it's got to look as if there's a connection between you, hasn't it? There's no point you requesting one particular girl because of her qualifications and interests and then you get face to face and think Jesus, I wouldn't touch her with someone else's barge pole."

I chuckle at her choice of words. "Yes, I suppose so."

"Okay. I'll let you know when the first one arrives." She walks out, and I let my gaze linger on her butt until she disappears around the corner.

I sigh. This won't get any work done. The business world still revolves in spite of what's happening in my private life.

I devote a couple of hours to emails and phone calls, then get bored and decide to see what Rich is up to. I wander down to the first floor, finding him as usual amidst the chaos of the game development pod. It's dark in here, the blinds drawn and the only light coming from the screens of the thirty or so guys huddled over their keyboards. We're not sexist—it's just that so far no girl has shown any interest in the freakish world of designing zombies and wizards that for some reason always want to destroy the Earth.

Rich is in his favorite spot in the corner, playing *World of Warcraft*.

"Working hard, I see." I pull up a chair next to him.

"I'm trying out my new Demon Hunter." His eyes are fixed on the screen while his fingers dance across the keyboard. "Checking out the competition." He's in the process of designing characters for a new game he's developing, so I know he'll see what works and what doesn't in various games and apply that knowledge to his own designs.

"And?"

"Yeah, it's cool. I like the double jump feature." He illustrates what he means, accidentally leaps off a cliff, and his character dies. "Fuck." He taps his mouse to resurrect the toon.

"If only it was that easy in real life," I say.

He sighs. "Yeah."

I know that many people—especially women—think gaming is a boys' thing, a hobby for geeks and losers. But those who don't play have no idea how wonderful it is to lose oneself in a game. It's the same as watching a great movie or reading a fantastic book—in gaming you envelop yourself in another world, and you become a hero, vanquishing evil and even challenging death, which can be comforting when life is treating you rough.

Rich, Will, and I got into gaming around the time we went to high school. We lived up in the Northland back then. Rich and Will were identical, and although I could always tell them apart, everyone else at school mixed them up all the time. The three of us guys used to meet up online and game during the evening—around doing our homework, of course. Teddi joined in where she could. She always had a thing for Will and it didn't surprise me when they started dating. He was devoted to her, and I know they would have been together forever. If he hadn't died.

That year, we all went through several levels of hell. Teddi just cried all the time—as much as she's able to with her artificial eyes. Frustrated at not being able to help, I drove Natalie to distraction by losing myself in work and being completely anti-sociable, a point I haven't really rectified since.

On the surface of it, for the first year Rich looked as if he was coping. But on the Christmas Eve after Will died, unable to reach Rich by phone, I called by his house to find him two-thirds into a bottle of whisky. He talked for hours about feeling like half a person, and at that point all I could do was nod and sympathize and make sure he was safe in bed when he passed out. Since then, and in spite of Teddi's and my attempts to get him to stay with us, he's gone away for Christmas and New Year, and I'm sure he's spent the entire two weeks in an alcoholic stupor.

When he's sober—which is most of the time because I know he doesn't like that dark place he ends up in when he's drinking—he doesn't want to talk about it. But every time he resurrects a character in a game, I'm sure I see a wry smile on his face.

"I hear Meg's organized a few girls to come in this afternoon." Rich pushes his keyboard away. He turns to face me, finishing off a cup of what's probably stone-cold coffee, because he winces as he swallows.

"Yeah. You want to join in with the interviews? You might find one you like."

He snorts. "No thanks."

I sigh and wonder why the two of us have had such trouble with women. Rich has gone from relationship to relationship without finding the woman of his dreams. Neither of us believes in true love anymore, or soul mates, or any of that crap. We're thirty-four and single, and relationships are too difficult, women too demanding. Neither of us thinks there are girls out there who will be anything but hard work. Having money is great, but Meg was right when she said it's an attraction, and both Rich and I are convinced the jangle of coins is far louder than the thud of Cupid's arrows where women are concerned. How can we be sure any potential girlfriend doesn't just want us for our money? Our lawyers have advised us it will be necessary to draw up a pre-nup when the time comes for marriage, but to be honest I can't see either of us ever getting that far.

"It's a fucking stupid idea," Rich says. "This fake fiancée thing. You know that, right?"

I shrug. "I've got to get her off my back somehow. Do you have any better ideas?"

"Tell the FBI she's a terrorist."

I laugh. "Yeah. Maybe. But at least I'll have a date for Christmas."

"Even if you are paying her to stand next to you."

"Yeah, well. My other idea is to have a vasectomy. I'm saving that as a last resort."

Rich stares at me. He knows me well enough to understand that I'm not joking.

We're guys—we don't normally talk about this sort of thing. Our conversations rarely delve deeper than discussing games, movies, and sports cars. Gestures of affection extend to a slap on the arm or, at most, a manly bear hug. We don't do in-depth analyses of each other's motives or meanings, and we certainly don't talk about anything personal.

But this time Rich frowns and doesn't immediately make a joke of it the way he normally would. "You're not serious?"

"It would be proof that I don't want kids. And she really wants them, Rich. It's all she talked about. She wants the whole pregnancy experience, and she'd never consider marrying a guy who couldn't give her what she wanted." I know I'm being unfair. Possibly. Natalie always talked about 'us' having kids—she used to say she wanted to share that with me, and have a little piece of me growing inside her. I don't know if that's true or if it's bullshit and all she wants is the status symbol of a beautiful baby to show her friends, but she's a woman who's used to getting what she wants, and she's determined that given enough time she can talk me round.

"A vasectomy's a bit final," Rich says.

"That's the point."

He tips his head to the side. "What if you change your mind?"

"I won't."

"You might meet a girl you do love who wants kids, and then you might decide it's worth the risk."

"I won't, because this isn't about anyone else except me. It's fucking selfish, I know that, but it's what I want. Come on, we're thirty-four—we know better than to think there's one person out there we're meant to be with. If I meet a girl I like but she wants kids and won't adopt, I'll back off. It seems to me that a woman should love me for who I am rather than who she wants me to be."

Rich stares at me, and I feel as if I should ask him if he wants to paint my nails and braid my hair. What are we, fourteen-year-old girls? Since when do we talk like this?

But then maybe that's a benefit of age. You can talk about feelings and shit and not worry that it means you're turning gay.

"I've changed my mind," Rich says. "Go for the fiancée thing. If there's even a chance of it working, you've got to give it a go before you put your balls on the operating table."

I chuckle and stand. "Thanks for your support."

"Don't mention it. I just know that if you have a vasectomy, I'll have to put up with all the moaning about the pain for the next six months."

He's not wrong there. I wince and have to fight not to rub myself as I walk out of the room and back up the stairs to my office.

*

Meg announces the arrival of the first candidate just before two.

"Get in here," I tell my PA when she tries to sidle out of the door. "I need moral support."

She sighs and brings in the first girl. I'm sitting in one of the armchairs, but I rise as they walk in.

I find it difficult not to stare at the candidate. She's small and slim with platinum blonde hair cut in a bob that's so sharp I'm sure it's a wig. She's wearing a helluva lot of makeup, and her black dress is like plastic wrap, it's so tight.

Hiding my surprise, I pin a smile on my face and hold out a hand. "Welcome, Arabella. Thank you for coming." Suddenly, I'm convinced that's not her real name.

"Hi," she says, sliding her hand into mine. Her nails are false and bright red.

"Please, take a seat." I gesture at the sofa, and she lowers herself gracefully onto it. She's wearing really, really high heels. They're kinda sexy, but her outfit's not what I expected considering she's here for an interview. I recall the dark-gray suit Meg wore to hers, her elegant hair. That's the sort of girl I'm looking for.

Meg sits in the other armchair. I glance at her, but she's busy flicking through her notes. I suspect it's a ploy so she doesn't have to meet my eyes.

I clear my throat. "So... I believe my PA has explained my situation and what I'm looking for?"

Arabella nods. "Yes, sir."

"Please, call me Stratton."

"Yes, Stratton." She smiles then, and it's genuine enough and lights up her eyes. She's a pretty little thing, and as we start talking the real girl shines out from beneath the plastic Barbie doll she projects. She likes animals and wanted to be a vet when she was young. She enjoys keep fit classes and goes to the gym. She likes Mexican food and loves dancing.

We don't really have anything in common, but she's nice enough. She laughs at my jokes and she knows how to pay a guy attention— she barely looks at Meg, and she shakes back her hair every so often, pressing her lips together and looking up at me through her lashes.

"Okay," I say after about ten minutes of chat. "Do you have any questions?"

"So you're just looking for someone to pretend to be your fiancée?" she clarifies.

"That's right."

"To go to functions and act like a girlfriend."

"Yes." I have a sinking feeling that I know where this is going.

"And it means staying in your house and your hotel room when we're away."

Now I'm faced with it, it suddenly seems like a ridiculous idea. "Ah, yeah."

"What about any other services," she asks as if it's the most normal thing in the world. "I have a leaflet outlining what I offer, if you want to see it."

My gaze slides to Meg. She's looking out of the window, but I have the distinct feeling she's trying not to laugh.

I look back at Arabella. "That won't be necessary, but thank you."

"Okay." She jumps chirpily to her feet. "Well thank you for the opportunity."

I rise, and we shake hands again. "Nice to meet you," I say, somewhat faintly.

Meg shows her to the door while I return to the chair behind my desk. I sit and lean back, watching as Arabella disappears and Meg turns back to face me.

"Come here." I beckon her toward me.

She approaches the desk and stands there, clutching her clipboard.

"Is there any chance," I say, "that the firm you contacted was an escort agency?"

She scratches her nose. "Possibly."

I lean forward and rest my forehead on the desk. This day just can't get any worse.

Chapter Six

Meg

Finally, I give in to the laughter that's been threatening to spill over for some time. I cover my mouth with my hand as Stratton sits back and glares at me, but it doesn't stop the giggles.

"You're taking the piss," he says.

"I'm really not." I sit opposite him and struggle to compose myself. "I thought this would be best. The thing is, if you were to ask a model to act as your fiancée you'd only be inviting disaster. You'd run the risk of them falling for you. If your face wasn't enough of a lure, your money would be."

He continues to glare at me, although I can tell by the way he's flipping his pen through his fingers that he's considering my words. Somewhat sulkily, he says, "You think I have a nice face?"

I ignore him, not wanting to go down that road. "You run the same risk with an actress. At least with an escort girl, you know they're in it for the money."

"Call girls can fall for guys too, you know. Haven't you seen *Pretty Woman?*"

I laugh, relieved there's a glimmer of humor in his eyes. "Yeah, but it's an up-front business arrangement, and I would imagine it's less likely. This agency is very exclusive, and when I explained what you wanted, they were keen to insist that all the girls will protect your privacy."

"It's not really the point. I don't want a call girl."

"You're planning on paying whoever you hire—what difference does it make?"

"There's a difference, Meg. There just is."

I frown at him, genuinely puzzled. "I'm really sorry, I didn't think it would bother you. I thought you'd be used to it."

"Used to what?"

"Being around call girls."

He stares at me. "Meg, I've never paid for sex, if that's what you're insinuating."

My jaw drops. I suddenly realize I've made a huge mistake. "Oh. I just assumed that, in your position, with all the big business deals you do…" His face tells me what an error I've made.

Now he's amused. "I'm picking up by this that your previous boss had a… shall we say colorful social life?"

The CEO I'd worked for could definitely have been called colorful. Although he didn't possess Stratton's sense of humor, and he was about thirty years his senior, he'd partied like a twenty-year-old, and he'd enjoyed throwing his money around when important customers came to stay. Those customers were almost always men, and he would invariably ask me to organize a night at Cesare's, which sounds like an Italian restaurant but is actually a lap dancing club attached to—for all intents and purposes—a brothel.

"Yes, and all his customers seemed to think it was perfectly normal to frequent that type of place… I just assumed…"

"Was your previous boss in the Mafia? Honey, Rich and I are computer geeks. Can you imagine us in a house of ill repute? The nearest we've come to going with a prostitute was driving through the red light district in Amsterdam just to see what it looked like, and it scared the shit out of both of us. I've not even been to a strip club. I think I'd die if I did."

I'm not sure whether to find this whole situation hugely embarrassing or hugely funny. I opt for funny and subside into hysterical giggles until tears pour down my face and my sides ache. Luckily, Stratton joins in, although I think he's laughing more at my giggles than at the situation.

"I'm so sorry." I wipe my face with both hands. "It's just that you're so…"

He runs a hand through his hair, still shaking his head and smiling. "So what?"

I think of Teddi's stories about him and Natalie never getting out of bed. He's so sexy I assumed he'd had hundreds of partners, but maybe I was wrong. "A man of the world," I choose.

He gives me a wry look. "I'm not a monk, but I'm hardly that. Oh jeez. There are three more call girls coming for interviews, aren't there?"

His genuine alarm starts me laughing again. "Don't worry, I'll cancel them. Mind you… look on the bright side—if you do fancy one of them, you can just pay for sex and you'd have no worry about commitment issues."

"Meg…"

"I'd be interested to see what was on that leaflet Arabella offered. You might still end up with the happy ever after you hoped for."

He snorts. "It's called a happy ending, Meg, and for God's sake, can we talk about something else?" He rests his head on the back of his chair and stares up at the ceiling. "I haven't had sex for six months and all this talk is making me…" He struggles to think of a word.

"Horny?" I suggest.

That makes him laugh. "You really have gotten used to me, haven't you?"

"Sorry. I forget you're my boss sometimes."

"That's good. Successful working—and personal—relationships rely on knowing where the other person's boundaries are, and on understanding their sense of humor. I'm glad you're used to mine."

"I sometimes wonder what Natalie made of it."

His smile fades. "I don't think she ever got me. We were like two binary suns, always circling and destined never to meet in the middle."

Liking the analogy, I open my mouth to say something, and then I realize what he said. "Wait, you haven't had sex for six months?"

"I broke up with Natalie in May. So, technically, seven months I guess."

"You really haven't been out with anyone since?"

"No. Why's that so surprising?"

Because you're so gorgeous and sexy I'd assumed you'd have been with a different girl every night.

I don't say it though. He looks sad, and my heart goes out to him. I've never spoken to him about what happened with Natalie, but suddenly I feel the need to comfort him. "I'm sorry."

"For what?"

"For what happened with Natalie. I'm not surprised you're taking time out for a while."

He studies his pen. "I don't know if I'll ever get back in the dating game."

"Oh, I'm sure you will once time passes."

He shrugs. "Men seem to want different things out of a relationship than women. I can't imagine any girl being happy going into marriage knowing the guy doesn't want kids. Even if she says she doesn't, I can't help but think she'll be hoping to change my mind at some point."

"You might be surprised. Not every woman wants kids either."

"I haven't met any who don't."

"Maybe you're just mixing in the wrong circles. For young, rich women, having a husband and two-point-four kids is going to feel like the ultimate aim—it'll be expected of them, and they'll want to give birth without pain relief and have perfect babies they feed with home-made organic food and who are potty-trained before they're eighteen months old."

He raises an eyebrow. "I thought you hadn't met Natalie?"

I laugh. "I knew that's what she'd be like."

"So I'm mixing with the wrong women? Who are the right women?"

"I don't know—I'm not an expert. Older women, maybe, who've decided to dedicate their lives to their career and who don't want the complication of a family. Or women who already have children." My heart bangs on my ribs. Does he realize I'm half-referring to myself?

He rolls his eyes. "I don't want to inherit some other guy's squawking brats."

It's a problem that unfortunately I'm more than aware of—that generally guys don't enjoy taking on other men's children. My heart sinks a little. It's tough being a single mum.

I don't want to think about it now or I'm going to depress myself. I clear my throat. "So…" I sit back in the seat. "What are we going to do? You want me to get onto a real modelling agency?"

His smile fades. "I dunno. I guess it was a stupid idea."

My brow furrows. "It wasn't stupid. I know you just want Natalie to leave you alone, and you were right—it might work."

"I'll think about it." He straightens and pulls his laptop toward him. "So you'll cancel those appointments?"

"Yes. I'm sorry, Stratton."

He waves a hand and starts typing, not looking at me. "Don't worry about it."

I leave the room, clutching my clipboard, and return to my nearby office with a sigh.

I feel distinctly flat, and I sit at my desk and pick up my phone with little enthusiasm. I'm embarrassed to have to cancel the appointments, and I apologize profusely to the woman on the other end of the phone, who's not amused.

For the rest of the afternoon, I'm listless and unenthusiastic, and it's a relief when five-thirty approaches. Sometimes I stay late if Stratton needs me, but I haven't seen him all afternoon, and I suspect he's avoiding me after what I did.

I start packing up my things, glance at my computer screen, and smile when I see an email from Alyssa. She's a new friend I've made since moving to Auckland. We met at the local swimming pool and got on well, as we have a lot in common, including that we're both single mums with teenage boys.

In her email she chats about her family and her day job at the kindergarten. The email subject shows we have been back and forth about twenty times and the message is as long as my arm, so I start with a fresh one and begin telling her about my day. Not about the call girls—I decide to leave that part out—but I tell her a bit about work, just general chit chat.

Then, because he's on my mind, I tell her about Stratton.

I'm just crazy about him, I type. *He so gorgeous he makes my mouth water. I'll have to introduce you soon. He has thick dark hair touched with gray and the most amazing eyes—one blue, one green. A stunning smile. He's six foot three and a big guy, but he's very unassuming and self-deprecating. You'd like him a lot. It's not easy working for him every day. I find myself sitting in meetings and instead of typing minutes I daydream about covering him in melted chocolate—or whipped cream, it varies—and then licking it all off. It passes the time.*

I finish it with a smiley face, sign it Meg, click the arrow where it says 'To' and choose her name, then hit send. Briefly, I wonder whether the IT team ever monitors my emails, but it's too late now, it's gone, so I suppress a sudden feeling of unease and rise to get my bag, ready to go home for the day.

A ping tells me I've received another email, though, and I sink back down to check it. I stare for a moment as I realize it's the one I've just sent. What? Why would it come back to me? Has it bounced? Has Alyssa closed her email account or something?

I look at who I've sent it to, and my jaw drops. Cold filters through me. Disbelievingly, I quickly start up a new email and click the down arrow that shows me the list of people I send to regularly. Oh no. I thought I'd clicked on Alyssa's name. But I haven't. I've clicked on All Staff.

My head spins, and I feel faint with horror. I've just told everyone in the building about my secret fantasies. Everyone who works here will have gotten that email. And that's bad, but it's not the worst of it.

Rich will get it, and so will Teddi.

And it's currently pinging up in Stratton's inbox, too.

Panic washes over me. What have I done? I've ruined everything with one hit of a tiny button. What an idiot. What a fucking stupid idiot I am.

I can't stay here—I've got to get out before everyone reads it. At least it's Friday—I can take the weekend to work out how the hell I'm going to deal with this.

I grab my handbag and run out of my office. Head down, I stride through the large workroom housing the secretarial pool, heads turning as I pass. Nigel from accounts stops me to talk about an invoice and drones on and on, and in the end I tell him I have to leave and just walk away. I ignore the elevators and take the stairs, running down them, my high heels tapping. I'm not sure if I've breathed in yet, and my head's still spinning. I have to be careful not to fall and break my neck—and yet a little part of my brain muses that such an accident might be a relief.

Exiting into the foyer, I run across it. My face is hot and my eyes are stinging with tears. What have I done? Holy fuck. I'm going to be a laughing stock, and as for Stratton… He thinks I'm married. I don't know whether he's going to be flattered, amused, or angry. Maybe he'll think it's hilarious. Oh my God, I'll never be able to look him in the eye again.

I can't bear it. I want to die.

I'm halfway across the foyer when I hear him call my name. "Meg!"

God, no! Anyone but him! I don't stop and continue running.

"Meg, for Christ's sake. Stop her, Andy!"

Obediently, the security guard closes the glass door and refuses to let go as I reach it. I hit him with my handbag, almost sobbing in panic. "Let me out!"

"Meg, it's okay." Stratton catches up with me and tugs my arm. I wrench it away and stumble back. I can't bear to look at him. "It's okay," he says again, bending to try and catch my eye. "Come on, it's not the end of the world."

"Don't." My face must be scarlet, because it's burning as if I've been out in the hot sun all day. "Just… don't."

"Hey." He obviously realizes I'm genuinely distraught, takes my arm again, and leads me across to the side of the foyer. Luckily, there's only Andy to witness the scene, and he averts his gaze as he takes up his place by the doors again, although I know he's listening.

"Let me go." I dash away a tear that's run down my face.

"Meg, sweetheart, come on. It was a mistake. You clicked on the wrong name, didn't you? It happens."

I cover my face with my hands. "I can't believe I did it. I'm so embarrassed."

He gives a soft laugh, moving closer to me and resting his hands on my upper arms. He rubs them gently, trying to offer comfort. "It's all right. Did you think I didn't know how you felt?"

I still refuse to look at him. I want to curl in a corner and sob. "I can't believe I sent it to All Staff. Everyone will know. I can't stay here. I can't come back."

"Meg, come on. Let's get it in proportion. There's no way I'm losing the best PA I've ever had just because she has a thing about chocolate sauce."

Oh. My. God. My face could melt lead it's burning so badly.

"Oops," he said. "Too soon?"

"Please, just kill me now."

He laughs and wraps his arms around me. "Sweetheart, we're grownups, and we like each other. You're gorgeous—you don't think I wonder what you look like naked ten times a day?"

"Oh, Stratton, please, don't. You're just making it worse."

"I'm saying that it's normal when you fancy someone. It doesn't mean anything. And it's hardly a huge shock to me."

I press my hands against his shirt and bury my face in it. "I thought you might be angry."

"Jesus, why? You made my day." He kisses my hair.

"Because I'm… m-married."

He slides a hand beneath my chin and lifts my face so he can look into my eyes. For a moment I think he's going to kiss me, but instead his green and blue eyes search mine, as if he's in an attic rummaging around in a trunk. "Are you?" he says.

A breeze washes across my legs, but I'm only half aware that the front door has opened. It's when I hear my name called—my real name—that I realize someone's come in.

"Maggie?"

I turn my head, and for the second time in the space of about five minutes my heart stops. I inhale sharply, feel my eyes widen, my jaw drop, and I push away from Stratton and stumble back.

It's the first time I've seen Bruce for about five months, and it takes me a few seconds to recognize him. He looks different, and I realize it's because he's not angry, and he's not drunk. He's wearing a smart shirt and jeans, he's lost weight, and his hair's longer, which looks odd because he's had an army buzz cut ever since I've known him. Then I notice the biggest difference—his right shirt sleeve is no longer pinned at the elbow. He has a prosthetic arm. It's not flesh colored and rigid—it's metal and has jointed fingers. It looks like something out of *The Terminator*.

He reaches his left hand toward me, and his face fills with relief. "Maggie!" he says again. "Thank fuck. I thought I was never going to find you." He walks across the foyer toward me. Admiration lights his eyes. "Blonde," he says. "Wow, that's different."

My heart is hammering against my ribs! "No!" I snap, backing up even further. Hot rage sears through me—I can't believe he's found me.

Stratton is staring at Bruce, but as Bruce comes toward me, Stratton moves in to intercede.

"Wait." Stratton places a hand on Bruce's chest.

Bruce knocks it to one side and steps around him, and I move back even further.

"I just want to talk," Bruce says, glaring as Stratton once again moves to block his path.

"No!" I say again—I can't seem to find any other word in my vocabulary.

Bruce pushes at the man before him, angry now, and I wait for him to knock Stratton down—it wouldn't be the first time he's decked another man who's dared to talk to me. To my surprise, though, Stratton shoves him back, and in a second he has Bruce up against the wall, an arm across his throat, using his superior height and weight to keep the smaller man pinned there. Andy is already running over to help, but I can see that Stratton doesn't need it.

"Andy," Stratton says through gritted teeth. "Can you escort this gentleman off the premises, please?"

"Of course, sir." Andy is six-five and about two-hundred-and-forty pounds, and he lifts Bruce like a doll and drags him over to the door.

"I just want to talk," Bruce yells, twisting and turning to try to escape. Andy throws him out, though, and Bruce bangs on the glass before walking off, his face furious.

I can't process what's just happened. It's all too much. I'm shaking like a kicked puppy, and in seconds my legs give way and I slide down the wall to the floor.

Chapter Seven

Stratton

"Meg! Oh Jesus." My heart's going like a train, and I stride over to her and sink to my haunches. "Hey, it's okay. He's gone."

It only takes me seconds to work everything out. From the fact that he called her Maggie to the way she reacted to him—that was her ex and therefore presumably Oscar's dad. She must have run away from him with Oscar, and come here to Auckland to start over again. Holy shit. I thought she might have invented a husband for some reason, maybe to make herself seem like a respectable married woman to get the job. I didn't even consider that it could be anything like this.

"He's gone," I say again. She's not crying, but she's trembling. No doubt it has something to do with the trauma of sending the email, too. Jesus. What a day she's had.

She covers her face with her hands. I glance over at Andy, whose expression mirrors what I'm feeling—pity and anger and helplessness all rolled into one. When Natalie cried, she always wanted me to make a fuss of her, but Meg's posture is defensive, and anyway, she's not my girlfriend.

She can't stay here, though, or she'll attract the attention of the office staff who'll be leaving now it's five thirty.

I reach out to take her hand. "Meg," I say firmly. "Come on. I'm going to take you home."

She doesn't move. She's trembling as if it's thirty degrees in here even though it's so warm in the foyer that my shirt's damp under my arms.

"What if he's found out where I live?" Her voice is little more than a whisper. Then she looks up at me, alarmed. "Oscar!"

I know that her son stays with her friend until five thirty, and then he walks to their apartment.

"Right." I push up and hold out my hand. "Come on, we'll pick Oscar up and then you're coming over to my place." My keys and wallet are in my pocket—I can do without my jacket.

She looks up at me, wary, and I frown. "He won't know where I live, I'm sure. Once you're there, you can decide what you want to do. But let's go get Oscar."

To my relief, she nods and slides her hand into mine. I pull her to her feet, but keep hold of her hand as I lead her across the foyer toward the door to the underground car park. She doesn't try to pull free, just follows me mutely. I nod at Andy as I go—he'll file a report for the evening shift and will let me know if he sees the man again.

We go through the door and down the steps, then enter the cool atmosphere of the car park. Three or four girls are talking by a car and they glance over at us as we walk past, but I ignore them and usher Meg toward my Lexus, pressing the button on the key at the same time. I lead her to the passenger side and open the door, and I'm relieved when she slides in.

I walk around to the driver's side and get in, start the car, and head out.

Meg leans her head on the rest and covers her face with her hands. "I feel as if someone's sitting on my chest."

"Just breathe." I'm not surprised she's having a panic attack after everything that's happened in the last thirty minutes. "In and out. Nice and calm." I negotiate the busy traffic with one eye on her. "You're going to be all right. He's gone."

She lowers her hands and blows out a long breath. I pull up at some traffic lights, put the car in neutral, and glance over at her.

For the first time since she sent the email, she meets my gaze. "I'm sorry," she whispers.

She has the biggest, bluest eyes I've ever seen on a woman, and even like this—distraught, trembling, and filled with panic—she's the most beautiful thing I've ever seen. More beautiful than Natalie, I think with some surprise, because Meg's beauty is natural and shines from within her, whereas Natalie's is strictly external.

"Sorry for what?" I ask.

"Where do I start?" For the first time, a glimmer of a smile curves her lips.

"You don't have to be sorry for anything." I'm captivated by those blue eyes. I think about her email, about that moment when I first read it and felt a rush of pleasure and excitement at the thought that she desires me. Hot on its heels was shock at the fact that the whole building would be reading the email, and at that moment I'd known that she would want to leave. As I'd run down the stairs, it had crossed my mind that she was a married woman, but now it comes to me that she is probably free. Maybe the same thought is going through her mind, because our eyes lock, and for a brief moment I forget about everything except the fact that she wants me, and I want her.

Behind me, somebody honks their horn, and I hurriedly put the car into first gear and pull away.

"I do," she says, and I realize she's replying to my statement, *You don't have to be sorry for anything*. "I'm so sorry for sending that email and causing you any embarrassment."

I snort. "You've raised my street cred by a billion percent."

She doesn't smile. "Thank you for being gracious about it, but it was such a stupid thing to do. Everyone's going to read it, including Teddi and Rich…" She looks out of the window, her blush returning. At least she has some color now.

"Fuck everyone else," I say vehemently. "Get it in perspective, Meg. Nobody's died. It was just an email. What happened in the foyer—that's important, that's something that needs sorting out. The email was nothing. It was the equivalent of a wolf whistle, that's all."

"You could fire me for sexual harassment," she says.

I glance at her, relieved to see a flicker of humor in her eyes. "Yeah, like that's going to happen. It put a smile on my face and made my day."

"I'll never live it down," she murmurs, scratching at a mark on her skirt.

"It seems to me you have more than that to worry about at the moment."

She looks back out of the window. "Yeah."

I'm turning onto her road so we don't say anything more. I pull up outside her apartment, turn off the engine, and give her the keys. "I'll get Oscar. You stay here and lock the door when I get out." I don't want to risk that the guy's lurking around here. If he's found out where she works, I'm sure he can track down where she lives.

Without waiting for an answer, I get out and shut the door. I walk a few yards away, then turn and put my hands on my hips. The indicators flash, telling me she's locked it.

I run across the road and press the button for her apartment. It's only seconds before Oscar's voice comes through, slightly puzzled. "Hello?"

"Oscar? It's Stratton."

"Oh, hi Stratton. Mum's not home yet."

"Yeah, she's with me. Can you buzz me in?"

"Um, sure." He does so, and I go in and take the stairs two at a time up to their floor.

When I get there, the door's open, and Oscar leaning against the doorjamb. He's changed out of his school uniform, and he's in jeans and a *Hella* T-shirt.

"What's up?" he asks, backing into the apartment. I follow him in and shut the door behind me.

"Your mum's in the car." Suddenly I'm not sure how to describe what's happened. Meg hasn't explained yet who the guy was, so I'm taking a jump in making any assumptions. But I've got to say something, and I know that Meg's very open with her son.

"Look," I say, as gently as I can. "I'm not sure of the whole story, but a guy turned up at the offices—I'm assuming it was your dad."

Oscar's eyes widen and real fear appears on his face. "How did he find us?"

"I don't know, but I'm not sure if he's discovered where you live, so I thought I'd pick you up and take you both to my place for a while. When you're there your mum can decide whether you want to stay or go to a hotel or to a friend, but for now I just want to get you out, okay?"

Oscar nods. He doesn't argue at all, and that—and the look on his face—tell me more about his relationship with his dad than any words could have.

"Get a bag," I instruct, "and pack a few changes of clothes, and whatever you need for tonight."

"Okay." He runs off.

I hesitate, then follow him through the small apartment to his room. "I guess I should pack your mum some clothes?" I suggest.

He's busy stuffing things into a rucksack, but he leads me out and into the bedroom next door. It's small and neat—very Meg. A white

MY CHRISTMAS FIANCÉ

duvet features red tulips growing up toward the pillows. On the dressing table is a scatter of girly items—makeup, handcream, a hairbrush, a jewelry stand with necklaces and rings. To confirm that she's single, there's no sign of a male presence—no photos of her husband, no guy's aftershave or socks on the floor. Suddenly I feel as if I'm prying. This is like peering through her curtains and seeing her without her clothes, and I realize just what a private person she is, and how little I know about her.

Oscar walks over to the wardrobe, pulls out a smallish blue overnight bag, and dumps it on the bed. "Here you go." He leaves the room to continue with his own packing.

I look around, reluctant to paw through her things, but I remind myself of the unpleasant guy in the foyer and the reason why I'm doing this. I pull open some drawers, note there are no men's clothes in there, take out a pair of jeans, a pair of track pants, and a couple of T-shirts, grab the pajamas folded on the pillow, and place them in the bag. I add a pair of Converses and socks, realizing as I do so that I've never seen her in casual clothing. If we have met out of work, it's been at a function where she's looked as smart as she does at the office.

I open the top drawer and pause. I don't want her to be angry with me for going through her stuff. But I'm doing this as a friend—as her boss, someone who cares for her. My gaze lingers briefly on scraps of lace and silk before I pick up some cotton underwear and a bra and toss them quickly in the bag.

I find a smaller bag in the wardrobe and I put a few of the bottles from the dressing table in there with her hairbrush. There's a tiny case next to it, half unzipped, and I realize it's her makeup bag. It makes me smile—Natalie wouldn't have been able to get a tenth of her makeup in there. I put it in the overnight bag.

I go into the bathroom and pack her toothbrush. I open the bathroom cabinet. There are more bottles, tampons, some Panadol and other over-the-counter tablets, and a box whose label suggests it contains contraceptive pills. I sweep everything into the small bag, go back into the bedroom, and stuff it in the overnight bag.

I exit to the living room. Oscar's just packing a sketchpad and some pencils. I didn't know he was artistic.

"Anything you think your mum might need?" I ask.

He gestures at an iPad lying on the side of an armchair. "She'll be lost without that."

I pack it. "Anything else?"

He zips up his bag and glances around, then picks up a well-worn notebook that bears many hours of doodling. "Her poetry book." He slips that into the bag.

"She writes poetry?"

"Yeah. She's won loads of competitions. She's really good." He speaks with pride, which warms me through.

"Oscar…"

He pauses in the process of hitching his backpack onto his shoulder and walking to the door. "Yeah?"

"I know your mum doesn't want to talk about it, but it's obvious that you guys have been through some stuff. I'm sorry about that."

He scuffs the carpet with his toe. "Mum didn't want me to tell you. She was worried how you'd react. She really loves her job."

"I don't care what's happened in the past," I tell him. "She's a terrific PA, and whatever's happened in her personal life wouldn't change that. I'm hoping she'll talk to me later and confide in me, but if she doesn't, I just want you to know that if you ever want to talk about anything, you can always talk to me. I hope you know that I'll always be there for the two of you."

He swallows, still looking at his feet. I can remember being that age. All hormones and angst, desperate to be a man, but secretly wanting to hang on to being a boy too. I feel a sweep of pity for him.

He looks up at me then, and I'm surprised how cold his eyes are. "He hit her," he says. "He put her in hospital. If I see him again, I'll fucking kill him." He breathes heavily, fighting with his emotion.

I stare at him in shock. How any man can use his superior strength against someone weaker than him baffles me, but that a man could turn on kind, gentle Meg…

Jesus. It's much, much worse than I thought.

How can I comfort this young lad, who should be thinking about nothing else but video games and rugby and what homework he has to do? How can I offer him platitudes that we will both know are full of shit after what he's obviously been through?

Lost for words, I walk forward and put my arms around him.

Oscar stiffens, then relaxes and rests his forehead on my shoulder. We stand there for a moment, man and boy, sharing in that unspoken resentment and hatred for those members of our sex who let us down.

I tighten my arms briefly before I release him, and turn to pick up the bag. "Come on," I say roughly. "You can check out my gaming room."

"Do you have an X-box?" he asks as we leave.

"And a Playstation 4. And practically every game ever made for them both."

"Cool." His eyes light up, and I'm pleased to see the fear and hatred have faded from them.

But the memory stays with me, lighting a fire deep inside that I know is going to be there for a long, long time.

Chapter Eight

Meg

It's not long before the door to my apartment opens, and out walks Oscar, with Stratton only a few feet behind. Oscar scans the road, sees the Lexus, and crosses over. He's carrying his backpack. Stratton has my bag. What's he got in there? Has he been through my stuff?

Oscar approaches the car, and I expect him to get straight into the back, but he shocks me by opening my door. He bends down, meets my eyes, then leans in and puts his arms around me.

"Are you okay?" He moves back. His voice is fierce.

I nod, feeling a surge of emotion at his protectiveness. "I'm fine."

"He didn't touch you?"

I glance at Stratton, who's thrown the bag in the back and slid into his seat. He doesn't look at me, just puts the key in the ignition and starts up the car. He registers no surprise at Oscar's question.

"No." I ruffle Oscar's brown hair, the color of mine beneath the bleach. "Stratton rescued me."

My boy and my boss exchange a glance, and then Oscar nods and moves back. He shuts my door and climbs in behind me. As soon as he's got his seat belt on, Stratton pulls away.

None of us says anything.

What has Stratton said to Oscar? He's obviously mentioned Bruce's appearance at the office. What did Oscar say in return? I wonder if he explained who it was to Stratton, and why I reacted the way I did. I'd told Oscar not to tell him, but neither of us had foreseen this.

Stratton is quiet, with none of his usual light-hearted banter, and I look out at the shops and restaurants flashing past. Misery weighs heavy on me. I can't believe Bruce has found us. How? My parents would never have told him, and nobody else in Christchurch knows.

I've changed my name and my hair color. How has he tracked me down?

I remember how he touched my hair and said *Blonde. I like it*. That would have told Stratton that I haven't always been this color. Jesus, I've been such trouble for him today. Maybe his statement that he was taking me to his place is a ploy to get me to the airport and put me on a plane to Timbuktu. I can't say I'd blame him if he did.

Dully, I realize I'm going to have to start again. Move, get a job, get an apartment, make new friends. I'm going to have to leave my life behind. Reinvent myself one more time, and destroy Meg as well as Maggie. Who will I be next time? Redheaded Madge? Black-haired Marge?

Resentment washes over me. I don't want to start again. But what option do I have?

Stratton's mobile rings, making me jump. He answers it, and Rich's voice comes out of the speakers.

"Strat? Where are you?"

"In the car, and you're on speakerphone."

"Is Meg with you?"

I wonder whether he's calling about the email, or if he found out what happened in the foyer. Probably the latter. Security officers are supposed to type up a report as soon as a situation is resolved, and it would have pinged up on his and Teddi's computers.

"Yeah," Stratton said.

"Is she okay?"

"She's fine. I'm taking her and Oscar to my place. Can I call you later?"

"Sure. Let me know if there's anything I can do."

"Will do." He hangs up.

Humiliation and embarrassment wash over me. I've made such a fool of myself today. I've worked hard to keep my personal and professional lives separate, and the last thing I wanted was to be a burden on the people I work with. Bruce arriving was out of my hands, but that email… I curl up inside again like a poked spider as I think about what I said. He now knows I think about covering him in melted chocolate and licking it off. Oh Jesus. How am I ever going to look him in the eye again?

Stratton heads east through Parnell. We don't talk as he drives. Eventually, he indicates and turns onto his road, then pulls onto the long drive leading to his house, which overlooks Hobson Bay. He opens the double garage with his remote and parks the Lexus next to the BMW Z4 convertible he uses at weekends. We get out, and I glance around nervously. How much has Bruce found out about me? Does he know who Stratton is, where he lives? I'm relieved when Stratton closes the garage door, shutting out the world.

He opens the boot, and I lift out my bag. "Did you pack it?" I ask.

He glances down at it. "I thought you might need a change of clothes. I just grabbed what was on top. I hope that was okay."

My face flushes again as I think of him sliding his hand through my underwear. He's been in my bedroom. If he hadn't guessed already, he'd have seen there was no grown man living with me. He must have gathered by now that I've been lying to him the whole time.

I look down at my left hand. The wedding ring glints in the overhead light. It was my grandmother's, and I treasure it, but the way I've been using it sickens me. All of a sudden, furious and tearful, I want to remove it. I tug it hard—it's quite tight—but manage to slide it off my finger. I glare at it, wanting to throw it away from me as hard as I can, but it will just ping around the garage like a bullet.

Stratton holds out his hand, palm up. I stare at it, then lift my gaze to his. He's not smiling, but his expression is gentle. Swallowing hard, I reach out and place the ring on his palm. He curls his fingers around it and tucks it in the pocket of his trousers. I flex my fingers, my hand feeling light and odd without the ring. Is it my imagination, or have his lips curved up a tiny bit?

He opens the door and steps back to let us precede him.

We go along the corridor and turn into the living room. It's a gorgeous house. It's also very Stratton. The furnishings are rich and dark, oak and mahogany, reds and deep blues and purples. There are more books here—shelves and shelves of them, and another huge desk in the corner, covered with papers and magazines. A large TV is mounted on one wall, and he once told me he lies on the dark-red leather sofa and watches movies late at night here. But I know that if he wants to watch the All Blacks or other sport, or one of the James Bond/Jason Bourne-type movies that he loves, he goes to his playroom.

When he first told me he had a playroom, my eyes nearly fell out of my head as I pictured whips and floggers and scary masks. He'd chuckled at the look on my face. "No," he'd said, "nothing like that." He'd opened the door and shown me the gigantic 105-inch curved TV screen on the wall that I know retails for $150,000 because I looked it up, the range of top-notch consoles beneath it, the walls full of video games and DVDs including a whole wall of boxed sets, the row of La-Z-Boys with drinks holders and speakers in the headrests, and I just laughed. Oscar's going to be in seventh heaven when he sees that.

To my surprise, he has a Christmas tree in the corner. He sees me look at it, and goes over and switches on the lights. It's very neatly decorated, and I wonder whether he did it, or if someone did it for him.

Stratton drops my bag onto the sofa. I sink onto it, suddenly exhausted. I need to think about what I'm going to do, but I'm aware I'm shaking, and I can't get my brain to form a coherent thought.

"Come on," he says, "I'll show you to the spare room. Maybe you'd like to take a shower, or have a rest, whatever. I'll do dinner for seven. Oscar can explore the playroom."

I let him lead us to the guest rooms. Mine is simply furnished with a pale blue duvet and curtains. There's a soft white bathrobe in the otherwise empty built-in wardrobe. Through the open door to the bathroom, I can see a range of small bottles of shampoo and the like. I feel as if I'm in a hotel. Does he organize these rooms, or does someone else come in and do all this? I can't imagine him with a vacuum cleaner and duster, so I'm sure he must have staff to keep it clean.

"All right?" he says softly. His face is full of pity, and I can't bear it. I press my fingers to my lips as emotion washes over me.

He tosses my bag on the bed, walks up, and puts his arms around me. "Shhh, it's all right."

I fold my arms between us as I struggle to regain control. He's so tall—I'm wearing heels and yet my forehead only bumps against his chin.

"It's all right," he says again. "I won't let anything happen to you." He rubs my back. His arms are warm, and his shirt smells of his aftershave and the crisp smell of washed cotton. It's only the second time I've touched him properly other than an accidental brush, and I like being this close to him. I can't remember Bruce ever holding me like this—tenderly, and with affection. It's not sexual, but it's wonderful, and as I relax against Stratton, his arms tighten around me.

I want to stay there forever. I wish I could have met him years ago, before Bruce, before all the trouble started.

But then I wouldn't have Oscar. Whatever's happened, I can't wish away that part of my life.

I know my son is standing there watching us, so I pull back to wipe my face, and Stratton drops his arms. "I'm sorry," I whisper. "I'm okay, really. Just a bit overwhelmed. You're right—I'll have a shower and a rest."

"Okay." He moves back. "Is pasta all right for dinner? Just something light?"

"That would be lovely." I'm surprised he cooks. I thought he ate takeout all the time. "Don't worry," I say to my son, because he looks upset. "It was just a shock, that's all."

Stratton gently guides Oscar out, and then he catches the door handle. "See you later." His eyes meet mine briefly before he closes the door.

I sink slowly onto the bed.

Leaving Christchurch was hard. I'd had a few close friends and many acquaintances, and I had to leave all of them, as well as my parents and sister and all my nieces and nephews behind. I'd quite liked my job and even though my boss was a bit in-your-face, we'd gotten along okay, and it had been a wrench to go. And doing it the way I had—secretly, not telling anyone except my parents—had been the worst thing, because I'd known it would upset many people.

Starting again had been really hard, but somehow this is harder. I try to work out why, and then I realize. This time, I'm happy. I like Auckland. I like working at Katoa, I like the friends I've made—Alyssa, the other secretaries, Rich and Teddi. And Stratton. How could I leave Stratton, even after the humiliating email I sent?

I like this life. In Christchurch, I'd struggled to piece together an existence from the scraps that Bruce left behind, but here I've been able to be me. And I like me. I didn't think I would, but I do. Meg's more confident than Maggie, calmer, funnier. She's the person I always wanted to be but somehow couldn't in Christchurch. Maggie had been a bonsai tree, carefully constrained so she didn't outgrow her boundaries, ugly and dull. Meg's a lilac-colored jacaranda, spreading her branches and scattering petals wherever she wants. She's efficient at work, wears leggings and baggy jumpers at home, eats ice cream from the tub, dyes her hair, and writes crazy poetry from the heart that people seem to enjoy. I like Meg.

And I discover that I don't want to let her go.

Chapter Nine

Stratton

I show Oscar to another spare room in case he wants to rest or have a shower. He's about as interested in it as I would have been at thirteen. Then I take him down to the playroom. His eyes bulge when he walks in.

"Jesus." He stares at the big screen. "That's enormous!"

"Size isn't everything," I say without thinking, but he doesn't hear me—he's too caught up in looking around the room. I watch him stare at the DVDs and games, and for maybe the first time in my life, I think about what it might be like to have a son of my own. Having kids has never appealed to me. I don't find babies cute. Toddlers irritate me. Young children always seem like a pain in the arse. Everyone says it's different when the kid's your own, but I find it difficult to imagine.

From about the age of ten up, though, it's different, especially with boys. I speak their language. Ask them at any given point what they're thinking about, and it's usually either food, gaming, sport, or sex, and I'm fluent in all of those. It would be nice to be able to share the things I like with someone. I have Rich, of course, and other mates, but the notion of being able to pass on my knowledge and wisdom—such as it is—to someone younger who looks up to me is oddly appealing.

Knowing my luck, though, I'd probably end up with a girl. I imagine being stuck with a younger version of Natalie, all makeup and boy bands and sarcasm, and shudder. No thank you.

"You want to choose something to play?" I ask Oscar. "Or watch—anything you like."

"In a minute." He shoves his hands in his pockets. "Can I have a drink first?"

"Of course. Come on."

I take him back out to the kitchen. He hops onto a stool at the breakfast bar, and I open the fridge. "Coke Zero? Juice? Water? Whisky?"

He smiles. "Coke Zero, thanks."

I slide a can over to him. No teenage boy wants a glass and a straw. I remember that heartfelt yearning to be treated as a grownup, and the delight I felt in a restaurant at fourteen when a waitress asked my parents what they wanted to drink and then turned to me and said, "And for you, sir?"

I also get a box of cereal bars out of the cupboard and pass those to him. The 'it'll ruin your dinner' thing is a fallacy where teenage boys are concerned.

"Thanks," he says gratefully. He takes one out and starts eating.

He shows no sign of leaving, so I turn back to the fridge and retrieve some ingredients for dinner. Chicken, I think, and bacon, and a tomato sauce with Penne pasta. "You like olives?"

He shrugs.

Meg likes them. I bring them out. He can always leave them if he doesn't want them.

Munching on the cereal bar, Oscar drags over his bag and extracts his sketchpad. He sits at the end of the bar and continues with a drawing he must have started earlier. It's a cyborg figure, the human limbs interwoven with mechanical parts. I recognize the symbol on its chest from *Dark Robot*, which makes me smile.

He doesn't want to be alone. Touched that he's chosen to stay with me, I begin slicing up the chicken.

As I work, I think about Meg. I'm not sure whether to ask Oscar questions. I don't want her to be angry with him for being disloyal and talking behind her back. Equally, I'd like to talk to her later with some knowledge about their background so I don't put my foot in it.

"Is your real name Oscar?" I ask, deciding to focus on him.

His pencil pauses for a moment, and then continues. "Yeah. But we've changed our surname. It used to be Walters."

"So is Brown your mum's maiden name?"

"No, Walters is her maiden name. Brown is my gran's maiden name."

I stop slicing and raise my eyebrows at him. "So… she's not married to your dad now?" Does that mean they're divorced?

He carefully draws the shoulder of the cyborg. "They never got married."

I study him for a moment, then continue slicing. I wonder why they never married. The time has long gone—in New Zealand anyway—where it's frowned upon to have children out of wedlock, but I guess I'm an old fashioned kind of guy. If I were to get a girl pregnant, and especially if it wasn't an accident and we lived together, I would definitely propose. Especially to a girl as lovely as Meg. Why would Oscar's dad not have asked her to marry him?

I scoop the sliced chicken into a dish and start on the bacon. "It must have been hard, starting at a new school."

"Yeah. It's all right, though. It has its own swimming pool. And two music rooms."

"Do you play an instrument?"

"Yeah, the drums. I had a kit in Christchurch, but I had to leave it there." He surveys his drawing, then starts adding some detail to the cyborg's metal face.

"What kind of bands do you listen to?" I ask him.

We talk about music for a while. I recognize most of the bands he knows, and suggest a few more for him. He's impressed that I went to see the Foo Fighters. "They caused a small earthquake, they were so loud," I tell him.

He grins and finishes off his cereal bar.

"What sort of music does your mum like?" I don't know anything about Meg's likes and dislikes. I feel ashamed that I haven't gotten to know her better over the last four months. I've been wrapped up in my own life, and even though we spend a lot of time talking at work, it's usually about business.

He reels off a few names, no boy bands, I'm relieved to hear, mostly lazy blues or folksy-jazz artists like Jason Mraz, Jack Johnson, and Ben Harper.

"Nice," I say, making a mental note to find some on my phone to play her later.

He starts coloring the cyborg in. "Dad hated her music. She only ever listened to it when he wasn't around."

I bite my tongue to hold back what I really want to say, put the bacon into the dish with the chicken, then start dicing an onion. "What's your dad's name?"

"Bruce. Henderson."

Bruce Henderson. I'll remember that name.

I put the onion in another bowl and started on some mushrooms. "So why do you think he turned up today?" If he didn't marry her, I wonder why he feels he has a claim on her. Of course, he's Oscar's father, but he came to see Meg—he didn't turn up outside Oscar's school and try to whisk him away.

"He told her he'd never let her go. He says he loves her." Oscar pauses, his fingers tightening on the pencil for a moment before he carries on.

"Does she have a protection order against him?"

"No." He bends closer to the paper as he colors. "Did you see his arm?"

"Yes." The metal fingers had closed on my wrist and for a moment I'd wondered whether he had superhuman strength and would be able to snap it in two.

"That's why he left the army," Oscar explains. Then, as if the dam has burst, the words spill out from him. "He used to repair the trucks and tanks. One day, someone didn't leave the handbrake on a truck and it rolled across his wrist. He was embarrassed that he hadn't lost his arm in a bomb blast or something. He loved being a soldier, and he hated it when he came home. He kept saying he was half a man. He wouldn't get a job—he thought he was useless and nobody would want him. All he did was watch TV and drink vodka. He shouted a lot and threw stuff, and he made Mum cry." Oscar's lips thin, and he clenches his jaw.

I retrieve a packet of dry pasta from the cupboard and measure some out, giving him time to compose himself. "How long did this go on for?"

He rubs his nose. "I dunno. A year maybe? Mum tried really hard to help, but he was horrible to her. She tried to get him to see a therapist, but he said real men don't need counselling. He was angry all the time. Then, after he'd yelled and smashed stuff up, he'd cry and tell her he was sorry. I hated it when he did that. I just used to walk out."

He seems relieved to be talking about it. "So it gradually escalated?" He gives me a blank look. "Got worse," I clarify.

"Yeah. She was always very calm. She knew how to handle him most of the time. There was no point in shouting back, or telling him to stop when he had one of his rages. She'd sit him in front of the

TV and get him to watch one of his favorite shows. She'd cook him the food he wanted and try to massage his shoulders, because his arm always hurt. But sometimes it seemed to make him worse. He wanted her to yell back, I think. She told me she made him feel in… um…"

"Inadequate?"

"Yeah. I don't know why."

"She's very competent, your mother." I pour boiling water over the pasta and place it on the hob. "She would have learned to cope on her own while he was away. Maybe he felt she didn't need him anymore."

"Yeah, I guess. He started accusing her of seeing other guys. She didn't of course, she would never have done that."

"And that made him angry," I say.

"Yeah. One day he saw her talking to the husband of one of Mum's old friends in the garden. He'd been drinking all day. He hit the guy and dragged her inside. Yelling, accusing. Mum told me to go to my grandparents' place, but I didn't want to leave her. I begged her to come with me but she said they had to get things sorted. They argued, and she lost her temper. It's the only time I've ever seen her shout. She… she yelled at him, said he was letting himself down, and letting me down. And then…" He falls silent. His face is white.

"You don't have to tell me," I whisper.

But Oscar shakes his head, obviously wanting to talk. "He's never hit her before, so she wasn't expecting it. It wasn't a punch—it was more like he pushed her, but she stumbled and fell onto the coffee table. She cried out, and I knew she was hurt." His lip trembles, but he lifts his chin, determined not to cry. "Dad just stared at her. I helped her up. She got her handbag, held my hand, and led me to the door. Dad ran after us then, crying and begging her not to go. He kept saying he was sorry. But she just got in the car with me, locked the doors, and drove away."

"Where did you go?" I lean on the breakfast bar, the dinner forgotten.

"To Nan and Grandad's. Dad followed us in his car, but Grandad refused to let him in and threatened to ring the police, and eventually he went away. Grandad took her to hospital then. She'd broken a rib, and she had bruises for weeks." He takes a deep shaky breath.

I stare at the work surface for a long moment.

"Don't say anything to her." Oscar's voice is little more than a whisper. "She doesn't want you to know."

"I won't." I'm glad he's told me, glad to have the knowledge so I can help her, but I hate what she's been through. What they've both been through.

"What happened then?" I ask. "Did you leave straight away?"

"No. We lived with Nan and Grandad for a few months. But Dad kept coming around. He wanted us to move back with him. Mum tried to tell him it was over, but he refused to accept it. She was really unhappy. She didn't go out anymore—she didn't even like going to the supermarket in case she saw him. Her friends stopped calling, as if they didn't want to know her after what had happened." His face is puzzled, hurt. "I think some people blamed her. I remember one of her friends saying that she didn't understand what he was going through, and that she should be more patient with him."

I shake my head and give a humorless laugh. "Jesus."

"Yeah. It wasn't long afterward that she started talking about leaving. At first I didn't want to go—I liked my school, and was… you know…" He's embarrassed to admit it. "Scared about leaving. But I wanted her to be happy. And I'm glad we did now. She likes it here. She's a different person."

"Blonde," I say, and smile.

He grins. "She says that now if she does something ditzy she can use the excuse that she's blonde."

I laugh. "I can't imagine her dark."

"She's better blonde. It's as if the color makes her happy. She smiles all the time now, although I think that's because she's working with you." He stops suddenly, obviously afraid he's said too much.

My lips curve up. "When you see her, ask her about the email she sent today."

"Why? What did it say?"

"I'd better let her tell you." I push off the bar and turn to the hob. The pasta's bubbling merrily, so I heat some oil in the wok and throw in the onion.

Oscar starts talking about *World of Warcraft*, and I tell him what Rich said about the Demon Hunter and ask him his opinion, and soon we're talking about games like two nerdy guys at the local sci-fi convention.

"Mum says the Holy Paladin is good fun," Oscar says.

I stare at him. "Are you telling me your Mum plays WOW?"

"Yeah. She has three top level toons. She's a mean healer. We play together for an hour every evening. She plays *Dark Robot* too, although I always beat her at that."

All these months working together and I didn't know that Meg's a gamer. No wonder we get on so well. I should have guessed. "I wonder why she didn't tell me at her interview."

"She doesn't tell anyone in case they think she's weird. None of her friends has ever played. She calls it her escape hatch. It's how she relaxes. She plays when I go to bed sometimes, although she'd never admit it."

Shaking my head, I add the meat to the veggies and then the sauce, and before long the pasta is ready. I toss it all together, put it in an oven dish, add some grated cheese to the top, and place it in the oven. It'll keep there on low until Meg's ready to eat.

"Wanna play some *Dark Robot?*" I ask.

His eyes light up. "You'll play with me?"

"*Mano a mano*," I say. "Or together against the world—your choice."

"Together," he says immediately.

I smile. "Come on then." We head off to the playroom, and soon we're building robots and blasting aliens like there's no tomorrow.

Inside, though, a fierce, hot fire burns. I wish I'd hit her ex now. I wish I'd smashed his face in with a cricket bat and then jumped up and down on his dying corpse.

As I can't do that, I shoot another few aliens. It's not quite the same, but at least it won't put me behind bars.

Chapter Ten

Meg

I awake with a jump, afraid I've been asleep for hours, but it's still light and the clock only says 6:47 p.m., to my relief. I rise and go into the en suite bathroom, taking my bag with me. It's like a hotel room, pleasant but impersonal, and I can't imagine that Stratton's ever spent any time in here.

I look through my bag and note the things he's put in there. He's thoughtfully included my makeup bag and a couple of bits from my bathroom. I note my contraceptive pills and blush. I pull out the pair of track pants and a T-shirt. Half of me had expected him to pack some of the sexy lingerie I own, but he's chosen plain cotton.

Deciding not to think about him going through my underwear, I take a brief shower, cleansing my face free of any smudged mascara. I dress and pull my hair back into a ponytail. I suppose I should reapply my makeup, but I don't have the energy, and so I leave the room and pad up the corridor in my socks. It might be the height of summer but my feet are always cold.

The living room and kitchen are empty, although there's a lovely smell wafting around. I open the oven to see a pasta dish warming through. Leaving the living room, I walk back through, passing the dining room with its circular table and the huge windows overlooking the large garden, and head through to where I know they'll be.

Sure enough, they're in the playroom, sitting next to each other, both of them having slid halfway down the seat the way guys do, fingers flicking over their controllers, their eyes fixed to the screen. They're laughing, though, and I lean against the doorjamb and listen to them exclaim as they take down the enemy and dodge around the space station. I watch as Stratton lets Oscar's character precede him into the enemy's camp, giving him the chance to play the hero. "Flank left," he says, crouching behind a crate, and the two of them attack a guard in a pincer movement, bringing him down without a sound. Stratton lifts a hand, and Oscar high fives him. It's quite adorable, really.

Stratton glances at the door, and his eyebrows rise. Pleasure sweeps across his features, which gives me a glow inside. He pauses the game and rises. Oscar complains, then sees me and gets up too.

"Hey." Stratton's staring at me, I'm guessing because it's the first time he's seen me in casual clothes and without my hair and makeup done. I tuck a stray strand behind my ear self-consciously, wondering if he's thinking *Jesus Christ!*

He's changed too, though, into a similar outfit, an All Blacks top and black track pants. I've never seen him like this either. He looks completely different, younger, oddly, and the tight rugby top clings to a muscular chest and bulging biceps I hadn't realized lay beneath his cotton shirts. For the first time since I've met him, he has a hint of stubble on his jaw. Wow. I like casual Stratton.

"I'm sorry, I dozed off," I tell them.

"That's okay, I thought you might." Stratton saves their game and flicks off the screen. "Ready for dinner?"

I nod, and he gestures for me to precede him back through to the kitchen.

Oscar slides his arm around me as we walk, and I kiss his hair. "Having a good time?" I ask.

He nods. "That's the coolest room ever."

"It is," I agree as we walk into the kitchen. "Maybe later I'll have to take the two of you on in a match."

Stratton gives me a wry look. "Yes, I heard that you play WOW and Dark Robot."

"I do. And I have to say that gun you were using isn't half as good as the plasma rifle with the telescopic sight."

His lips curve up as he gets out some pasta dishes and lays them on the breakfast bar. "I should have guessed you played. Is there anything you can't do?"

Have a successful relationship, I think, but I just shrug and smile.

He dishes up the pasta, which looks gorgeous, then gestures at a bottle of red wine. I nod thankfully, desperate for some alcohol to numb my panic and embarrassment. He pours us both a glass of wine and Oscar a glass of orange juice, and we sit at the breakfast bar, Oscar and I along the side, Stratton sitting on the end.

"We can use the dining table if you like," he says. "There are great views across the garden."

"I'm good here," I say, and Oscar nods, so we stay.

We start eating, and I'm conscious of a growing silence. Oscar looks guilty, and I suspect the two of them have been talking. No doubt Oscar has given him the background to our situation. I can't blame him, and it's nice that he's able to talk to Stratton. My parents are always there if he needs to talk, but he never does, and although I took him to a therapist, I don't think she helped him much. This is what he needs—a decent guy to talk to. And there are few guys more decent than Stratton.

"What email did you send today?" Oscar asks.

Stratton coughs into his wine. I pause with a forkful of pasta halfway to my mouth. "What?"

Oscar looks at the man sitting next to him, who's trying to hide a smile, unsuccessfully. "He said you sent an email today, but he wouldn't tell me what it was."

I send them both an exasperated look, eat the pasta, and stab my fork into some chicken. "I meant to email Alyssa, but I mistakenly selected All Staff."

"What did it say?"

My eyes meet Stratton's. Highly amused, he sips his wine and raises his eyebrows.

"It was personal," I reply, my cheeks growing warm.

"So personal the whole office block knows," Oscar says. "Mum…"

"I mentioned that I find Stratton attractive and that I wanted to…" My face is burning. "Do things," I finish lamely.

"Oh." Oscar looks at the object of my affection. Stratton widens his eyes and gives him a shrug that says 'What are you gonna do?' and Oscar laughs.

"Yeah, yeah," I grumble, "feel free to mock me."

"At least you can blame it on being blonde," Stratton says.

I meet his gaze again, remembering that Bruce commented on my hair color, so Stratton must be aware that I dye it. "Blondes have more fun," I say. "Allegedly."

His smile is gentle. Again, I wonder what Oscar's told him.

He picks up some olives on his fork and then pauses. "Have you thought about what you want to do tonight? Are you happy staying here?"

I push my plate away. It's lovely, but I'm not hungry, and I've had enough. I sip my wine, which is expensive and rich, warm and smooth. "I'm not sure."

"Would you rather go? I'll take you anywhere you want, or I can call you a cab?"

I wipe up a drip of wine from the bar with my finger. "Would you rather we go? I don't want to… get in the way."

"It's a huge house, Meg, and there's only me here. You won't get in the way. Not only do you work for me, but I consider you my friend, and I'd rather you stay. But it's up to you, of course."

"We'll stay, then." I smile at Oscar, who gives me a thumbs up.

"Cool." Stratton looks relieved. He pushes his own empty plate away. "Do you want me to call anyone else for you? Do you want me to ring the police?"

"No. He hasn't really done anything wrong."

Stratton's eyelids lower to half-mast as if he disagrees with that, but he doesn't say so.

"I just need a bit of time," I say. "To decide what I'm going to do."

Oscar swallows his food and stares at me. "We're not leaving, are we?" He looks panicky. He was so wonderful when we left Christchurch. He's been by my side the whole time, and although it must have been difficult starting a new school at his age, he's worked hard to settle in. Even if I wanted to leave, I couldn't have said so after looking at his face.

My gaze slides to Stratton's. He's not smiling. Suddenly, I know that Oscar's told him everything. Back in Christchurch, I had my parents and my sister, but I had no male friends because Bruce wouldn't let me. The thought that I have Stratton here supporting me gives me the strength to reply.

"No," I say softly. "We're not running away this time."

Stratton's mismatched eyes soften, and he gives a short nod, as if to say *Good*. Oscar blows out a long breath, then finishes off his pasta.

"I thought you might like to watch a movie," Stratton says. "The new Bourne's on Netflix if you fancy it."

"Yeah!" Oscar's eyes light up. "In the playroom?"

"Of course." He gets up and clears away the dishes, rinsing them before placing them in the dishwasher. Then he opens the tall freezer, pulls out a drawer, and beckons Oscar toward him. "What do you fancy?"

Seeing the look on Oscar's face, I have to rise and walk over to look in there with him. It's full of small tubs of ice cream, all different flavors.

"Treats to Tempt You?" I read the name on the lid.

"A chocolate and coffee shop in the Northland," Stratton says. "It also does the best ice cream in New Zealand. I order a batch every few weeks." He raises an eyebrow as I grin. "What? I like ice cream."

I choose one called Christmas Pudding. Oscar has Chocolate Fudge Brownie, and Stratton picks Macadamia Crunch. We collect spoons, and another glass of wine, then head off to the playroom.

Stratton's told me before how he loves gaming and movies because he can escape. I've been a gamer for years, but for the first time tonight I really understand what he means as I lose myself in the movie. I curl up in the La-Z-Boy, eat my ice cream, and sip my wine, letting the action flow over me and not thinking about anything but the thrill of the chase and the exciting storyline.

Oscar sits between us, and he and Stratton chat occasionally, Oscar asking questions about the plot, and Stratton pointing out interesting facts about the hi-tech equipment. For the first time, it occurs to me that a friendship with Stratton will be a good thing for Oscar. I wouldn't expect the guys at Katoa to give Oscar a job just because he's my son, but it's possible that in the future, after he's gone to uni and got his qualifications, they might be open to giving him an internship.

When the movie finishes, it's almost nine-thirty, and Oscar's yawning. We take our glasses and rubbish back to the kitchen, and he spends another thirty minutes or so talking to Stratton about gaming before I finally prod him toward his room. I walk down there with him. It's been a while since I've put him to bed, but I feel in need of a cuddle, and he's happy to reciprocate.

"Thank you for being there," I whisper as I hug him.

"Are you okay?" He looks at me earnestly.

"I'm fine." I cup his face and kiss his forehead.

He clears his throat. "Are you going to talk to Stratton now?"

"Probably." A tingle runs down my spine at the thought of being alone with him.

"I... um... had a chat to him earlier, and... um..."

"It's all right." I kiss him again. "I know you've told him."

"I couldn't help it," he says, somewhat desperately. "It just came out."

"It doesn't matter. I'm sure he guessed most of it after what happened today anyway."

He rubs his nose. "Did you really send that email to everyone?"

"Yep. The whole office block."

"Saying that you fancied Stratton?"

"Yep."

"Jeez."

"Yeah."

"What did he say?"

"You know Stratton. He was very polite about it while secretly feeling quite smug and amused."

Oscar laughs. "He likes you."

I turn down his bed. "You think so?"

"Mmm. Hey, Mum?"

I straighten. "Yes?"

"You know that I don't mind if you... you know... hook up with someone. A guy. Right?"

I stare at him, startled. "Jeez."

"I'm just saying. I like Stratton. He's nice. I like the way he hugged you."

My face warms. "Me too. But I don't know if he thinks about me... like that."

"I think he does. He's always looking at your legs when you're not looking. Or your butt."

"Oh." I can't believe I'm talking to my son about this. "Well anyway, maybe you should go to bed."

"Yeah." He scrambles beneath the covers. "Night."

"Night, sweetheart." I turn off the big light. I know he'll be on his phone flicking through gaming websites for the next half an hour or so before he crashes out. With a smile, I think that Stratton probably does the same before he goes to sleep.

I close his door and walk back to the kitchen.

I hear music playing, and I'm surprised when I recognize the song as John Mayer's *Gravity*, one of my favorites.

"Oscar," I say to Stratton, who's in the process of checking his emails on a laptop while a machine prepares steaming hot coffee in the corner.

He grins and closes the laptop. "Yeah."

"Did he tell you everything about me while I was asleep?"

"All your secrets." He smiles.

I wonder if that's true, and how far Oscar went with his confessions. Stratton's not always an easy man to read. Sometimes, like now, I think I can guess his mood, but I don't know him well enough to know if I'm right. I sense an underlying fury simmering away—not toward me, but toward Bruce, no doubt. Stratton's not going to voice it, though. As my boss, he has no right to act as my protector, and he knows it, but that doesn't stop him wanting to go *Dark Robot* on my ex's ass. It makes me smile.

He gestures at the machine. "Coffee? Or another glass of wine?"

"Coffee, please." The two glasses of wine have relaxed me, but it's only ten, and I don't want to be asleep by ten fifteen.

I tap his laptop as I perch on the stool. "Do you have work to do? Don't let me stop you if you're busy."

"No, it's okay. I just emailed Rich and Teddi to let them know you're all right. They're worried." He glances at me, then goes back to preparing the coffee.

I feel a rush of emotion at the thought of these people feeling concern for me, and have to swallow hard to contain it. "Did they joke about the email?" I ask in a small voice.

"Didn't even mention it." He brings the mugs over.

I look into the milky coffee and take a deep shaky breath.

"Come and sit down," Stratton says gently.

"Okay." I follow him into the living room. He sits in one of the armchairs, and I curl up on the sofa, just across from him.

Mayer's voice washes over me like Aloe vera, and I exhale, letting the tension ebb away. The coffee's hot and with a touch of caramel—how did he know I like a caramel shot in mine? The sun's set, although the sky is still touched with pinks and purples to the west, but he's switched on a couple of lamps that give the room a warm glow, and the Christmas lights sparkle on the tree.

"So," he says, and sips his coffee. "I have a question to ask you."

I wonder what it will be. *Why did you stay with Bruce so long?* Or *How could you let a man treat you like that?* My throat tightens, some of the tension returning. "Okay."

His blue and green eyes meet mine, and I watch the corners of his mouth curve up. "Will you marry me?"

Chapter Eleven

Stratton

Meg's jaw drops, and she stares at me for a full ten seconds before she says, ever so politely, "Pardon?"

I chuckle. "I should clarify. I mean fake marry. I think you should be my fake fiancée for Christmas."

She closes her jaw and, now she understands, gives me a wry look. "I see. And why has this idea sprung into your head?"

"It makes perfect sense. From my point of view, Natalie knows we work together. It's feasible that a relationship could have developed between us that we would want to keep secret from everyone. It makes much more sense than some random chick turning up."

"I suppose. And from my point of view?"

I shrug. "You tell Bruce you're marrying me. That should shut him up."

She stares at me. "You're serious."

"I'm perfectly serious. We're in the same position, Meg. You still want me to call you Meg? Or would you rather go back to Maggie?"

Her gaze drops to her coffee again. "Meg. I left Maggie behind. She was weak."

"She doesn't sound weak. She sounds like a very loyal woman who worked incredibly hard to make her relationship work, and who finally reached the end of her tether and decided it was time to move on."

She stares into her coffee. I watch her bottom lip tremble.

"Aw." I put my mug on the coffee table. "I'm sorry. I've said the wrong thing."

"No." She puts her mug down too and leans forward, resting her elbows on her knees and her face in her hands. "That was very much the right thing to say." She starts crying.

Thinking that it doesn't look like the right thing, I rise and sit beside her, lean back, and pull her gently toward me. She resists for a moment, but I try again, and finally she turns and curls up to me, burying her face in my chest. I put one arm around her and rub her back, murmuring things like "It'll be okay."

For a while she sniffles and snuffles, and I rest my head on the back of the sofa and look out at the last threads of copper weaving through the darkening sky.

It's strange to have another woman in my arms. She's bigger than Natalie, who has a girlish figure, fine boned, slim to the point of being skinny, with small breasts and narrow hips. I was always worried I was going to break her. Meg's hardly fat, but she's tall and goes in and out in all the right places, with generous breasts and wide hips. I know she's given birth and she's not likely to have Natalie's flat stomach, but it doesn't bother me. I like that she's a woman, not a girl. Natalie might have had a few tricks up her sleeve in the bedroom, but, in spite of being a mother, and being very competent in the workplace, Meg has an innocence about her that appeals to me. In my twenties, I was looking for sex. Now… well, I'm still looking for sex, but also something more. I'm not quite sure what, but I have a strange feeling that Meg will help me work out what it is.

She fishes in the pocket of her track pants for a tissue and pushes herself upright without pulling away from me, so I leave my arm around her, and she doesn't complain. She blows her nose, keeping her gaze averted, and wipes beneath her eyes. She has no makeup on that I can see. I'm hardly an expert on these matters, but I'd grown used to watching Natalie apply her face in the mornings when I stayed over at her place. Foundation, powder, blush, eyeliner, eyebrow pencil, eyeshadow, mascara… The whole process used to take her thirty minutes to an hour of blotting and smudging and reapplying. I once told her she was gilding the lily, and she just rolled her eyes. She didn't have a clue what I meant.

Meg normally wears some, I'm sure—she usually has attractive dark pink lips that makes me want to kiss them. But tonight her skin is clear, her lips a light, natural pink. Her eyebrows and lashes are dark brown, and I wonder if that's her natural hair color. Her big blue eyes meet mine, and although they're red-rimmed, they're still beautiful.

She swallows hard and lifts her chin, intent on regaining her dignity. I melt a little inside. I love that blend of vulnerability and determination. She's so... womanly.

"I'm sorry," she whispers. "To do this to you."

"I don't mind." It's the truth. Ordinarily, I'm not one for crying women. Natalie wept and wailed theatrically and refused to be consoled until I exclaimed in exasperation, at which point she just sobbed even more. I like Meg's calm, quiet sorrow. I can deal with that.

"Still," she says, "it's not fair."

I just shrug.

She brings her feet up onto the edge of the sofa and wraps her arms around her knees. I'm not hugging her now, but my arm is still along the back, and she's flush to me, taking comfort, I think, from being near.

"We're oddly similar," I say. "Both caught in relationships we can't seem to end."

"I guess. Do you think we're too soft?"

"Maybe. It's more difficult to break off a relationship when you still have feelings for the person."

"You still have feelings for Natalie?"

I inhale deeply, then blow the breath out. "I was with her a long time. She drove me crazy in many ways, but I was in it for the long haul—at first. Breaking up was hard. It wasn't like either of us did something wrong—there weren't months of arguments or anything. There was just sadness and incompatibility. She couldn't understand why I wouldn't give her the one thing she wanted more than anything. She said if I loved her, I'd do anything for her, and maybe she was right."

"That works both ways, Stratton. She should at least have understood why you don't want kids."

"I suppose. Society leads men to believe that it's our duty to make women happy. There aren't many people who sympathize with my plight. Everyone thinks I'm being too harsh, and that it was unfair to tell my partner that I wouldn't have a child with her, even though there was a risk of blindness. Even Teddi thinks I did the wrong thing, although I know she doesn't like Natalie."

Meg shrugs. "That's sisters for you. And I would think she's going to have a different view of being blind to the rest of us. I don't want to put words in her mouth, and obviously you know her better than me, but I would think she wouldn't see it as the curse that sighted people see it. I presume that if you suffered from that kind of condition, you'd have to train yourself not to think of it as a disability, or to use it as an excuse for not doing things, or you wouldn't be able to get out of bed in the morning."

I tuck a strand of hair that's escaped from her ponytail behind her ear. "You're very perceptive and thoughtful. I like that." She's so different to Natalie, who didn't have the ability to put herself in someone else's skin and feel what they were feeling. There's a phrase in *To Kill A Mockingbird* where Atticus says that you never understand a person until you stand in his shoes and walk around in them. Natalie would never stand in someone else's shoes unless they were Manolo Blahniks.

Meg tips her head as if she's about to press her cheek to my hand, but catches herself and stops.

The song changes, and it's Bic Runga's *She Left on a Monday*, moody and sad, and Meg's face reflects this.

"Do you still love Bruce?" I ask.

She leans back, her head resting on my arm, and stares up at the ceiling. "No. I did. There was something magnetic about him when he was young—he had some kind of hold over me. When he was away, I'd sometimes think about leaving him, but whenever he came back it was like he was the sun and he just put everything else in shadow. But I stopped loving him a long time ago. I stayed with him out of duty, because that's what I thought a good person should do. I felt sorry for him when he lost his arm, and I tried hard to be understanding and supportive. I know it took away his feelings of self-worth. I would have stayed with him and helped him through it. I didn't expect it to be immediate. I could have coped with his indifference, his moodiness. But I couldn't cope with his outright anger and even hatred of me."

"I'm sure he didn't hate you," I say, but I'm not sure I believe that.

"Maybe not." Her eyes are distant. "But he certainly didn't love me. He said he did, but how he acted… that's not what you do when you love someone. Love should be tender, affectionate, caring, supportive. All I ever felt from him at the end was jealousy and resentment."

"Why didn't he ask you to marry him?"

Her expression turns wry. "He did. I was the one who said no. I didn't want to be an army wife. I didn't want Oscar to have to move from school to school, country to country. If we weren't married, they wouldn't give us married quarters, so I kept telling him I wasn't ready. It gave me an excuse to stay in New Zealand."

"You don't think that looking for an excuse not to be with him was a sign that something wasn't right?"

"I guess. It's not as black and white as that, though."

I want to move the subject away from feelings, because her eyes are glassing over again, and I can feel that she doesn't want to relive it. "So what happened after…"

"After he put me in hospital?" Her eyes meet mine for a long moment. I wonder if she's waiting for any sign of shock, and seeing none there confirms to her that Oscar did tell me everything. She looks down at her hands. "He wouldn't leave me alone. He hung around Oscar's school and pestered him when he came out. It was so hard for Oscar. In spite of what happened, I didn't want to come between him and his dad, and I told him that if he wanted to see his dad, I wouldn't stop him, but Oscar's stood by my side through all of this. He refused to talk to his father and would just walk away."

"Did you ever consider a protection order?"

"Yes." She sighs. "I told him I'd get one if he didn't leave Oscar alone, and he stopped bothering him at school. But you're right, it is like you and Natalie. I loved him—once. And I pitied him. He'd been through hell. He'd seen mates get blown up and killed. He was in a lot of pain, physically and emotionally, and he was on high doses of painkillers. An injury like that is going to affect a man's self-worth, especially a soldier's, because they rely on physical strength and fitness. What happened that night when he pushed me—it was unforgivable, but it was an accident. He didn't mean to hurt me. I didn't want to punish him for it. I just wanted him to leave me alone."

I say nothing, although I don't agree with her. There's no excuse for a man striking a woman, no matter what he's been through. Nobody's perfect, and everyone has faults and weaknesses, but I have zero respect for any guy who loses his temper and takes it out on a woman. Natalie drove me insane at times, but when I'd had enough, I walked away. That's what I did at the end. Just walked away. Maybe it would have been easier for her to accept it was over if I had struck out at her, but the thought makes my blood cold run cold. I don't care what they say about all men being inherently violent and potential rapists, that's bollocks. That's not me—I won't let it be me. But I suppose not every man has my self-control.

Meg gives me a small smile. "You don't agree."

"No. But I respect your right to your opinion."

She chuckles, then sighs. "I don't suppose I could have another glass of wine?"

"Of course. I'll get us both one."

A little reluctantly, I lift my arm from around her shoulder, go into the kitchen, and pour us a glass. When I come back, she's curled into the corner of the sofa—an unspoken signal that our intimate moment is over. Surprised at the disappointment I feel, I give her the glass and sit on the other end of the sofa, but I'm rewarded when she turns and stretches out along it, tucking her feet under my thigh.

"Are your feet cold?" I ask. "You're wearing socks and it's seventy-five degrees in here."

"My feet are always cold. I can be wearing a bikini and still have socks on." She purses her lips as I raise my eyebrows. "Scratch that. It's not the kind of thing I should be telling my future husband."

My lips curve up. "So what do you think about my proposal?"

She sips her wine. "I think I need a few more details first."

I slip down in the seat a little, stretch out my legs, and rest one hand on her ankles. Her eyes meet mine. There's a flicker of humor in them.

"It would be a business arrangement," I say. "You and Oscar would stay here. You'd come with me to the ball in Wellington, and you'd pretend to be my fiancée. That's it."

"And afterward?"

I shrug. "We'll call it off. But hopefully by then both Natalie and Bruce will have gotten the idea that our relationships with them are over, and that we've moved on."

It sounds perfect to me. I can't imagine why she wouldn't be interested.

She sips her wine again. "The part about pretending to be your fiancée…"

"Yeah?"

"What would this involve, exactly?"

I swirl the Merlot around in my glass.

Stay in my room, I want to say. *Sleep in my bed. Let me make love to you every night until Christmas Eve, and let's see at the end whether we still want to call it off.*

But am I brave enough to say the words?

Chapter Twelve

Meg

Stratton sips his wine. The song's changed to an artist I don't know, some guy with a husky, breathy voice singing about seducing his lady, and it sends shivers down my spine.

I'm having trouble reading Stratton at the moment. His look has turned sultry, but I'm not sure if it's just the wine and the warm evening that's making his eyelids slip to half-mast.

I feel all mixed up and confused. I don't know what I want. Well, I do, but my desires mix with my common sense. I'm not sure what's going to win. *Coulda, shoulda, woulda, Meg.* I note that I'm finally calling myself Meg in my head. Perhaps I've truly become that woman I'd always hoped I would be—confident, sexy, not afraid to confront and explore her own sexuality.

Then I remind myself that I'm still Maggie inside. It deflates me like a balloon.

I try to turn my thoughts away from sex. This isn't personal. Stratton's my boss, and even though his idea of us pretending to be engaged sounds like a ridiculous one, a tiny part of me realizes that it's possible it might work.

He's still not saying anything, so, as usual, I resort to humor. "Do you want a list of what I offer? I have a leaflet."

That makes him laugh. He tips back his head and laughs from his chest, big, hearty chuckles that make me laugh too. When he drops his head again, he's smiling, and jeez, he has such a sexy, naughty smile—he has straight white teeth with canines slightly longer than the others, making him look a bit like a vampire, or a tiger. I imagine him leaning forward and pressing those teeth against my neck. I'd let my head fall to one side so I could feel the scrape of them, followed by his warm tongue over my skin.

I blink. His look has turned a tad wry.

MY CHRISTMAS FIANCÉ

"What?" I say.

He shakes his head and takes another mouthful of wine.

It comes to me then. "You're thinking about the melted chocolate, aren't you?"

He chuckles. "It crossed my mind."

We survey each other for a while, and I guess his thoughts are going down the same route as mine. He leans an elbow on the arm of the sofa and rests his head on his hand, still watching me.

I think back to when he caught up with me in the foyer. It didn't register at the time, but now I'm calmer, I recall his words.

"In the foyer, you said 'Did you think I didn't know how you feel?'" I flex my toes beneath his thigh. He's warm and solid, grounding my swirling emotions. "How did you know?"

His hand still rests on my ankles, and he tightens it, squeezing my feet. "I wasn't certain. I did think you were married, after all."

"But you suspected?"

"Mmm."

"You're not going to elaborate?"

"I'm not great at explaining myself."

I change tack. "You still haven't answered my question. I'd like to know what acting as your fiancée would involve."

"You wrote the email to the agency. You know what I'm looking for."

"Yeah, but it's a bit different knowing I might be the one actually doing it."

"I want to get Natalie off my back. So I want someone to pretend we're an item. That means living here, staying with me when we go away, acting as if we're…" He searches for a word. "Compatible," he settles for.

"Compatible?"

He shrugs.

"Stratton…"

"I want us to look like an item. How much clearer do I have to make it?"

"A few more sentences should do it."

"Okay. When we're in public, we need to act like we're in love. That's all."

I think about what that entails. Looking up into his eyes as if I'm crazy about him... Hanging on his every word... I pretty much do all of that already.

"And in private?" I ask.

He tips his head to the side and just looks at me.

"I'm just clarifying," I say.

"You'd have your own room here," he says softly.

"And when we're in the hotel?"

"I'll take the couch."

He's not going to bite—literally or metaphorically—and suddenly I wonder if I've read him wrong. Maybe he is just being a good, kind boss, and he's not interested in me in that way. It was me who sent the email, after all, not the other way around.

"Hey." He rubs my feet. "What is it? Your eyes are like the sky—it's so easy to see your moods pass across them like clouds."

I give a little shake of my head, feeling emotional again. I'm being stupid thinking there could be anything between Stratton and me. But I want him so badly. He holds my gaze, and I'm unable to hide the longing that sweeps through me. I know it's not just physical, and that it's probably something to do with what happened with Bruce. I'm looking for comfort, for solace, and it would be stupid to have a fling with him. Do I really want to lose my job? Of course I don't. But I want him. I really, really want him.

"Meg," he says gently, "I'm offering a business deal. It doesn't have to be anything more than that. You work for me, and I enjoy having you as my PA, and I don't want to lose you. But you should know that when you look at me like that, I have to fight with every bone in my body not to lift you onto my lap and kiss you senseless."

I stare at him. My heart seems to stop, then bangs painfully against my ribs. He doesn't look embarrassed or regretful at what he's said. He means it.

Holy moly.

"I..." My voice comes out as a croak. I swallow and try again. "That's... um... nice to know. But... um..." My face is burning. "I don't think you'd... um... find me very..."

He raises his eyebrows.

"Interesting," I say, rather lamely.

His lips curve up. "I beg to differ."

"I mean it. You're used to Nympho Natalie, and I'm sure she swung from the chandeliers and used... things."

He's smiling now, possibly at my nickname for his girlfriend, although maybe at my choice of words. "Things?"

"You know. Toys and stuff."

"I can swear to you that I'd never let her anywhere near my Lego."

"Stratton!" It comes to me that I probably shouldn't have any more to drink, because my mouth won't stop moving. "I mean bedroom toys. Like... um..." I say the first thing that comes into my head. "Whips."

Now he's most amused. "Meg, I don't know what kind of idea you have about me, but I'm not kinky." His gaze slips down me, soft and sensual as a feather, and he sips his wine. "Not much."

I shiver, my mind whirling. "Not much? What does that mean? You see, I have no idea. Just because I have a child doesn't mean I'm experienced."

"Well you've been with Bruce for at least thirteen years, surely?"

"Yeah, but..." I don't know how to phrase it. "He wasn't very..."

I don't need to finish the sentence. I can see that Stratton's guessed.

Bruce wasn't all bad. We were both nineteen when we met, and he was like any young bloke, I suspect—randy and desperate for sex as often as he could get it. He'd only had a couple of girlfriends before me, and I'd only been with one other guy, so neither of us was particularly experienced. Sex was okay. With him it was all about the destination, and, as he could achieve that quite easily, he wasn't into foreplay. He had no interest in spending a whole evening gazing into my eyes before rubbing me gently with oil and taking hours to tease me to ecstasy. If I had an orgasm, it was more by luck than planning. Later, after his accident, his self-image was shot so much that if we did attempt it, he sometimes had trouble achieving an erection. I did my best to be patient. But when a man not only has trouble making love but for some reason seems to blame you for it, it kind of kills any passion that exists between you.

"So I'm very dull," I conclude. "Not of interest to you at all. I'm nothing like Natalie."

He scratches his cheek, and I hear the unusual rasp of stubble. "You're assuming that a man always wants the same meal two nights in a row."

I think about that while Stratton studies me, amusement in his eyes.

Something seems to be settling in the air around us. It's nearly Christmas, and the tinsel on the tree sparkles in the light from the lamps, lending a magical glitter to the evening.

My panic and tension is gradually fading. I'm enjoying talking like this with him. It's intimate and sexy and a little naughty—a bit like Stratton himself—but not too dangerous, not yet. I'm not leading him on, I don't think. In fact, he seems to be enjoying it too. It's like we're new partners on the dance floor, gradually learning how the other moves. I've never done this before, not really, not since I was a teen anyway, flirting with the guys at school, and back then I was even more innocent than I am now, which is saying something. It's a different experience, doing it as a grown up. The promise of this developing into something is exciting—I feel as if it's Christmas Eve and I can see the presents glittering under the tree.

"You don't mind me talking like this?" I want to check in case I'm making him uncomfortable. He is my boss, after all.

"I love you talking like this. It's fun and sexy, and I've wanted you since the first moment I laid eyes on you and you admitted you locked yourself in the loo. But I need you to understand something." His eyes are suddenly serious. "You've had a rough day, and we've had a few drinks, and I want you to relax and enjoy yourself and forget about that idiot in the foyer. But it doesn't have to mean anything, unless you want it to. Does that make sense?"

"Not really."

"We can flirt, Meg, and talk about sex until the cows come home, and you can take up my offer of pretending to be my fiancée, and live here, and stay in my room at the hotel, and even fool around for a bit. Whatever you want. But there needs to be an understanding between us."

"No commitment," I say, thinking I know where he's going with this. He doesn't want a repeat of the Natalie situation.

He tips his head from side to side. "That wasn't what I was going to say. More no expectations. On either side. Just because you flirt with me, I'm not going to assume we'll end up in bed together. And just because I'm asking you to marry me, I'm not asking you to marry me."

That makes me smile. "All right."

"Cards on the table," he says. "At all times. Okay?"

"You can look at my hand anytime you like."

He laughs. "Okay. So… are you going to take me up on my offer? I'm serious when I say it will benefit us both. I promise not to leave your side while Bruce is around. I'll make sure he doesn't hurt you again."

His eyes are hard. He's such a teddy bear of a man—gentle, funny, sexy—and also geeky in a gorgeous kind of way, that in the past whenever he's joked about punching someone I've had trouble imagining it. And I'm certainly not looking for another violent, envious man. But that's not what's showing in his eyes. That look isn't possessive or jealous. He's not trying to stake a claim or mark his territory the way a dog pees around his kennel. He likes me. He feels affection for me. I'm his employee and his friend, and the look in his eyes is protective. He wants to look after me and make sure nobody hurts me. And that makes me want to cry all over again.

I already know I'm going to take him up on his offer. I want to be around this man, and even if it doesn't lead to anything, I'm looking forward to spending time with him, getting to know him socially. I want more evenings like this one, cooking dinner together, watching TV, drinking wine, listening to music, talking. I want to share my life with someone—even for a little while—who's not going to make demands on me, who's going to be gentle and kind, who'll listen to my point of view and laugh at my jokes, who'll respect me and not think I'm put on this Earth to make his life easier.

And if it leads to something more? I study his mismatched eyes. The hard look has vanished, to be replaced by something softer, sexier. He knows I'm thinking about going to bed with him.

I'm not stupid—I've seen movies and read books, and I know that my love life with Bruce left a lot to be desired. I can't be sure that Stratton is any better, but I'd bet every cent I own that he is. He's a sensual guy—he smells nice, he likes silk ties and expensive suits, he loves ice cream and quality food. He's going to enjoy lovemaking, and something tells me that when he takes a girl to bed, it's not all over in minutes.

I want him. Badly. But I'm not going to tell him yet. I decide that I want to play a bit longer.

"So," I say, settling down a little on the sofa, sliding my feet further beneath his solid thigh. "You're only a little bit kinky. Tell me more about that."

Chapter Thirteen

Stratton

"I'm going to have a whisky." I get up and go over to the drinks cabinet, take out a heavy-bottomed glass, and gesture to Meg.

She nods. "Yes, please."

Meg's tipsy, and she probably shouldn't have any more to drink, but she's had a hell of a day, and if there was ever a time to get drunk, it's after your mad ex shows up. I speak from experience. Besides which, she's safe with me. We're having fun, but I won't let anything else happen. I just want her to relax and enjoy herself, and it seems to be working.

I pour us both a generous measure of a superb seventeen-year-old Caol Ila, add ice, and return to the couch. After I've sat, Meg tucks her feet under my thigh again. I like the connection, and find it sexy and oddly comforting too. Natalie and I rarely played the old married couple like this. If she ever stayed over, which was unusual, we'd have dinner, go to bed, and then I'd end up working while she watched reality TV shows.

"I'm waiting," Meg says, and sips the whisky. I wait for her to shudder and exclaim with horror, but she murmurs her approval, so she must be used to the smoky finish of an Islay malt. This one has strong toffee notes with allspice and a touch of anise—one of my favorites. It strikes me that Meg's like a good Scotch—I have a feeling she's improved with age, and I bet she tastes really good on the tongue.

It's only when she raises an eyebrow that I realize my chuckle wasn't silent. "Sorry. I was comparing you in my head to a good Scotch."

She grins. "I'd rather be compared to Scotch than cheese."

I smile, knowing she's picked up on the metaphor of improving with age. I like the fact that she's almost the same age as me. Most of my mates despaired when they turned thirty, thinking their youth was behind them, but I wasn't one of them. I like being thirty-four. Old enough to know what you're doing, young enough to enjoy it.

"Come on then," she says mischievously. "Define mildly kinky."

She wants to play, and I'm fine with that. I won't be the one who gets embarrassed.

I consider her for a moment, pondering on what she said about her ex. It doesn't surprise me that the idiot was bad in bed. I wonder whether he ever gave her a decent orgasm. If he did, it was probably by mistake.

Thinking about Meg and orgasms in the same sentence is probably a bad idea. Now I'm thinking about how she'd look with her eyelids fluttering shut, her head tipped back, her bottom lip caught between her teeth as she murmurs with pleasure. I can imagine how it would feel to slide inside her, to feel her tense around me until she can't hold it in anymore and comes hard with short, fast gasps. Mmm. I like that fantasy.

She blushes. "Jeez."

"What?"

"You're looking at me like you're thinking about something X-rated."

"I am. Of course I am. You're *sexy as*, Miss Meg. And you've just informed me you're single. My male brain is going to add two and two and make sixty-nine."

She giggles. "That's one definition of your mild kinkiness, is it?"

Aw. If she defines a sixty-nine as being kinky, she really hasn't had much experience.

"Why don't you tell me what you consider kinky?" I suggest.

She snorts. "Anything that isn't missionary." She sips the whisky, swallows, then runs her tongue across her teeth. "Bruce liked me on all fours. That was about the extent of his inventiveness." She meets my eyes, then looks away.

I make a mental note of that comment. As much as the thought of sliding into Meg from behind like that gives me goose bumps, that will be one position that won't be on my list for the foreseeable future.

She's a little embarrassed by her frankness, but I get the feeling she's actually enjoying speaking to someone about sex. I've heard that some women talk openly about their love lives, but I'm sure that isn't the case for everyone. It's the same for guys—when I was young and with my mates, we might have joked about who we'd done and in what position, but once we grew up, sex became a topic rarely discussed. It's oddly refreshing to talk like this. She's taken the cards-on-the-table analogy to heart. I like that she feels able to talk to me.

I slip down a little on the sofa like she has, getting comfortable. I can hold my drink, but I'm starting to feel mellow and a tad reckless, so I know the alcohol's getting to me. *Careful*, I warn myself.

"So," I say, "let's rephrase the question. What would you put on your sex bucket list?"

She laughs. "That sounds a lot more fun than an ordinary one."

"Damn straight."

She sips her whisky. "I'm a bit embarrassed to say. You'll think I'm terribly tame."

"I think you're incredibly sweet. C'mon, tell me. I won't laugh. I want to know."

She studies me as if wondering if I'm telling the truth, and obviously sees sincerity in my eyes, because she rests the rim of the glass against her lips, thinking. "I'd like to take time over lovemaking. That's something we didn't do very often, if at all."

"That's fair. So… you have a whole evening in which you're going to do nothing but spend time with the man you love. What do you do?"

She presses her lips together, considering. "Take a long, hot bath together."

"Nice. I hope you scrub his back."

She chuckles. "Of course. I'd like to… um… wash him all over."

"And can he wash you all over in return?"

She sips her whisky. "If he wants to."

Oh… he does.

Slowly, she runs her tongue around her lips. I don't think she's aware she's doing it, and she's probably collecting drops of whisky, but it makes me shiver. "I'd quite like to make love in the bath," she says. "Or try anyway. You see it in the movies. Is it possible?"

I smile in answer. "Just make sure the dude takes the tap end."

She laughs. "Maybe the shower would be better," she says, warming up. "I bet that would be fun."

"Now we're getting to the good stuff." Meg wet and slippery in my arms. Yeah, that would be fun. "What else?"

"Different positions."

"Well that goes without saying."

"For you it might. But I want to understand what's so good about doing it in other ways. Selfishly, I mean—what's good for me." Her eyes flash. It's a good sign—her spirit's returning.

"What else?" I prompt. She's turning me on, and I want to know more.

"Everything," she says. "I want to try everything. I want to understand what all the fuss is about. I want to try oral properly, and massage and toys."

I wonder what 'oral properly' means. I'd certainly be happy to help her find out.

She looks deep into my eyes. "I want to be with someone who's gentle and who'll help me explore. Does that make sense?"

I melt inside at her sincerity. "Yes."

"I don't know if I'll like everything, but you don't know until you try, do you?"

"That's true."

"Everyone talks about things like… um… vibrators, and role play, and I want to at least try it all before I grow old and die." She speaks vehemently.

I blow out a long breath. I've had a hard-on for about ten minutes now, and it won't go down anytime soon if she carries on like this.

Her lips curve up. "Your face is a picture."

"If you expect me to remain unaffected while you're talking about vibrators, I'm afraid you're going to be disappointed."

Our eyes meet, and our gazes lock.

"Don't you think you'll find me boring?" she whispers.

"No."

"I'm not sure I believe you. You must have done all this before. With…" She doesn't say, but I know she's thinking about Natalie. Damn Teddi for telling her about my ex. I understand why Meg's eyes show a glint of envy, but she doesn't need to be jealous. It doesn't work like that.

I don't release her gaze. "Imagine that I've taken a round-the-world cruise. And then you tell me that you'd like to take one with me. Do you think I'd find it boring to take you to all the cities? To show you the sights, and watch your face as you see everything for the first time?"

MY CHRISTMAS FIANCÉ

She smiles slowly. "I suppose. So tell me. If you were to take your innocent fiancée to the bed for the first time… What would you do with her?"

I'm tempted to slide my hand up her calf, then up her thigh, and then even higher, and explore her with my fingers. I'm sure she wouldn't push me away.

Self-control, Stratton, I scold myself. She's your PA, and she's had a bad day.

Still, there's no harm in a little sexy talk.

I swirl the whisky over the ice. "Maybe we'd start with a shower. I like the idea of getting her naked, having her all wet and slippery and shiny."

Meg leans an elbow on the back of the sofa and rests her head on a hand. Her eyes take on a dreamy look. "Mmm. And then?"

"I'd wash her all over." I'm getting in the swing of it now. "Taking my time to slide my hands over her skin. I'd linger on her breasts, because I'd know that her wet nipples would be super sensitive."

Meg's eyes widen a little, and I think I've shocked her with my openness, but all she says is, "And then?"

I shift on the sofa, trying without being obvious to readjust my growing erection. "While I kissed her, I'd slide my hands down between her legs and arouse her there, until she's swollen and sighing."

Her lips part. "What would you do then?"

I'm hypnotized by her blue eyes, which are glazed with longing, and I can't look away. "I'd drop to my knees, part her legs, and slide my tongue into her folds."

"Oh…" Her eyebrows raise a little and she gives me a helpless look. "I bet she'd like that."

"She would," I say firmly. "She'd bury her hands in my hair and moan out loud while I lick and suck and explore her with my fingers."

"Stratton…"

"I'd tease her right to the edge, and then I'd stand and lift her knee to wrap her leg around me. I'd guide myself underneath her, and she'd be so swollen and slippery that I'd have no trouble entering her. I'd continue to kiss her as I slid inside, moving slowly until I'm right up to the hilt."

She closes her eyes.

"I'd take my time," I murmur, enjoying watching her, knowing I'm arousing her just with my words, which is so fucking hot I'm pretty sure we could both come without even touching. "I'd thrust slowly, touching her breasts, kissing her, until I knew she was close to coming."

"How would you know?" she whispers, opening her eyes a fraction to stare at me through a whisky-induced sexual haze.

"Her breathing would change. It would grow deep and ragged, her cheeks would flush, her eyelids would flutter. She'd whisper my name, and she'd moan every time I brushed against her clit until she'd start to clench around me."

She swallows, breathing fast. Her pupils have dilated so much there's hardly any blue left. "And then?"

"I'd steady myself on the tiles and I'd thrust harder. I'd sweep us both away beneath the hot water, and I'd capture her cries of pleasure with my mouth, and thrust until I came inside her, filling her up…"

I trail off, blinking, somewhat bemused. I hadn't meant to get quite so detailed. But Meg doesn't look as if she's going to complain. She looks as if she's holding her breath. Her eyes are wide, and her lips are parted.

"Is that real or a fantasy?" she whispers.

"It's a real fantasy." It's the truth. I've daydreamed about that scenario, and I would be happy to put it into practice.

"Holy shit," she says, and starts laughing.

I give her a wry look as her husky chuckles erupt. "I'd prefer it if she didn't giggle straight afterward. It can kind of kill the mood."

"I'm sorry." She covers her mouth with a hand, but her eyes are dancing. "It's nervous laughter. Stratton, that was so…"

I raise an eyebrow. I'm all sexed up now and with nobody to take it out on. I give her a somewhat sulky look.

Her lips curve up, and to my surprise she shifts a bit closer on the sofa. "So fucking hot," she whispers.

My heart races. "Meg…" I say in a cautious tone, but I don't move. I want her to touch me more than anything in the world. I want her to slide her hands into my track pants and stroke me to a climax, maybe even take me in her mouth… Jesus. I'm going to need a cold shower after this.

MY CHRISTMAS FIANCÉ

"I know." But she doesn't move back. Her gaze settles on my lips, and doesn't move as she sips her whisky and then licks up the drips. "But will you kiss me?"

I swallow hard. "I don't think that's a good idea."

"Please?"

"Sweetheart, I don't want to do anything you'll regret in the morning. I don't want you to be angry with me."

"Angry?" That surprises her. "I could never be angry with you. It takes two to tango."

"Yeah, but I'm the guy. I need to exercise self-control."

She moves a little closer. "I won't regret it. And I won't be angry."

"You're my employee. You could sue me for sexual harassment."

"Stratton..." Her gaze lifts briefly to my eyes before returning to my lips. "Come on. Don't you want to kiss me?"

This is like the temptation of St. Anthony. I'm only human, for fuck's sake, and I've had three glasses of wine and a glass of whisky.

"Just one," I say.

Her soft pink lips curve up. "Just one," she agrees. "I promise."

Chapter Fourteen

Meg

Stratton's lips curved up a little when I promised it will only be one kiss, but he doesn't move toward me yet.

We survey each other for a moment. The song changes, and I realize it's Marvin Gaye's *Sexual Healing*. Stratton chuckles, and I smile.

God, he's so sexy. My head's still spinning from his description of how he'd make love to me. He's such a strange dichotomy of personality traits. On the one hand he's geeky and boyish and mischievous. I keep expecting him to blush and admit he's never kissed a girl before.

But on the other hand, he's very, very much a man. He talked about his fantasy without batting an eyelid, and his eyes tell me that he's thinking about doing some very naughty things to me. His cheek and jaw have a five o'clock shadow, which brings me out into goose bumps on its own. I'm close enough to him now to smell his aftershave, and I know that when he kisses me he'll taste of whisky and ice cream.

I want to scrape my fingernails along his stubble. I want to slide a hand up under his tight rugby top and see if his abs are as hard and flat as they look. I want to find out if he's all talk, or if he really is as good in bed as he's implying.

I know it won't go that far, though. He's wavering on the kiss, but he won't take me to bed, not tonight. Even though we've drunk too much, we're both old enough and wise enough that we can't pretend we don't know what we're doing, or that we're not aware that actions have consequences. I've been at his side for the past four months, and I know he has high principles and considers himself a man of integrity. He doesn't like the idea of sleeping with his PA, and he certainly won't take me to bed after the kind of day I've had.

But he wants to kiss me.

I take his glass and place it with mine on the table. His arm rests on the back of the sofa, and so I shuffle a little closer to him and curl up by his side. I'm not touching him, not yet, but I'm damn close, and I can feel the heat from his body.

"So, are you going to be my fake fiancée?" he asks, his tone playful.

I rest my gaze on his mouth. "If you kiss me, I'll consider it."

His lips curve up. "Blackmail, Ms. Brown?"

"Encouragement, Mr. Parker," I correct him.

He chuckles. I feel his hand slip into my hair, and he runs a strand of it through my fingers.

"What's your real color?" he murmurs.

"Dark brown." I feel embarrassed to admit it, conscious that I've been lying to him about who I really am.

He doesn't seem annoyed, though. He pulls the strand of hair straight and tugs it gently. "Do the collar and cuffs match?" he teases.

My face heats, but I try to stay sassy. "You'll have to wait to find out."

He smiles and touches the back of his fingers to my cheeks. "How old are you?"

"Thirty-three."

"You blush like a fifteen-year-old."

"And you like teasing me," I say, blushing even more.

"I do. I've not had this effect on a woman before."

And suddenly I realize that's why he likes my semi-innocence. Presumably his previous girlfriends have been very experienced, and the idea of initiating me into the delights of sex appeals to him.

Until that moment, because he hadn't immediately kissed me, I'd begun to wonder whether he felt bashful, or if he was as worried about making a fool of himself as I am. But with some surprise I realize he's neither of those things. He's enjoying the moment, the anticipation. The Christmas Eve sensation. He has more confidence than I thought, and boy, is that sexy.

Sliding his hand to the nape of my neck, he holds me there and finally lowers his lips to mine.

For a long moment, I hold my breath as he kisses me. I don't want to miss one second of this, and although the world's a little hazy around me, blurred by the whisky and the fairy lights on the tree, I feel as if every cell in my body is focused on the point where his lips touch mine.

Gradually, however, I realize that even though I promised it would only be one kiss, he appears to be taking that to mean one kissing session rather than one press of his lips, and he's not stopping anytime soon. I exhale, and he murmurs his approval as my breath whispers across his lips, and he tightens his arm around me, pulling me closer.

Letting him, I raise a hand to his face, and I'm granted one of my wishes as my nails scrape across his stubble. He shivers, and then I feel the tip of his tongue touch my lips, a gentle request to let him in.

Shyly, I open my mouth, and he brushes his tongue inside. He's gentle, tender, as if he's comforting a wounded animal. Knowing I'm in good hands, I finally close my eyes and give myself over to the kiss.

Christmas Eve might hold promise, but Christmas Day always fails to live up to expectations and is never as good as I expect or hope it will be.

This kiss is, though. Oh… it's heavenly. It's been so long since I kissed a man, and I don't remember ever kissing one like this. Bruce was never this gentle or considerate. But Stratton is everything he promised, and everything I've been dreaming of these past four months, as I've lain awake at night, imagining how it would feel to have his lips on mine.

He tips his head to change the angle of our mouths and delves his tongue a little deeper. My nipples tighten in my bra, and my exhale turns into a soft moan as I clench deep inside. Stratton groans in response, a sexy tiger growl, and I slide my hand into his short hair, loving being able to touch him.

The song changes again. It's Joan Armatrading's *Love and Affection*, and her husky, sensual voice sends shivers down my spine. It's the ideal song to drink whisky to on a warm Christmas night, the perfect song to make out to, I think with an exultant inner smile. Stratton seems to think the same, because he slides a hand under my thigh and lifts me, and before I know it I'm sitting astride him, sinking both hands into his hair as he kisses me properly. Wow, that was smoothly done. I like this confident, sure side to my boss.

He fans his hands out across my back, and I wonder whether he's going to slide them under my T-shirt, and if he'll touch my breasts. I want him to—they ache to be warmed by his large hands—but he doesn't. He does stroke my back, though, and he slips one hand to the nape of my neck, holding me there as if afraid I'm going to pull away and end the kiss.

I have no plans to do that any time soon. I'm in seventh heaven. I feel as if someone's given me a huge tub of ice cream topped with melted chocolate and told me it's all mine and I can take as long as I want to eat it. I feel spoiled and decadent and special, being given this opportunity, and I don't want to waste it.

I lift my head a little and cup his face with my hands. His eyes open a fraction to watch me, and his lips curve up when I brush my thumbs across his cheeks, feeling the stubble.

"Very manly," I whisper.

"Very womanly," he counters, his hands skimming down my ribs, dipping into my waist, smoothing over my hips.

He's enjoying this too. It's a revelation to me, that a guy could enjoy kissing without expecting more, without it merely being the amber light before the green to go. He just wants to kiss me tonight. I know he wants to comfort me, and to show me that not all men are like my ex, but I hope there's more to it than that. I hope he desires me.

Almost as if he's reading my mind, he tightens his hands on my hips and pulls me toward him an inch or two. I feel it then—his erection pressing against my mound, long and firm through the soft material of our track pants. I catch my breath, and his eyes meet mine, amused and sultry. This isn't all about comforting me. He's trying to tell me he wants me.

Thrilled, almost tearful with relief, I lift my head half an inch, hovering my lips over his. He lifts to meet them, and I move back another inch, out of his reach. He smiles wryly and rests back, and I kiss his face, touching my lips to his nose, his cheekbones, his eyebrows, his eyelids, his jaw, before kissing back to his mouth, soft light kisses from one corner to the other. He lets me, his lips still curved, but they part when I touch my tongue to them.

This time I kiss him, exploring his mouth, delving my tongue inside. His fingers tighten on my hips, and I think maybe he's fighting with himself not to touch my breasts. He wants to, but he's promised himself he won't, not tonight, and now I begin to wonder if I'm teasing him, leading him on, trying to push him over the edge.

So I lift my head, and this time I wrap my arms around his neck and rest my cheek on his shoulder. He sighs and hugs me, and I love how warm he is, and how safe I feel in his arms.

"Thank you," I mumble.

He chuckles, and I feel him kiss my hair. "Thank *you*." He rubs my back. "Do you feel better now?"

"Mmm." I don't want to move, ever. I think I could sleep like this. But from the photo of him with Natalie I know she can only be around five-feet-four, and she looked as if she weighs as much as one of my thighs. "I don't want to squash you," I say, and start to push myself up.

In answer, Stratton suddenly stands, still holding me, and I squeal and wrap my legs around his waist. He laughs and kisses me again, then slowly lets my legs drop, and I slide down him until my feet reach the ground.

"Light as a feather," he says, linking his hands behind my back.

I rest mine on his chest. "You're full of surprises."

"I hope so. Otherwise life would be very dull."

I look up at him, into his eyes. "When are we getting married then?"

He grins. "Let's set a date for… June?"

"Okay."

"You'll have to give me some background info. I know very little about you."

I nibble my bottom lip. I've purposely not said much about my past, but he's right—if we're going to pretend to be engaged, he needs to know a little about me. I nod, and he smiles and finally—reluctantly, I think—releases me. "Come on."

He takes my hand and leads me through the house, turning off the lights as he goes, down the corridor to the bedrooms. Outside mine, he stops and turns once again to face me. "We'll talk more in the morning, okay?"

I nod.

He studies me for a long moment, maybe arguing with himself, then eventually leans down and presses his lips once more to mine. "Goodnight."

"Night." I go into the room and give him one final look over my shoulder before I shut the door.

Only then do I let myself breathe out. I go into the bathroom, and when I've finished there and changed into the pajamas Stratton thoughtfully packed for me, I climb beneath the duvet and turn on my side.

The curtains are open, and I can see the stars of the Southern Cross glittering like fairy lights on black velvet. Even the sky's getting ready for Christmas. The thought makes me smile.

I have to be careful. Stratton was right—I am vulnerable at the moment, and I could easily fall for him, if I haven't already. But right now, I don't care. I've just had the best evening I've experienced in years. Maybe ever. And all we did was kiss.

I feel that I ought to lie there and think about the consequences of my actions for a while, but the whisky is having an effect, and it's only seconds before I fall asleep.

Chapter Fifteen

Stratton

When Meg comes out the next morning, I'm in the middle of making Oscar breakfast.

I pause in the process of frying eggs and bacon, and glance over my shoulder as she approaches the breakfast bar and greets her son where he sits on a stool, playing a game on his very old and decrepit phone.

She kisses Oscar's forehead, but her gaze meets mine over the top of his head. She looks a little wary, which doesn't surprise me. I was certain that when she awoke, she'd be thinking about what happened last night, because I'd done the same.

As soon as I'd opened my eyes, I'd remembered Meg sitting on my lap. The way she'd cupped my face in her hands and looked at me with such wonder it had made me catch my breath. How her lips had felt when she'd kissed me, and how my blood had fired around my body when she'd slipped her tongue in my mouth.

I'd started by thinking I should regret what had happened, but the thing is… I don't. I wanted to kiss her. She wanted to kiss me. So where's the big problem? She's not married. We're both single. Yeah, she's my employee, but we can work around that.

Meg's gaze locks with mine, and I can almost see her holding her breath as she waits to see how I'll react. Will I look away, embarrassed or angry? Or will I give her a worried smile that shows her I wish it hadn't happened?

I do neither. Instead, I wink at her.

Immediately, her lips curve and her eyes crease in a smile. She lowers her gaze to Oscar, but not before I've seen the relief on her face.

"I was going to ask if you wanted to go for a swim," she says to him, "but I can see that's a stupid question if bacon's in the offing."

"Yep," Oscar says.

I laugh. "I'll save you a sandwich," I tell her.

She hesitates. "Is it okay if I use the pool?"

"Of course. Towels are in the cupboard in the hallway."

She goes out. As she does, I wonder what she's going to wear, as I didn't pack a costume for her. Maybe she won't wear anything. I pause in the process of flipping the bacon, and my eyes glaze over for a moment before I continue.

"Did you and Mum have a nice evening?" Oscar asks.

I prod the bacon with the spatula, and for a brief, horrific second I wonder whether he came out of his room and saw us on the sofa. I glance over my shoulder at him, but his face is neutral—it's a genuine question.

"Yeah, thanks. We had a few glasses of wine and listened to some music." I bring the loaf of bread over to the breakfast bar and start buttering six slices. "I think the day finished better than it started."

"What are we going to do today?" He plays with a fork, examining the tines. "Are you going to take us home?"

I finish the bread and remove the frying pan from the heat. If my mother were here, she'd carefully drain the bacon on some kitchen towel to mop up the excess oil, but she's not, so I place the gleaming, crispy slices on three slices of bread and top them each with an egg.

I'm not sure whether I should discuss this with him. My instinct is that Meg would prefer to be the one to talk it over with him. But she's not here, and it's clear that Oscar feels some connection with me, and trusts me.

"Well…" I put the other slice of bread on top of his sandwich and push it over to him, then do the same to mine and Meg's while he adds some ketchup. I wrap Meg's in foil, then take a seat opposite him. "Your mum told you about my plan, didn't she?"

"To find a fake fiancée?" He laughs and takes a bite of the sandwich. "She doesn't think it would work." Egg drips down his chin. He wipes it off with a dreamy look on his face. "Mmm."

I smile and bite into my own sandwich. Yeah—that hits the spot. "She might have been right if it had been a stranger. But we've come up with a plan. Your mum's going to play the part."

His eyebrows rise. "Oh, I didn't think she'd go for it. I said she should," he explains at my curious look. "She likes you," he adds, taking another bite.

"That certainly helps if we're getting engaged."

He laughs. "So what does it mean? Will we stay here?" His eyes light up.

"Well, we need to speak to your mum about the details." I'm touched by his excitement, but I don't want to overstep the mark and put words in Meg's mouth. "I came up with the plan to try to convince Natalie—my ex—that we're over, but I also thought it would be good for your mum. She might be able to use it to convince your dad it's over, too. I don't know how you feel about that."

I'm sure I can guess, and I discover I'm right when his brow lowers and he takes another bite of sandwich. "I'm fine with that. She'll be safe with both of us looking after her."

I hide a smile at his protectiveness. "That's the plan. So I thought you could stay here. The only problem is that Wednesday night I have to go to Wellington, and I'm hoping your mum would come with me."

"I could stay at Alyssa's," he offers. "I'll probably be going there while mum's at work next week anyway. She's mum's friend. The one she meant to send the email to." He grins.

I laugh. "That was a real blonde moment."

"Yeah. Although she had those even when she wasn't blonde. Don't tell her I said that."

I chuckle and finish my sandwich. Then I pause. "So, Oscar, you don't mind us pretending to be engaged? You're the man in her life now, the most important person to her. You've had a real tough time of it, and I don't want to make things worse for you."

He scoops up some ketchup with his finger. "I don't mind."

I bend my head to catch his eye. "I think we're mates, right? And we both want your mum to be happy. I'd much rather know what you're thinking than try to guess and worry I've got something wrong. So do you promise to be honest with me?"

He nods. "I promise."

"Okay."

"Stratton..."

I stand and carry my plate over to the dishwasher. "Yeah?"

"I don't mind if you and mum... you know."

I turn to stare at him. "If we what?"

He shrugs. "If it's not all fake. That's all. She likes you a lot. I know guys don't always like women who've got kids. I just want you to know that I wouldn't… you know… get in the way, or make a fuss."

"That's very thoughtful," I say softly. "Let's just play it by ear, okay? I like your mum too, but she does work for me, and she's had a tough time. Relationships are hard, and it's best not to go too quickly. You have to try each other on, see if you fit. But Oscar, the fact that she has a son doesn't worry me at all, okay? You're a great kid, and you care about your mum. I like that. You're a bonus, if anything. No guy worth his salt would walk the other way because of you."

He stares at his sandwich and swallows hard. The past few years must have been tough on him too. Seeing his dad angry all the time, and watching him be mean to his mum. I think about Bruce and what he's gone through—the hard life of soldiering, the humiliation of being wounded and feeling less than a man. It doesn't excuse his actions or his attitude toward Meg, but nobody exists in a vacuum, and the guy is only the sum of the experiences he's had over the past few years.

The older I get, the more I realize that it's pure luck whether a couple grows together or apart. People change as they age. Sometimes love deepens and turns into a strong bond that cannot be broken no matter what life throws at them—I've seen this with my parents, who are fortunate enough to have a rock-solid marriage that has never shown any signs of faltering. But for others, the love fades. Meg and Bruce's relationship underwent some pretty heavy trials. It could have brought them together and made them stronger, but unfortunately their relationship decayed, the same way mine and Natalie's did, resentment and bitterness corroding what had once been bright and exciting, the way seawater corrodes a copper pipe. It makes me sad.

"I'm going to take your mum a cup of coffee," I say, because Oscar's struggling not to show any emotion at my compliment, and us dudes don't generally do the comfort hug thing unless it's really bad. "You want to go in the playroom?"

"Can I?"

"Of course. You don't have to ask. Just make sure you don't spend more time on the machines than your mum allows."

He nods and runs off. I smile, put his plate in the dishwasher, and make Meg and myself a cup of coffee.

I take them outside into the bright summer morning. It's in the low sixties and the air feels a tad fresh, but the pool has solar heating, and I know it will be mid-to-high seventies in the water. I cross the deck and descend to the fence, open the gate awkwardly with one hand as I'm carrying the cups, and enter the pool area. Meg's swimming lengths. I put the cups on the table, sit on a lounger, lower my sunglasses, and watch her for a while, sipping my coffee.

It's unusual for a Kiwi not to be able to swim, and, like most Kiwi girls, Meg looks as if she was born in the water. Her strokes are long and confident, and she plows up and down the pool, doing a proper tumble and turn at the end.

After a few minutes she stops for a breather, smoothing her hair back, and I have the pleasure of seeing her face light up when her gaze falls on me. Through the rippling water I can see that she's not naked—it looks as if she's wearing a bra and panties.

"You could have gone skinny dipping," I say, and hold out her cup. "I wouldn't have complained."

She laughs and swim across to take it. "Thank you. And I have to admit, I did consider it. You're not exactly overlooked here, are you?"

I glance around. The house is surrounded by bush on either side, and we have a beautiful view of Hobson Bay to the east. "No, not really."

"It's a gorgeous house, Stratton. You're very lucky."

"I know." I smile. My parents aren't dirt poor, but they're both teachers, so they're not exactly rolling in it. Coming from a relatively modest background does mean that Teddi and I both appreciate what we have.

Meg sips her coffee and puts the cup on the side. "Are you coming in?"

"My mum said I shouldn't swim on a full stomach."

She laughs and twirls in the water. "Do you always do what your mum tells you?"

"Very rarely." The water—and Meg—are too tempting, so I stand, remove my sunglasses, and tug my T-shirt over my head. I'm not wearing swim shorts, but I have boxer-briefs that will do. I toss the T-shirt onto the lounger and slide off my track pants, then walk to the edge of the pool.

It's a glorious morning, and I tip my head back, stretch my arms, and enjoy the sun on my skin for a moment. I'm conscious of excitement building deep inside me, the kind I used to get when I was a kid in December. It could be because Christmas is only just over a week away, but I know that's not all it is. This thing with Meg—it's energizing me, giving me something to look forward to, which hasn't happened in a long time. I look down at her, and see her gaze locked on me, her lips parted as she admires my almost-naked form. I give her a second to drink her fill, wanting to fire her up, so that by the time we make it to the bedroom, she's sure of what she wants.

Then, because I know I'm going to get an erection if she keeps looking at me like that, I lean forward and dive neatly into the pool.

Chapter Sixteen

Meg

Stratton cleaves through the water, surfacing just in front of me. I back up against the edge of the pool, more so I can admire him than because I want to get out of his way. Standing on the tiles before he dived in, he took my breath away. He's a fine figure of a man, tall and toned, and I'm having trouble believing there's a chance the two of us could be a thing. I've never been that lucky.

He swims up beside me, puts one hand on the edge, and runs a hand through his hair. It's gone dark and spiky, and droplets run down his face, making his skin shine. I want to lean close and catch them with my tongue, feel where his pulse beats in his neck.

I don't, though. But I do reach out and run a finger along his jaw, which is smooth again, recently shaved. He glances down, and he obviously knows I'm wearing my bra and panties. He doesn't comment, though. He just smiles and says, "You swim well."

"I was a champion at school. Held the record in most styles. I like swimming. I feel… free."

He pushes away, swimming on his back, and I follow him, doing breaststroke. "That's an interesting word to choose," he says.

"I've felt… claustrophobic for many years." I like the word—it describes exactly how I felt. "I love my parents, but they were quite old when they had me and my sister, and very traditional. They didn't have much money, and there was no expectation for us to go to university or get a career. Mum was a secretary and I followed in her footsteps. All she and my dad wanted for me was the security of a good marriage. I know I disappointed them by not tying the knot with him."

We reach the other end of the pool, and reverse positions, Stratton tipping onto his front, me onto my back, and we begin to swim to the other end again.

"Was Bruce in the army when you met him?"

"Yes. We were both nineteen. He was young, good looking, a bit of a bad boy, but I found that attractive at the time. I got pregnant quickly, after one stupid night when we forgot to use a condom, and that kind of cemented us together, I suppose. We got on well enough, for the first few years anyway. He was away a lot, and that helped. I made my own friends, lived my own life, pretty much. I suppose as we got into our late twenties, I began to realize things weren't going to get any better. I matured and began to want more out of life. I started studying law through a distance learning course and dreamt one day of going to university, but Bruce was very dismissive of that. His life was the army, his mates, and the pub, and he didn't want the sort of partner who made him look and feel inadequate."

My tone is harsher than I mean it to be. Stratton doesn't say anything, but when we reach the other end of the pool, he gestures with his head, and we swim to the side. We rest our arms on the tiles, looking down at the beautiful view of Hobson Bay.

He glances at me. "I think you deserve nothing but admiration for how hard you tried to make your relationship work, considering. Not all women would have been that patient."

"Or that dumb."

"Meg..."

"Sorry, but I do feel it sometimes. I was so miserable. I cried so much. Poor Oscar used to come into my room and climb on the bed, put his arms around me, and say 'Please don't cry, Mummy.' No child should have to watch that."

"I don't know, I think there are worse things than teaching a child that his mum's human and that not all relationships are perfect. I know what you mean, but Oscar won't go into his own relationships with rose-tinted glasses thinking everything's going to be wonderful all the time. He'll realize that both parties have to work at it, and that sometimes it's okay to say this isn't going to work."

Stratton always knows how to make me feel better. I bump shoulders with him, and he smiles.

"I'll have to tell Oscar we're staying," I say, joining up a group of drips on the tiles with a finger.

"Er... I've mentioned it already," Stratton admits. "I hope that's okay. He asked if you were going back home this morning."

"Oh." My face warms as his mismatched eyes survey me. He always looks at me as if he's thinking about me with no clothes on. Maybe he is. I wouldn't put it past him. "What did he say?"

His lips curve up. "He gave me permission to date you."

My face flames. Oscar! "Oh, goodness. I'm sorry."

Stratton just laughs. "It was quite touching, actually. He's worried that you having a teenager will put guys off you, and he wanted me to know he won't get in the way." He chuckles.

Oh, poor Oscar. I've not even come close to dating anyone else since breaking up with Bruce, but my son's getting to that age where he might be starting to think about girls himself, and it's bound to cross his mind that I might want to meet someone one day.

"What did you say?" I whisper.

"I told him that we'll play it by ear, because it takes time to see if two people fit, and it's important to both of us not to rush anything. I'm not assuming anything, but equally I didn't want to discount the possibility because... well, I want you." His eyes bore into mine, and the desire in them makes my heart hammer against my ribs.

Then he smiles, reaches out, and touches the back of his fingers to my hot cheek. "I hope that was okay."

I nod. "Yes," I squeak, turning to jelly at the thought that Stratton wants me.

"Can I suggest something?" he says. "I'm a very up front kind of guy—I think you've probably gathered that after working with me for the last four months. And we did say cards on the table at all times."

"Okay."

"I'm single, you're single, and we're engaged, so things are looking pretty hopeful."

I laugh. "I suppose."

"Things are going to be up and down over the next few weeks. Bruce and Natalie are going to find out about us being engaged, and we'll both have to deal with whatever that brings. It's not going to be easy, I'm sure. The thing is, Meg, I really like you, and I don't want whatever we have—or could have—to get tangled up in the past. It would be the easiest thing in the world to go to bed together tonight, and to make this all about sex. And I can't say I'm not considering it." His lips twist. "But we hardly know each other, not really. I'd like to spend some time getting to know you. So how about we put sex aside for now, and concentrate on just spending time together?"

I can't deny that I feel disappointment at his words. I want him badly, and part of me wants him to say *Fuck everyone else!* and whisk me off to the bedroom where he makes mad, passionate love to me from here until the New Year.

But I know he's right. Oscar's here, for one thing, and even though the sweet boy has given us permission, I can't just sleep in Stratton's room straight off the bat. It wouldn't feel right, and I don't want to give Oscar the impression that it's okay to have casual sex with your boss.

But I get a warm glow inside at the fact that Stratton's suggesting this not because he doesn't want me, but because he thinks there could be more than just sex. He's an astute businessman, and he's thinking about long-term investments, not short-term thrills.

He's smiling now. "You're pouting," he says with amusement.

"No I'm not."

"Yes you are."

"All right I am, but I know you're right that we should take it slow. We don't want to make any stupid mistakes, do we?"

His gaze drops to my mouth, and I get the feeling that part of him doesn't care if we make a mistake—he wants me, and he's finding it difficult to fight his desire. I'm excited and a little bit terrified by that at the same time.

He says, "No, that's right." But his lips curve up, and I hold my breath as he leans forward and touches his lips to mine. It's such a small kiss, hardly X-rated, but it's like an hour before midnight on Christmas Eve—it's the glitter of parcels and a glimpse of Santa's sleigh in the sky. It's the promise of magic, and I'm so excited I want to burst.

*

After our swim, when I've eaten my bacon sandwich and I've dressed and readied myself for the day, Stratton takes Oscar and me back to our house and practically stands guard while we pack some more clothes and whatever else we think we'll need for a week or two away.

I come into the living room to see Stratton looking out of the window, down at the street. "I feel like I have a bodyguard," I say, amused.

He lets the curtain drop and smiles. "You have."

I quite like that idea. I felt very nervous at the thought of coming back to the apartment knowing that Bruce might have discovered where I live. So far, there's no sign of him, but I still breathe a sigh of relief when we leave and head back to Stratton's car.

"I'll have to pick my car up at some stage," I say.

"Maybe after work one day." He doesn't want me to drive on my own, not yet. I know he's really worried about what Bruce might do to me.

I think about that as he drives back through the busy Saturday Auckland streets. Stratton doesn't realize that Bruce doesn't want to hurt me. He wants me back. What happened in Christchurch was an accident. I know he pushed me, but I tripped and fell. It wasn't as if he took a baseball bat to me or anything. He didn't mean to hurt me. I'm not stupid—it doesn't make it right, and I'm not making excuses for him. But I truly don't believe that at heart Bruce is a violent man.

Clearly, though, Stratton's not taking any chances.

I haven't been thinking about where we are, and I'm surprised when Stratton pulls over and parks in the middle of some shops.

"Do you need some groceries?" I ask.

He gives me an amused look, and I remember that he told me he has a housekeeper who gets food for him, as well as keeping the house clean. "No," he says. "We're going shopping."

I stare at him. "For what?"

"For clothes, Meg. I'm guessing you'd like something new to wear to the ball in Wellington?"

My jaw drops, and I study the shop opposite us. Its window shows two long gowns and a variety of accessories. It looks elegant and exclusive and very, very expensive.

My cheeks warm. "Stratton, it's very kind of you, but I couldn't possibly afford to shop somewhere like that."

He gives me an exasperated look. "I told you that the successful candidate would have a clothes budget." He fishes out his wallet. "Come on."

I don't move. He pauses with his hand on the door and studies me. Then he leans back in the seat. "What?"

"You've seen *Pretty Woman*. What does it make me if I take money off you?" Especially if we have sex. I don't say the words because Oscar's in the back, but I can see that Stratton's guessed what I'm thinking.

His gaze flicks to Oscar. Oscar's not seen the movie, though, and he looks baffled as to why I'm refusing money.

Stratton's gaze comes back to mine. "That's not what this is," he says softly.

I know it's not. His reaction to Arabella told me that he spoke the truth when he said he'd never paid for sex. And that's not what's happening here. If I'm going to the Wellington ball with him, I do need a dress because I don't have a single suitable thing to wear in my wardrobe, and that's not female pride talking—I really don't have anything, unless faded track pants are the in-thing in fashion at the moment.

Still, I hesitate. He would have paid Arabella if she'd agreed to pretend to be his fiancée, but then they wouldn't have had sex—probably—so it would have been more of a job. But what if we do sleep together? Why does this make me feel so awkward?

Stratton's smiling at me. "I forgot," he says easily. "I haven't given you your Christmas bonus yet." He waves his wallet, as if he's trying to tempt a dog out of its kennel with a meaty treat.

It's my turn to give him an exasperated look. "A Christmas bonus? Are all your employees this lucky?"

"Only those who've worked really hard."

I chew my bottom lip. The poorer you are, the prouder you are, and I've never accepted money from anyone in my life.

"Meg," he says softly, "can't I give the best PA I've ever had a present?" He looks boyishly earnest all of a sudden.

I soften like a marshmallow dropped into hot chocolate. "Aw, you're such a smooth talker."

"Come on, Mum," Oscar says impatiently. "It's only a dress."

"Okay." The truth is, I'm excited at the thought of buying something new, especially something as exotic and rare as a ball gown that I'll probably only ever wear once. I've never been to anything like a ball before, and I'm nervous and ecstatic at the same time. I feel like Cinderella.

"Good." Stratton grins at me, pleased that I've folded. I stick my tongue out at him. I don't want him to think he'll be able to get his own way with me all the time. He just laughs though, and we get out of the car and cross to the shop.

Inside, he's as easy and confident as he is with his customers at Katoa. This is what money does for you. I feel intimidated, as if the girls working there will somehow know I can't afford to buy even a handbag at their prices. But Stratton goes straight up to the oldest assistant and explains to her that I'm accompanying him to a charity function and that I need a dress and accessories, and whatever else I fancy. I watch him give the woman his credit card and murmur something to her, and she pockets it discreetly.

He comes over to me. "Lucy will take care of you—she knows the kind of thing you need. Do you want me and Oscar to stay? You can give us a fashion parade."

I know Oscar will be bored out of his brain if he has to look at clothes for more than two minutes, beside which I want to take my time. "No, you can go."

"All right. We'll meet you in the café just up the road when you're done. Take your time." He slides a finger under my chin and lifts it to look into my eyes. "Get whatever you want for the day, okay?"

I nod. "Okay."

He smiles at Lucy and leaves with Oscar, who gives me a big thumbs-up before closing the door behind him.

I blow out a breath and turn to Lucy.

"A ball!" she says without an ounce of attitude. "How exciting."

"I have no idea what to wear," I admit, conscious of my scruffy jeans and faded T-shirt.

"That's okay—we'll work it out together. But please, no black. Okay?"

My shoulders droop. "I'd hoped for something black so that I don't stand out."

"My dear, I think the one thing he wants is for you to stand out. Now come on. I have the very thing."

Chapter Seventeen

Stratton

Oscar and I call into a shop or two, then have a coffee and a doughnut in the café until Meg turns up. She refuses to show me what she's bought, but her eyes are glittering and her cheeks are flushed, and it looks as if she's had a good time.

She gives me my credit card back, and I put it in my wallet. I know she didn't like me buying her clothes, but I don't see what the problem is. If I was hiring someone to paint the office, I'd expect to pay for the paint, even if he brought his own ladders.

I do get the *Pretty Woman* analogy, but Meg hasn't slept with me yet, and there's no guarantee she's going to. If she did, I wouldn't pay her for it. And I want her to go to the ball with me, so I'm done with worrying about it.

I drive them home, and we spend the rest of the day indoors. In the afternoon I do some work while Meg and Oscar have a swim in the pool, and then Meg announces it's her turn to prepare dinner, so Oscar and I play *Dark Robot* until she calls us in. She's prepared a fantastic crispy chili beef with noodles, and we take it to the dining table this time, and drink red wine while we eat and talk.

After that we watch a movie, and then all three of us play *Little Big Planet* until Meg announces it's time for Oscar to go to bed.

He comes up to me and holds his hand out in an awkward but grownup gesture while he says, "Thanks for a nice day."

"You're welcome." I catch his hand, then pull him in with my other arm for a bear hug. I ruffle his hair, and he laughs and pushes me away. I catch Meg's eye before she follows him out, but I can't read what she's thinking. Maybe she doesn't like me getting too close to Oscar. I muse on that as I go along the corridor to my study, and stare down at my desk.

I'm working on a better controller for the blind. My first invention, which—together with Rich's version of *Dark Robot* for the blind—won numerous awards and spring boarded us into the top three technology manufacturers and the top game manufacturer in New Zealand, was revolutionary, but I know I can do better. I've been working a lot with Teddi, as well as reading the latest research on how the brain reprograms itself when a person loses his or her sight, and I have an idea for a controller that has a better response time, and that reacts to a person's movement almost like a VR headset for the blind. It would have to be bigger than a standard controller, but that would mean it could have a larger touchpad and a couple more buttons. I want to improve the text-to-speech option, because Teddi says the original one is brilliant for helping her to connect with her friends online but it's too limited, and it would be helpful if it worked for all the menus on the game. I have lots of ideas, and I run my fingers over my initial sketches on the desk, hopeful that it will help.

"What's that?" Meg comes up to stand beside me. Her arm presses against mine as if she wants to touch me but doesn't want to be too forward.

"A new controller." I explain what I've just been thinking about. When we lean close to look at the drawings, I can't help but rest my hand in the small of her back. She doesn't push me away, and when we straighten, I let my hand linger as long as I can before I let it drop.

"Do you want to work this evening?" she asks. "I'm happy to read or watch a movie on my own—I don't expect you to entertain me all the time."

"Going to work on your poetry?" I tease.

Her eyes widen, then narrow as she realizes how I know. "Oscar."

"I'd like to hear some," I say. "He told me you've won prizes."

"I can't imagine that you're the kind of guy who likes poetry," she scoffs.

"I don't know much about it," I admit, "but I'd like to know more. I don't know much about art, but I like it when someone who does walks me through a gallery and explains the paintings."

She meets my gaze, her big blue eyes shining. "Okay. I'll read one to you later."

I slide my hands into the pockets of my jeans. "I have something for you."

"Oh?"

I gesture with my head for her to follow me, and lead the way into the living room and over to the windows. She stands before me, expectant, puzzled, and a little wary of accepting another gift. There's no point in trying to explain, so I just pull the box out of my pocket and open it.

She stares at it, then looks up at me.

"It was my great grandmother's." I extract it from the box. "From Hatton Garden in London. She married in 1941. Both my grandmother and my mother were very young when they had their first child. We've squeezed a lot of generations into this century."

"Stratton…"

"There were restrictions on the use of gold and platinum because of the war, so it's made from palladium."

"Palladium?"

"It has the lowest melting point of all the metals."

Meg gives a short laugh.

I smile. "Sorry. Science brain kicking in there. The diamond's only a carat, so it's not worth a fortune."

"Only a carat." She laughs again. "It's beautiful, Stratton."

I turn my other hand palm up, requesting she place hers in it. "I had it altered to fit."

She stares at me. "When?"

"I nipped out this morning before I did breakfast." Normally it takes a few days to get a ring altered, but it's amazing what a bit of extra cash will encourage someone to do.

Her eyes are wide. "How did you know what size I was?"

"I still have the wedding ring you were wearing."

"Oh."

I let my other hand drop. "You don't have to wear it all the time. But you'll need it for Monday when we go to work. I thought I'd announce it at the morning meeting. It will explain your email, and word will start getting around."

Slowly, Meg reaches out and takes the ring. "Yes, I suppose you're right." She examines it, looking at the diamond, turning it around to catch the light. Then, almost shyly, she pushes it onto her ring finger. It fits perfectly.

I close the box and slide it back into my jeans pocket. "Never thought I'd do that."

She laughs then. "I'm waiting for the proposal."

"Do you want me to get down on one knee?"

"Oh, I think our story is going to be much more exciting than that." She looks up, thinking. "You took me out to the most expensive restaurant in Auckland, and the waiter brought it over with the dessert."

I catch hold of her hand and lead her into the kitchen. "I'd never propose in public in case she said no."

"No woman would ever say no to you, Stratton."

Her compliment warms me through. "Well, thank you, but even so, the fear of humiliation would be too great. If I *were* to propose…" I take the half-filled bottle of red wine and pour some into two glasses. Just a small amount—last night I think we both overdid it. "I'd do it out of the blue. When she didn't expect it. Somewhere quiet and romantic." I hand her a glass. "Let's say I did it on the beach at midnight. Up in the Bay of Islands."

Meg looks suddenly alarmed. "That's where your parents live."

"Yeah, well, I'll have to pretend we visited them a few months ago."

"You're going to tell them you have a fake fiancée?"

"Ah, not yet. But I'm sure they'll be fine about it," I say, more confidently than I feel. My parents have always been there for me and Teddi, and they're incredibly supportive, but I'm certain they're going to think I'm nuts when I tell them what I've done. "I'd like you to meet them," I say. "They'd like you." They never said so until we'd broken up, but I knew that they didn't like Natalie. Mum thought she was shallow and sometimes cruel, and Dad thought she was after my money. Unfortunately, all of their observations are probably true, to some extent.

Meg takes a large gulp of wine. "I couldn't meet your parents." She looks horrified. "What will they think of me for pretending to be engaged to you?"

"They'll think you're wonderful, Meg, because you are." I move closer to her, loving the range of expressions that cross her face, her honesty, her integrity. She takes a step back but meets the counter, and it means I can move up close to her, until I can feel her pressed against me, her breasts soft against my chest.

I know it's stupid. We're not really engaged, and, until now, even though I've admired others who've made this commitment, I've always thought marriage isn't for me. But she's wearing my ring. I feel as if I've stamped the word *Mine* onto her forehead. When Bruce or indeed any other guy looks at her now, they'll know she belongs to me.

For some reason, I like that feeling.

I lower my lips to hers. She inhales sharply, but she doesn't move away and just closes her eyes. I pause a second, smiling as her lips part automatically and her cheeks flush with an attractive pink. Then I kiss her.

She's already had some wine, and when I brush my tongue into her mouth, I taste plum and blackberry. Everything about this woman is rich and sweet. Her mouth is so soft—it makes me hard in seconds, and I can't help but push my hips to hers. In response, she gives a sexy little moan, and I sigh and delve deeper, enjoying the sensations of being intimate with her, of using all my senses to explore her.

When I eventually raise my head, she has a dreamy look in her eyes, and she presses the rim of the glass to her lips, looking at me with a bashful smile.

"You're a naughty boy," she murmurs.

I laugh. "Come on." I lead her into the living room. I tend to work in the evenings or watch movies because I don't go to bed early, and it can be lonely with hours of time to yourself. I don't mind my own company, but I don't know many men who are happy doing nothing, and I like to fill my time with something productive.

But tonight, like last night, I sit and chat to Meg while we listen to music, and the hours roll away as we talk about everything under the sun. We learn about each other's pasts, where we grew up, what we were like at school, who we dated and who our best friends were. I tell her about Rich and Will. We talk about Teddi, and I tell her more than I've ever told anyone about how hard it's been for her, for all of us, having to deal with her blindness.

I'm enjoying this exploration of her life, finding out more about the Meg beneath the PA I've gotten to know quite well. She says she has lots of faults, but I'm having difficulty seeing them. She's kind and generous, funny and hardworking. She admits she can be a bit OCD with organization, but then that's what makes her such a good PA. She says she's too soft on Oscar, but I haven't seen that—he's growing up into a great lad, and I tell her so, which earns me a lovely warm smile that will stay with me for a long time.

We talk about her poetry, and finally I persuade her to read one out to me.

"It's called 'Beckett's Offspring,'" she says, and begins to read.

"Bursting with life, in the cemetery,
I stand and muse on how meaningful it would be
to 'give birth astride of a grave'. How eloquent
to deliver onto freshly turned earth
blood and mucus to mix with the mud
a truly natural birth.
People would think: how inappropriate!
But I can't imagine a more evocative place
to nurture a seed.
It's so peaceful here. I can feel
the breath of creation in the trees
the river of life running below,
ferrying souls to and fro,
and I know that the bones of the dead
would donate their flowers for the newborn's head.'"

She finishes and looks up at me warily.

"Wow," I say. "That was amazing."

Her look turns wry. "Yeah, right. You have no idea what it was about, do you?"

"I do," I protest. "That's a quote from Samuel Beckett's *Waiting for Godot*. I love the way you ended with a rhyming couplet."

Her smile is amazing. "You really liked it? It won first prize in a competition, although when it was printed I actually had someone write and say how inappropriate the subject matter was." She pulls a face.

I frown. "I don't get that. I can see what you were trying to say, about how life is a circle, and how energy flows from birth to death to birth again. I think it was beautiful."

She doesn't say anything else, but I can see she's touched by my words.

It's very late before we admit we're tired and that we really should go to bed. We place our glasses in the dishwasher and walk down to our bedrooms, and I bend to kiss her cheek before we part.

I go into my room and lie on the bed for a while, looking out at the dark sky. I don't know what's going to happen between us. I want to do this right, and I don't want to fuck it up. I can only go by instinct, and that's not always worked for me in the past. But I know Meg likes me. More than that—she wants me, it's clear in her eyes and the sighs she gives when I kiss her. If I were to knock on her door now, she'd welcome me in and in less than five minutes we'd be making love on her bed. I want to. But something stops me. She's better than that. She's been through a lot, and she deserves more than a brief fling.

I don't know what I'm willing to offer her yet, but I do know it's more than that.

I look out at the stars. Am I being foolish? She's not been with a guy for some time, by the sounds of it, and I know that it's not only men who can have sex without any emotional commitment. Maybe all she wants is a fling.

I don't think that's the case, though. I might be wrong. All I know is that she didn't take my ring off all evening, and it was still on her finger when she went to bed.

Chapter Eighteen

Meg

On Monday morning, I dress with a strange mixture of nerves and excitement.

Saturday and Sunday passed slowly, and I don't think I'm over-exaggerating when I say it was the nicest weekend I've ever spent.

Stratton seemed to understand that I needed some peace and quiet, and he left me to my own devices for much of Sunday while he worked in his office on his new designs. I swam several times, played games and watched movies with Oscar, and then in the evening Oscar and I cooked Shepherd's Pie for us all. After that, we sat together in the living room like any family would do, Oscar drawing and listening to music, Stratton and I reading and chatting occasionally.

I felt at peace in a way I have never felt with anyone save Oscar. Stratton's so easy. It's only now that I realize how high maintenance Bruce was. He was always prickly, like a hedgehog, and I spent most of my time with him trying to work out what mood he was in, and what I'd said to offend him this time. Stratton doesn't seem moody at all. Teddi has told me that he's not been himself since he broke up with Natalie, but to be honest I certainly haven't seen much sign of that over the last few days. He's thoughtful sometimes, but he's even-tempered, patient, and he never has a cross word for Oscar.

I try to be realistic—I've only been with the man two days. When you have guests in the house it's natural to be on your best behavior, and it's entirely probable that if I lived with him for any length of time I'd discover that he has good and bad days the same as any normal person. But it's just a relief not to feel as if I have to be on my guard the whole time. He's warm and funny, considerate and thoughtful. I've worked with him for four months, day in, day out, so I know he's not putting on a show. Yeah, he's still naughty—he has a wicked sense of humor and loves to tease me, but the more I'm with him, the more I'm able to relax and give as good as I get, and he loves that. It turns him on, I think, our back and forth banter, especially when it's a bit near the knuckle. As much as I'm conscious that he's still my boss, this is a very unusual situation, and whatever happens over the next few weeks, things are going to change at work.

I don't want to think about the future now, though, because I have the present to deal with. We've dropped Oscar off at Alyssa's—she'll take the boys to the local sports center later, where they can wear themselves out playing tennis and swimming all day—and now Stratton and I are heading to work.

"What about Andy?" I ask, remembering he'd been there when Bruce had shown up. "What will he say when he hears about our 'engagement'?"

"Rich has spoken to him," Stratton announces, heading to the car park beneath the office building. "He's the only one who knows what's going on, and he's very discreet—he won't tell anyone. And by the way, I hope you won't be using air quotes when you tell anyone that we're engaged." He sends me a wry look.

I'm too nervous to smile back. "And what about Rich and Teddi?" I'm worried they're upset with me. They both thought Stratton's plan to hire a fake fiancée was a stupid one, and I can only imagine what they must think of me for agreeing to go along with it.

"They'll be fine." Stratton doesn't elaborate—he just drives into a parking space and turns off the engine. "Ready?"

I look down at the ring on my left hand. I still can't believe he's given it to me. Well, loaned it to me, obviously. But even though it's not permanent, I'm still touched at the gesture. For a start, he went to the trouble of getting it resized. His own great-grandmother's ring! It makes me want to cry. Every time I look at it, I go all gooey inside. Stupid, I know, but gestures matter.

"Come on." He gets out of the car, comes around to my side, and holds out his hand. I place mine in it, and he pulls me to my feet and shuts the car door.

Then he moves closer, pinning me to the side of the car.

"This is allowed now," he murmurs, dropping his head so his lips brush mine. "We're engaged."

"There's nobody to see," I protest weakly, as the car park is empty.

"So?" He gives me that tiger-grin, then kisses me. Just a touch of his lips to mine, but it makes my knees go weak.

Oh dear, I think as he pulls back and smirks before leading me across to the elevator. This isn't going to be easy.

*

As it happens, the first bit is incredibly easy. Stratton announces it to everyone in the top office. By the end of his speech, even I'm convinced that we've fallen madly in love and can't wait to tie the knot.

Everyone crowds around, eager to congratulate us and give us their best wishes. I note that Teddi and Rich have returned to the board room, where we'll continue in a few minutes with the daily meeting. I haven't spoken to them yet, and I'm not sure how they're going to react to me.

Butterflies in my stomach, I nod and smile, relieved when everyone starts to leave to return to their offices.

"When's the big day going to be?" Ella, the head of the typing pool, lingers curiously.

"Next June," I tell her. Stratton and I have already prepared our answers to questions like these. "We thought we'd go for a winter wedding, and we need some time to prepare."

"Of course." Ella glances at Stratton, who's busy talking to a couple of the other managers in the office, although I have a feeling he has one ear on what we're saying. She leans closer to me conspiratorially. "We all knew there was something going on between you two."

I blush, sure he's listening. "Oh, really?"

"We could spot it a mile away. You should see the way he looks at you when you don't realize he's watching. He can't take his eyes off you. He's been the same ever since you started here."

I glance at Stratton—yes, he's listening. He raises an eyebrow. I blush even more. "Oh, goodness. Well, that's nice to know."

"It happened very quickly, didn't it?" Ella persists.

Whatever I say is going to get around the office, and Stratton warned me that Ella also sees Natalie socially sometimes, so I have to be very careful what I say here. I hope she doesn't mistake my blush for lying. "Yes," I agree, "I suppose it did, but we both fell in love at first sight. Because we work together, we kept it very quiet. But neither of us sees any point in waiting. We're not getting any younger."

She nods and smiles. "Well, I hope you'll be very happy. He's quite a catch." She grins and makes that rubbing movement with her thumb and fingers that indicates he's loaded.

I go still, indignant and offended, even though we're not really engaged. "His money has nothing to do with it," I snap, but even to me it sounds slightly ridiculous. The guy's a billionaire. We're engaged within four months of me starting work here. Of course everyone's going to think I'm after his money.

"Sure," Ella says, "sorry," and she gives me an awkward, apologetic smile and walks away. I know she's going to get straight on her mobile and telephone Natalie, and tell her that her ex has been snapped up by a gold digger. For some reason, that gets to me more than anything.

Across from me, Stratton excuses himself and comes over. "Everything all right?"

I nod, although I'm flustered and upset, and annoyed that I'm flustered and upset. Why should it matter what anyone thinks of me for doing this? But it does matter, because I do like him, and now it's making me question whether there is even a small part of me that is drawn to his bank account.

He pulls me to one side. "What is it?"

I look down at my feet. "It's nothing, it's stupid… It's just that I know everyone's thinking that I'm after your money."

To my surprise, he laughs. "Little do they know that I had to force you to take my card the other day."

"It's not funny," I protest.

"No." He sobers, but his eyes are still alight with humor. "Let's show them it's not about the money, shall we?"

"What…" I taper off as he moves closer and cups my face with a hand. Oh jeez, he's going to kiss me, in front of everyone. I put my hands on his chest, intending to push him away, but at the last minute I think *Ah, what the heck*, and I let him lower his lips to mine.

I close my eyes, shutting out the room, and concentrate on Stratton, his mouth, his warm hand, just being near to him. A cheer goes up, and it continues around the room as everyone obviously turns to look. I know that Ella's going to be watching. *Take that,*

Natalie, I think, smiling as Stratton finally laughs and pulls back, then takes a bow to the room.

I glance over at the boardroom to see Rich leaning against the door, arms folded. I'm relieved to see him smiling, and when he speaks over his shoulder, I know that he's relaying what's happened to Teddi.

"Come on," Stratton says, taking my hand, and he leads me to the boardroom.

I close the door behind me, and take my usual seat at the end. Stratton sits on my left, Teddi and Rich on my right. I hear a sigh as Bella the Labrador lies at Teddi's feet beneath the table.

"So…" Rich begins, tipping back his chair and surveying us with amusement. "That was some acting out there."

Stratton says nothing, just plays with his pen and glances at me as if to check that I'm not upset still. I decide to make fun of the situation.

"Thanks," I say to Rich. "Apparently I'm up for an Emmy."

He laughs, Stratton grins, and the tension lifts around the table.

"Stratton told us what happened in the foyer," Teddi says.

I hesitate and then give a long sigh. "About that… I want to apologize for lying to you all. I'm very sorry I didn't tell you the truth at the beginning. It's just… I couldn't." I swallow hard.

"It's all right," Teddi says softly. "We understand."

"And I'm sorry about the whole fake relationship thing." This is even more embarrassing. "Normally, I would never have done something like this, and I have to admit that I thought it was a daft idea at the beginning, but when Bruce showed up, suddenly I understood why Stratton had come up with the idea. I thought that maybe Bruce might finally leave me alone if he thinks I'm getting married to someone else."

"That's true," Teddi says.

"The thing is…" Suddenly it's very important to me that they understand. "I've never considered myself a victim. I've had to cope on my own for a long time. I like to think I'm independent and strong. I know it doesn't look like that—after all, why did I stay with him so long? But I tried to make it work. And even though I'm not frightened of him, not physically, having Stratton around…" I don't know how to put it into words. I don't think Bruce is a violent man at heart, and I can stand up for myself... And I feel very strongly that I am not a woman in need of being rescued...

But being with Stratton makes me feel safe. Or at least, he gives me confidence in my own ability to stand up for myself. I've made mistakes in the past, I know that. And sometimes I wish I'd done things differently. But I'm done apologizing for my actions.

"There's nothing else to be said," Teddi states. "We'll back the two of you up, of course. And I hope it works out for you." She taps the special tablet she has for the blind, the surface of which is covered with the raised dots of Braille. "I'd like to raise the subject of booking adverts and promotions for your next game, Rich, ahead of time. Do you have any preferences where you'd like me to start?"

Relieved that she's changed the subject, I give her a thankful glance, then realize she can't see it and murmur, "Thank you." I open my laptop and start taking minutes, relieved that neither Rich nor Teddi have given us a hard time.

Stratton winks at me before turning his attention to the subject under discussion. It makes me think of the kiss he's just given me.

And now I'm back to thinking about melted chocolate. Some things never change.

Chapter Nineteen

Stratton

It takes just under thirty minutes for my mobile to ring and show the name of one of Natalie's friends. I'm amazed it's taken that long. News on the office grapevine moves faster than Usain Bolt when he has a plane to catch.

We've just finished the morning meeting and returned to our offices. I stare at the phone for a moment. When I first broke up with Natalie, she called and texted me incessantly, and eventually I blocked her number. Since then, she's used her friend's mobiles. I could block them all, I guess, but she has a lot of friends.

Most of the time, I just cancel the call. But I'm going to have to do this at some point, so I rise from my chair, walk over to the window that looks down over the waterfront, and answer it.

"Hello?"

"Stratton?" She sounds surprised—she didn't think I'd answer. "It's me."

I was tempted to say "Sorry, who?" but I restrain myself. I might want her out of my life, but I once cared for her, and I know she's hurting.

"Hey," I say, making my voice softer than it wants to be.

"I've just heard something very strange." In contrast, her voice is loud, angry. "Someone told me that you announced you're engaged. To your PA."

I watch a boat making its way out of the harbor. The sun glitters on the water like tinsel, making my eyes water.

"Good news travels fast," I say.

There's a long silence. Partway through, I hear a noise at the door and turn to see Meg coming in with a takeaway latte and an armful of files. She walks up to my desk before seeing that I'm on the phone. She places the coffee and folders on the table with a gesture of apology at interrupting, and then her eyes widen as she sees the look on my face.

"Natalie?" she mouths. I nod. She pulls an *eek* face, which makes me want to laugh, even though my stomach's in a knot. She goes to walk out, but I catch her arm and ask her to sit. Oddly, I'm comforted by having her there, even though I'm talking to my ex. I want her to hear me tell Natalie that we're done. She lowers herself gracefully into the seat, looking wary.

I turn back to the view. "Are you still there?" I ask, wondering if she's hung up. Or if she's fainted.

"I'm here."

I can imagine the look on her face. Her light green eyes will be blazing, her pretty lips pursed in fury. I remember trying to divert an argument between the two of us once—she'd had that look on her face, and I'd lifted her up and carried her into the bedroom, where I'd kissed her and made love to her until she'd given in. I'd been triumphant, but I'd discovered afterward that I hadn't stopped the argument, only delayed it. It makes me uncomfortable to think about it now, and I push the memory away.

"Meg," she says. "Really?"

"Really."

"How long have you known her? Three months?"

"Four," I correct.

"Oh, sorry, four months," she says sarcastically. "What, did she refuse to go to bed with you until you popped the question?"

Various options flash through my mind—I want to be sarcastic and cruel, to yell at her, to make her promise to leave me alone. She has a habit of bringing me down to her level. But part of me senses that she wants an emotional confrontation, and for once I refuse to give it to her.

"I'm not talking to you about Meg. What do you want, Natalie?"

"To tell you not to make a stupid mistake. You know you're on the rebound, right? Is this about making me jealous? Is this all part of a plan to get me back?" Her voice is sharp, but I can hear the misery behind it, as well as a glimmer of hope.

Suddenly, I'm overwhelmed with pity. This is a stupid thing I've done. I've hurt her badly, and I'm not the type of guy who can do that easily to a woman. Why can't she accept it's over? Why did she have to drive me to lies and deceit?

"Not everything's about you," I tell her quietly. "We broke up seven months ago, and I'm moving on, that's all. I wish you'd do the same. We're over."

"We're not," she snaps. "We're perfect for each other, but you're too stupid to see it."

Impatience flickers inside me. "Natalie…"

"What's she like in bed? Does she know all your secrets? Does she let you do all the things you like to do to a girl? Not every woman's as accommodating as me, Stratton. Not every girl will let you fuck them the way you fucked me."

I haven't blushed since I tripped up the steps onto the stage at prize giving when I was thirteen, but, conscious of Meg watching me, I feel my face grow hot. I glance at her, and she raises her eyebrows. I hope she can't hear anything from the other side of the desk. Thank God I didn't put the call on speakerphone.

"You're embarrassing yourself," I snap at my ex, angry now. "Stop it."

But she's too far gone to stop. She's almost yelling now. "Do you really think you can give up what we had? Tell me you don't think about that night in Brisbane. Does Meg let you do that? Does she know what an incredibly dirty man is inside that smart, geeky guy?"

"Natalie—"

"I love you." She's crying now. "I'll do anything if you'll come back to me. I won't mention marriage or children again—I don't care if I don't have kids, or if we adopt—I just want you."

"It doesn't matter." My voice is like a switchblade, made so by sheer frustration. This is the first time she's told me that she'll give up having kids for me. But she's too late. She's destroyed whatever I felt for her, and I could never go back to her, not now. "You're not listening to me. I don't love you anymore. I don't know if I ever did. I want you to leave me and Meg alone. Find yourself some other man to obsess over, Natalie. We're done."

"Does she want children?" Her words slice through me. "Have you asked her? Is she willing to give them up for you?"

I hang up. It takes every ounce of willpower I own not to throw the phone across the room until it shatters against the wall.

I glare out of the window, furious at her and at myself for having a conversation with her, almost shaking with frustration. I wish I hadn't asked Meg to stay. I don't want her to see me like this.

I feel her hand touch the small of my back. Then, to my surprise, her arms slip around my waist, and she hugs me.

Emotion sweeps over me, and I take a deep, shuddery breath. I can't remember the last time I cried, but tears prick my eyes, and I have to swallow hard to make sure they don't fall.

"Fuck," I yell.

I feel Meg give a short laugh. "Eloquent as ever," she murmurs. She rests a hand on my chest, over my heart.

I exhale, then bring up my hands to cover hers. I become aware of her breasts pressed against my back, her cheek resting between my shoulder blades. She's warm, and her very touch is comforting, and calms me. This is what being with a real lover should be like, I think, not missing the irony that we're not actually lovers. I can't remember Natalie ever hugging me like this. It occurs to me that our interactions consisted of two distinct situations—either we were fucking or fighting. How could I ever have thought that could be the basis of a lasting relationship?

I turn and put my arms around Meg, and rest my lips on the top of her head.

"We're really screwed up, aren't we?" she murmurs.

"Yeah." I kiss her hair. "At least we're screwed up together."

She chuckles. Then she moves back a little and looks up at me. Her expression turns mischievous. "So… you're an incredibly dirty man?"

I close my eyes. *Shit.* She overheard Natalie.

Meg laughs. "Don't tell me that Stratton Parker is embarrassed? I never thought I'd live to see the day."

"Well, it's not every day your fiancée overhears your ex talking about what you were like in bed." I kiss her nose. "I'm sorry."

"Oh Stratton, she didn't say anything I didn't already know. You think I wasn't aware that you're a very naughty boy inside?"

My lips curve up. "You make me sound like Dennis the Menace."

"That's the perfect description for you. I'm going to call you that from now on."

I chuckle. "I am sorry you had to hear it, though."

"I don't mind. I'm… intrigued." Her eyes meet mine. They're alight with curiosity and desire. A tingle runs from the nape of my neck down to my tailbone.

"I see." Heat floods through me at the thought of educating Meg in various sexual pleasures.

Leaving her for a moment, I walk over to the door and close it. Then I come back to where she stands by my desk. I move up close to her, and she takes a step back, but the desk stops her retreat. She slips her hands behind her butt and draws up her shoulders as if she's nervous, but her eyes are wide with excitement, her lips parted.

This woman does something to me. I don't quite know why. At the time, Natalie hooked me in with her experience in the bedroom. I've never been particularly drawn to innocent girls, and the blushing virgin does little for me. I liked that Natalie had been with other guys and wasn't afraid to experiment. I enjoyed the way we showed each other what we knew, and uncovered a few more things between us. She was fun, and that was all I needed for several years, while I was busy with work and didn't have the time for an elaborate courtship.

I haven't realized it before, but now I understand that I'm ready for something more. Quite what, I'm not sure. But there's something about Meg that's lighting my candle in a way no other girl has for a very long time. She's naive, but not innocent. Sassy, but not nasty. Confident, but not arrogant. And she's fucking hot, and I'm not going to be able to hold back for much longer, because it seems that all I think about is taking off her clothes, lowering her to the bed, and sliding inside her.

I cup her head with a hand and claim her mouth with mine, and I don't bother about holding back this time, hoping to show her how much I want her. Meg gasps, her mouth opening, and I take full advantage of it and delve my tongue inside, wanting to taste her, to brand her as mine. Her left hand comes up to rest on my chest, and I take it, interlinking our fingers. I can feel my great-grandmother's ring, and a surge of almost primal smugness runs through me that Bruce lost her, and I've got her now. I want to make love to her until she forgets that idiot, until I wipe all memories of him from her brain. I don't want her ever to think of him again.

I lift my head to look at her, and her eyes slowly open. Her cheeks are flushed, and I've kissed all her lipstick off.

"You're so wicked," she murmurs. "Anyone could walk in."

"Don't care, we're engaged." I kiss her again. I could kiss her all day.

But I have phone calls to make and reports to write, and eventually I move back and release her with a sigh. "I suppose I should let you get to work."

"Yes, you should." She moves reluctantly, though, straightening her white blouse and navy skirt, and casting me an exasperated glance when she touches her lips to find them bare. "Everyone's going to know what we've been doing."

"Good." I sit behind my desk. "I want them to know."

She rolls her eyes and walks to the door, giving me a final, wry glance before she exits.

I turn my chair and look out over the harbor. Clouds have crossed the sun, and the sea no longer sparkles, like an old Christmas bauble that's lost its glitter. Natalie had a thing about them—every year she would buy new decorations, because she said old ones made her sad. I think that was probably because she had a difficult childhood, with her father being blind and unable to find work much of the time—she never liked to talk about the past. Maybe that's why she wants kids so much. Just like Bruce, she doesn't exist in a vacuum, and it's a culmination of experiences that have made her the way she is.

I have to take the blame for some of that. Much of her current bitterness is due to me. It's rare for a woman not to want a family, and it's not always something you discuss before you begin a relationship. By the time you discover one of you doesn't want them, it's too late—you've already stood in the bear trap.

Does she want children? Have you asked her? Is she willing to give them up for you?

It's irrelevant, I tell myself—I've not even dated Meg properly yet. We're hardly at the stage where we're talking about the future. We're not really engaged!

But I feel a ripple of unease. She has a child, of course, a teenager, and she's thirty-three, four years older than Natalie. While that's hardly old, it's possible she's not interested in having any more kids.

But she might want them. I have to consider that. What if I begin a thing with her, only to discover that, like Natalie, she wants a baby?

I turn the chair away from the view and start up my laptop. It's pointless to try to second guess everything. I'm going to have this problem no matter who I date.

Irritably, I bring up the report I need to work on and stare at it gloomily. Natalie's words are like flies buzzing around a dead creature. I swat at them, but they won't go away.

I understand that we are only animals, and our reason for being is procreation and continuing the human race. But social media tells us that everyone should want children. We're made to feel odd and unusual if we don't. I was shocked when I looked up the statistics and discovered that 47.6 percent—nearly half!—of women in the U.S. aged between fifteen and forty-four have never had children, and I suspect it's a similar figure in New Zealand. Of course that doesn't differentiate between those who don't want them and those who can't, whether it's due to fertility or not having a partner. But it irritates me when people I've met who can't have kids are angry with me because I've chosen not to. As if I've won a holiday to somewhere they desperately want to go, and I've turned my nose up at it.

It's not that I don't understand the attraction of having a child. If I think about it too hard, I get a hollowness inside and feel a strange wistfulness at the thought that I won't continue the family line, and there will never be a little piece of me running around. But I can't. I just can't. If my partner got pregnant I'd have to put her through the stress and upset of having the fetus tested, and if we discovered it had the mutated gene we'd have to have it delivered early so it could have its eyes operated on. How could I ever try for a baby with that hanging over my head? If ever there was something to trigger impotency in me, that might be it. I don't want to do it, and I'm sick of being made to feel abnormal because of my decision.

I pick up the coffee Meg brought me in and sip it, and think about how her lips felt beneath mine. We're not even really engaged. And I'm not going to worry about it anymore. I have other things to think about. Such as, it's Christmas, and I need to buy my fake stepson a present.

Lips curving, I pull my laptop toward me and start to type into Google.

Chapter Twenty

Meg

The next couple of days pass quickly. To my relief, there's no sign of Bruce. I admit I'm a little more cautious than normal, and I haven't wandered around the shops like I usually do in my lunch hour, nor have I gone to the local swimming pool, which I tend to do several times a week. Instead, I've swum in Stratton's pool every day, and we've taken lunch together, usually in his office because he's so busy, although we did manage to sneak out yesterday to visit a café.

I don't like this feeling of constantly looking over my shoulder. I'm going to have to face up to the fear at some point, whether that involves meeting up with Bruce and trying to convince him I've moved on, or, if he won't listen, finally getting a protection order.

But I'm not going to think about it now, because it's Wednesday afternoon, Midsummer Day, and we've left Bruce behind in Auckland somewhere and we're on our way to Wellington for the NZAB Solstice Ball.

It may sound stupid, but I've not really given much thought to what it means that Stratton has money. I know he owns his own company with Rich and Teddi. I've read all the articles about how it made major breakthroughs, and how successful it is. My jaw dropped when I first walked into his house, and I'm aware that his suits are tailor-made and expensive, that he has all the most modern gadgets, and that he enjoys the finer things in life, like good food and the best whiskies.

But… well… he's Stratton. At my interview, I was shocked how young all three of them are. And not just that, but none of them are arrogant or superior because of the position they've found themselves in. Maybe that's because they don't come from money, or maybe they're just nice people, but when I'm with them, as well as with Stratton alone, I don't think about it.

I know he's a billionaire, though. As his PA, I've seen his bank accounts, and I nearly passed out at the sight of all those zeroes. And now, travelling with him for the first time, I realize exactly what it means to have that kind of money.

For a start, we fly down in a private jet. Holy shit! He looks surprised when I express my disbelief at not having to travel cattle class with all the holidaymakers. I wonder when he last had to do that.

There are Christmas decorations in the first class lounge, and carols playing on the loudspeakers. It crosses my mind that Christmas is only days away, and I have no idea what I'm doing for it. My parents have asked whether I'd like to go back to Christchurch to spend it with them, but I'm not keen on doing that. It will be safer considering that Bruce is probably still in Auckland, but this is my home now. Plus, Stratton's original suggestion was that we play the fiancée game for a few weeks over the Christmas period. Maybe I should have given that more thought. What does he intend to do on Christmas Day? Does he go up to his family in the Bay of Islands? If so, is he expecting me to go with him, or to stay here on my own with Oscar?

I resolve to worry about it later, and on the plane I concentrate instead on drinking the best Champagne I've ever had—no, let's be honest, the only Champagne with a capital C I've ever had because it's the real stuff from France, not just fizzy wine—and enjoying the lovely canapés the flight assistant brings us. Stratton is busy making calls and catching up on last minute work on his laptop, so I pretend to read, but actually I spend the time looking around me and marveling that I'm actually there.

When we arrived in Wellington, rather than having to make our way to the taxi rank, we're picked up by a driver in a limo who delivers us in style to Carlton's, the upmarket hotel where the ball is taking place.

It's all like being in a play where I'm Cinderella who's been asked—literally—to go to the ball. But it's only when we check in and the receptionist tells us that we're in a Premier Suite that I start to think I'm dreaming.

"I hope it's okay," Stratton says when we walk into the suite. "It seemed a bit odd coming to a charity ball and booking the Penthouse, so I settled for the Premier."

"You *settled* for the Premier." I walk around, mouth open at the sight of the red leather sofas, the plush carpets, the expensive wooden dining suite, the state-of-the-art kitchen. It has two bedrooms, both huge, and each of them has an en suite bathroom. The walls bear expensive-looking paintings, and there are fresh flowers everywhere, interspersed with elegant Christmas decorations that look as if they've cost more than a week's rent. I'm utterly dumbfounded.

Stratton checks his phone. "We have a couple of hours before dinner. I really ought to go to the AGM before the ball. Is it okay if I leave you here to get ready? You're welcome to come with me, but it's going to be boring."

"I think I'll be all right," I say, imagining how wonderful it's going to be to have a bath in the huge tub while sipping a glass of the wine that's currently sitting in an ice bucket.

He hesitates, as if he's about to say something, but in the end he just smiles. He's been quiet over the last few days, ever since Natalie's phone call. We've had nice evenings, and we've talked a lot, but he's still not made a move on me. I'm not sure whether he's regretting breaking up with her, or if something else upset him. Or it could be that he's decided he's not interested in me, for whatever reason—maybe my lack of experience in the bedroom has put him off, or perhaps he's come to the conclusion that a thirty-three-year-old with a kid and a psycho ex isn't what he's looking for. The thought makes me sad, but I'd understand if it was the case.

"Will Natalie be at this meeting?" I ask as nonchalantly as I can.

"Yes, she'll be there, but there will be a lot of people around, and I'll do my best to avoid her." He pauses by the door to check his appearance in the mirror. I know he's not vain, so I'm surprised to see him run a hand through his hair. He's worried what Natalie will think.

I come to stand beside him and look up at him. He's so gorgeous. Today, he's wearing a smart, expensive-looking navy suit, a white shirt, and the tie I bought him for his birthday, *sans* coffee stain, which makes me smile. I know he's brought a tux with him for tonight, and I can't wait to see him in it, although a small part of me misses the Stratton from home who wears an All Blacks top and his track pants.

"Stratton," I say.

He adjusts his tie, distracted. "Mmm?"

"I just wanted to say…"

He looks at me, and I'm momentarily speechless as I fall under his blue and green-eyed gaze. He waits, then raises an eyebrow.

"Um…" I try to gather my wits, like scooping up frozen peas from a split bag. "I hope… I hope that I'm not in the way here."

He frowns. "What do you mean?"

"With Natalie." This has been building for a few days and, wanting to get the words out, I start to speak quickly. "You've been quiet since that phone call you had with her in your office, a bit distant, and I knew it shook you up. I wondered whether you've been regretting breaking up with her, and if you've been thinking about getting back with her again. I just want to say, if that's what you want, please don't worry about me. If you want me to stay in one bedroom and you take the other, or even if you want to go back to her room tonight to talk or to… you know… make up with her, it's okay, I understand, and I'll be fine, I mean I'll be disappointed, but I'm not expecting anything. I mean, I was hoping, but that's not the same as expecting, and I get why you might not be interested in me. I'm only supposed to be your fake fiancée anyway, it's not like we're really engaged, I do know that, and I'm not here to make demands on you. I don't want you to feel beholden to me, because you asked me to come. I'm your PA first, and I'm thinking of this as part of the job, so if you've changed your mind about us, that's okay, I won't make a fuss…"

My voice trails off. He's looking at me with a mixture of bewilderment and amusement.

Keeping his gaze fixed on mine, he moves closer, pinning me against the wall.

"How long have you been bottling that up?" He rests his forearm on the wall above my head and leans in close. I've taken off my heels, and jeez, he's tall. He towers over me, all height and breadth and dark glowering gorgeousity.

"A few days," I admit, and swallow nervously.

He surveys me for a long moment, his gaze skimming down me, then coming back up to rest on my mouth.

"I don't want to get back with Natalie," he says.

I blink a few times. "Oh. Okay. Only I thought—"

A frown flickers on his face. "I have been thinking about… things, but not in that way. I'm sorry if I've been quiet—I didn't want to bore you or hurt your feelings in any way by talking about my previous relationship. But that conversation I had with Natalie made me realize that the relationship I had with her wasn't what I thought it was. It made me sad—I should have worked out earlier that we weren't right for each other. I feel guilty that I wasted time for her, time she could have spent looking for a partner who would give her what she wanted—marriage and children."

"It's partly her fault too, Stratton. If she'd accepted it earlier, rather than keep thinking she could change you, she'd be over you by now." I think about it. "Probably. I don't think you'd be an easy man to get over."

His eyes bore into mine. "Don't you?"

"Um…" I chew my lip nervously. "I don't know what you mean by that. I can't tell if you want to yell at me or kiss me."

His gaze drops to my lips. "I'm sorry I've been distant. And I'm sorry if it made you think I've changed my mind. Because I most definitely want to kiss you."

"Oh."

"And more."

I'm melting inside at the look in his eyes. "M-more?"

"Yes, more, Miss Meg. I know I shouldn't. We're not really engaged, and you're my PA, and there's all sorts of conversations we should have before we get involved, but the truth is that I can't wait any longer."

My lips part, but I can't exhale because someone's stolen all the air from my lungs. "Can't you?"

He gives a little shake of his head. Desire rolls off him in waves. "I want you," he murmurs, bending his head so I can almost—but not quite—feel his lips touch mine. "And tonight, I plan to take you into that bedroom and fuck you senseless."

I look up into his eyes. They're hot and amused, waiting for my reaction.

Holy shit. I can't think what to say. My brain's turned to mush. My heart's banging on my ribs, trying to get out. I'm terribly inexperienced at dealing with this kind of man. I feel excited and turned on and panicky all rolled into one.

As usual, when words desert me, I opt for humor. "That doesn't sound very romantic."

Something flickers across his expression—regret, maybe, or even shame. "I'm sorry," he murmurs. "I haven't done this in a while." He kisses my cheek, a tender apology that makes me sigh. "I want to make love to you again and again, until you're exhausted from all the orgasms. Until your body aches and your lips are sore and you're drenched in sweat. Until you beg me to stop because you can't take any more pleasure." He brushes his lips against mine, and at the same time I feel his right hand close over my left, touching the engagement ring. "Until you can think of no one else but me."

I open my mouth to groan, but I don't get a chance because he kisses me, and I'm swept away on a wave of desire that leaves me shivering in its wake. I don't know which bit of that conversation is making me shake more, the general he wants to fuck me senseless bit, or the detailed description of what he wants to do to me. Both are really, really hot, and I can't believe he still wants me.

He kisses me until I've completely lost the plot, until my legs are trembling and my heart is racing and my chest is heaving because I'm trying so hard to keep breathing. When he eventually lifts his head, I worry that I'll slide down the wall and collapse as if all my bones have been removed. I managed to stay on my feet, but only just.

He studies me with his sizzling eyes and a sexy smile on his face. "I'll be back around six," he says, "in time for a shower and to get changed. I look forward to seeing your gown."

I nod, because I can't speak, and he pushes off the wall. His eyes tell me that he knows perfectly well what he's done to me, and he likes it, very much. He walks out, and the door swings shut behind him.

I just manage to make it to one of the beds before my legs give way.

I flop onto the mattress and stare up at the ceiling. What the hell am I doing? I have a perfect job and an almost perfect life, and here I am putting it all in jeopardy by sleeping with my boss.

I should say no. I should write a note and say that this was all a stupid idea. I ought to get my bags, call a taxi, go right back to the airport, and pretend that I'm actually a professional PA who has morals.

Coulda, shoulda, woulda, Meg.

MY CHRISTMAS FIANCÉ

I hold up my hand and watch the ring glitter in the early evening light.

I don't want to go. I'm excited to be here. I want to play Cinderella. I want to wear my dress, I want to go to the ball, I want to be with Stratton and pretend we're in love, because I think that, actually, that might be the truth, and it'll be fun to pretend he feels the same way about me.

And a small part of me... a tiny, little, miniscule part... believes in fairy godmothers.

Chapter Twenty-One

Stratton

The AGM's long and tedious, and I'm relieved when it gets close to six and we have to stop so everyone has time to get ready for the ball.

Natalie's here. I haven't seen her for a few months, and I have to admit she looks good. She wasn't fat to start with, but she's lost weight, and she's model-thin. Even in high heels, she's tiny compared to Meg, her skin so pale she looks as if she's made of porcelain. She's very, very beautiful, but she's the moon to Meg's sun, so cold that I have to suppress a shiver.

She ignores me for the length of the meeting, but as it starts wrapping up, she glances over. When people start rising and heading for the door, she intersects my exit.

"Hi," she says.

"Hello, Natalie."

She moves toward me and offers her cheek. I'm conscious of a few people in the room watching us while pretending not to—no doubt our breakup and my sudden engagement are still doing the rounds and causing some curiosity.

Not wanting to embarrass her in front of everyone, I bend and touch my lips to her cheek, surprising myself by feeling disloyal to Meg as I do so. When I straighten, Natalie rests a hand on the lapel of my jacket, then slides her index finger behind it and brushes down as she looks at me somewhat coyly. It's an intimate gesture, something a lover does to her partner, and all of a sudden I'm irritated.

"Did you see the new financial secretary?" she murmurs, leaning close conspiratorially. "I thought John Merrick had walked into the room."

The poor guy is rather ugly, and Natalie has always been able to pick on people's flaws and make fun of them to get me to laugh. Part of me does find the comment funny, and I hate myself for that. Why does she always make me feel as if I'm looking into a warped mirror? I don't like the reflection I see of myself when she's around. I don't like who I am when I'm with her.

I step back and go to move around her. "Excuse me."

"Wait." She holds my arm. "What's the rush?"

"My fiancée's waiting for me."

That wipes the smile from her face. Her coy look turns hard and her green eyes blaze—this is the Natalie I know.

"That was spiteful," she says.

"I'm sorry if the truth hurts."

She lifts her chin and changes the subject. "Are you pleased at the total raised this year?"

To anyone listening, it sounds as if she's genuinely interested in my thoughts on the matter, but I know her better. Nothing about Natalie is as it seems. Whenever she speaks, I've learned to look beneath the surface at whatever's lurking beneath. This time, she's trying to make a connection between us. She's reminding me that we both have relatives who are blind, implying that Meg can't understand me the way she does.

Well I'm not in the mood to play. In the past, I would have countered with a witty remark, which she would have returned with a sharp retort, and we would have continued like that, as if we were playing verbal tennis. This is what she wants, a reaction from me.

"Excuse me, I have to go." I step around her and leave without looking back.

I walk through the foyer to the elevators, half expecting to feel her hand on my arm again, restraining me. She doesn't, though, and for that I'm thankful. Still, I'm sure it's not over. She knows that displays of emotion embarrass me, and that I'll do anything to stop a scene taking place. I'm convinced she's going to do something, maybe over dinner, or later, during the dancing, but I'm not sure what. I have a sinking feeling it will involve Meg in some way—it wouldn't surprise me at all if Natalie tried to humiliate her as punishment for daring to love me.

To *pretend* to love me. I frown as I enter the elevator carriage and press the button for my floor. Pretending to be engaged to someone

I actually like was a big mistake. Still, at least it means I have Meg to myself for the night.

I wince as I remember the startled look on her face when I told her I wanted to fuck her senseless. I'd forgotten who I was talking to—Natalie preferred me to talk dirty than hearts and flowers, and I'd gotten used to being frank and filthy. But Meg's not Natalie. She's cut from a different cloth. She really likes me, but she's been faithful to Bruce, and she's going to need a tender hand in the bedroom.

I'm surprised to discover I'm looking forward to romancing her.

Suddenly, I wish we weren't going to the ball. I wish I'd organized a night somewhere far away, so we could share a quiet, romantic dinner, then return to our room for an evening of sensual lovemaking, without having to worry about a formal dinner and dance, and an ex who was threatening to go psycho.

Then I remind myself that the whole reason for 'hiring' Meg as my fiancée was to sort out my psycho ex, not to get my leg over. I keep forgetting.

The elevator pings and the doors slide open, and I make my way along the corridor to our suite. Meg's face when she saw the room was a picture, and it's not even that fancy a hotel. I'd love to take her somewhere really swish. Maybe I will. I need to think about what we're going to do for Christmas, and I decide there and then to schedule some time away over the festive season with Meg somewhere nice.

I arrived at our suite, insert my key card in the door, and go in. The living room's empty, and the door to one of the bedrooms is closed. I smile as I think of her explaining that we can have separate rooms if I want to. I feel guilty that I've been so caught up in my own problems over the past few days that she thinks I've changed my mind. It wasn't that at all. It was a peculiar mixture—of being preoccupied about Natalie, of being conscious that Oscar was in the house, and of wanting to give Meg time to make sure she's interested in taking this further, plus, because of what happened to Will on Boxing Day, I always feel odd at this time of year.

I'm done with waiting, though. Tonight we'll be on our own, and I fully intend to make the most of it.

I knock on the closed door, wondering if I'll be gifted a glimpse of her in sexy underwear. "Meg?"

"Don't come in!" She sounds alarmed. "I'm getting ready."

MY CHRISTMAS FIANCÉ

"You know we're not getting married tonight, right?"

Her husky laugh filters through the door. "Don't be cheeky. I want you to see the finished effect."

"Fair enough."

"I put your bags in the other room so you can get ready there."

I sigh. "Yeah, okay. See you in a bit." Somewhat sulkily, I go into the other room.

I watch TV for twenty minutes to catch up on the news, then finally summon the energy to go into the bathroom. I take a hot shower, making sure I'm clean in all the important places, shave as close as I dare so there's no chance of me giving her stubble burn in *her* important places, wince as I splash aftershave on, and then get dressed.

I like wearing a tux, and mine is exceptional, even though I say it myself. From an exclusive range by an up-and-coming Kiwi designer, it's made from Soft Super 130's Wool, slim fit, single-breasted, and non-vented, with a satin shawl collar. Accompanied by a white shirt and a black bow tie, it makes me feel like James Bond and a catwalk model rolled into one.

I run a comb through my hair, which does what it wants regardless, put on my cufflinks and watch, slip on my shoes and jacket, and survey myself in the mirror. If I can't get Meg into bed looking like this, there's no hope for me.

After picking up a small box from my case, I make my way out of the room and into the living room.

Like my office in Auckland, the view is of the harbor, although the water here looks different. In Auckland the bay is relatively calm and usually sparkling blue. In windy Wellington the water's gray and choppy, and I watch with a wry smile as the passenger ferry heads out toward the Cook Strait, bouncing about on the waves. I'm not a great sailor—I'd be hanging over the side by the time it reaches the South Island. The sky's fantastic though, the setting sun turning the clouds striking shades of tangerine and cherry red. It makes me want to paint, even though I don't know one end of a brush from the other. I pull out my phone and take a photo for Oscar, who's doing a project on color palettes in his Art class at school.

There's a sound behind me, and I turn as Meg's door opens and she comes out. She's in the process of applying an earring, but the hands that are fumbling at her lobe stop as she sees me.

We stare at each other for a long, long time.

I'm not sure what I expected her to be wearing. I know she's conscious of her curvy figure because she jokes about it sometimes, so I thought she'd choose black, as most women do when they want to hide the bits they don't like about themselves.

Meg's dress is the same color as the sunset—a deep cherry red. It has a V-neck, double spaghetti straps, and a long skirt that, as she walks, reveals a split all the way up to the top of her thigh. She turns full circle as she crosses the carpet to reveal it has an open back. She's obviously not wearing a bra. The satin clings to her waist and falls over her hips in flattering folds.

It's gorgeous.

She's gorgeous.

She stops a few feet from me. She's taller than she was when I left her so I know she has heels on, and when I look down I see a pair of sexy sandals the same color as her dress peeping out from beneath the skirt.

I drag my gaze back up, seeing that she's pinned her hair in an elegant chignon that bears a simple small red flower. Her makeup, although heavier than usual, is still on the light side compared to Natalie, and her lipstick matches her gown.

"Whoa," she says. "I didn't think you could look any sexier, but holy moly, that's one hell of a suit."

I can't take my eyes off her. "Meg, you look amazing."

She glances at her dress, then back up at me, her cheeks flushing. "You like it?"

"It's perfect. You're perfect."

"Aw." She gives her nose a little rub. "Are you trying to make me cry?"

I chuckle and pull the box out of my pocket. She's wearing a silver necklace and earrings that look fine with the dress, but it needs a little extra something. "For you," I say as I open the box and show her the matching set. The platinum pendant showcases a three-carat round diamond, and the earrings each have a two-carat. The set cost me a pretty penny, the most I've ever spent on jewelry for a woman. Which is weird, now I come to think about it, considering I went out with Natalie for five years, and Meg and I are only fake engaged.

Meg stares at the box. "Holy shit. Are they real?"

"No, I got them out of a cracker." I take them out and lead her over to the mirror. Turning her to face it, I stand behind her and remove the other necklace while she takes out the earrings, then place the new one around her neck and fasten it. She slides the earrings through her lobes and then stares at her reflection.

She's quiet for so long that I begin to have doubts. "Do you like them?" I adjust the necklace a little. "You don't have to wear them, if you'd rather wear your silver set."

"Stratton, they're beautiful. It's just… when you say they're a present…"

"They're yours," I tell her softly. "They're not on loan."

She touches them reverently, the way she might if she were an archaeologist who'd discovered a rare Roman mosaic. Her eyes glitter.

"Please don't tell me you can't accept them." I rest my hands on her shoulders, and my fingers tighten. "I'm so glad it's you here with me and not some hooker."

That makes her laugh. "I'm glad too."

"I mean it, Meg. I can't tell you how good it feels to have you with me. I don't know why, but even though this engagement thing is only a sham, it feels right to have you by my side. You make me feel… stronger. More complete." I'm making a hash of this. I'm only eloquent when I'm talking about computer games. How can I put what I'm feeling into words? "I just wanted to show my appreciation, that's all."

She lifts her hands to rest on mine, and meets my gaze in the mirror. "Thank you. I accept your generous gift."

My breath leaves me in a rush. "Okay. I guess we'd better make our way downstairs then."

Meg collects her clutch bag, and we head out to the elevator. There are several couples waiting, and when we enter the carriage, she stands close to me. Automatically, I slip an arm around her waist. She doesn't object.

"How was Natalie?" she murmurs as some of the others strike up a conversation together.

"Usual." I don't want to talk about my ex, I want to concentrate on Meg, but I think she deserves to know what's going on. "She's still pushing me. It wouldn't surprise me if she makes a scene tonight."

"Let her," Meg says, surprisingly vehement. "Much good it will do her."

"That's the spirit." From my high vantage point I can see down her front, confirming that she's not wearing a bra. Something strikes me, and, suspicious, I slide a hand down from her waist over her hip.

"Meg?"

"Mmm?" She gives me an innocent look.

"Are you wearing *any* underwear?"

She holds my gaze and her lips curve up in answer. I stare at her, and she giggles.

"That's unfair," I murmur into her ear. "How am I going to concentrate all evening?"

"I thought you needed something to take your mind off things." Her eyes are dancing—she's enjoying my reaction.

I desperately try to steer my brain away from the fact that she's naked beneath the scrap of material she's wearing, but it refuses to be distracted, and I'm unable to stop my erection springing to life. I groan and turn to face her to hide it from anyone in the elevator who might be looking, and I begin to laugh as Meg's giggles become infectious.

"You minx." I rest my lips on her hair and attempt to count my thirteen times table to compensate for the rising desire inside me. "You'll pay for that later."

"Oh, I hope so."

I look down at her, smiling, and it strikes me that Natalie is going to be unprepared for how the two of us are together. She might not suspect that the engagement is a fake, but she'll assume this relationship is less intense than what we had. She won't be expecting this intimacy, or the fact that desire is coming off from us both like steam from tarmac on a hot day. I almost pity her.

"I hope you don't find this evening too boring," I say, and touch my lips to hers, lightly so as not to smudge her lipstick.

"It'll be great just being with you," she says. And to my surprise, I believe her.

Chapter Twenty-Two

Meg

The first few hours of the evening pass in a blur of new faces, fine food and wine, speeches and clapping.

Stratton is worried I'll get bored, but I'm so excited to be there that I spend every minute taking mental pictures so I'll be able to remember everything when I get back. The ballroom is amazing—fairy lights have been strung from a point in the middle of the ceiling to all four walls, and there's a huge Christmas tree in one corner that sparkles all through the evening. Round tables with white cloths surround a large dance floor. The tables bear centerpieces with candles and baubles. The guys are all black tie and the girls are in their best dresses, and there's a distinctly Christmassy feel to the whole affair.

Or maybe the excitement is inside me. I still can't believe Stratton gave me the jewelry. I find myself fingering the necklace throughout the evening, and when he catches me doing it, he grins, obviously happy that I like my present. I felt guilty at accepting it at first, but he looked so worried that I was going to turn his generous gift down, and besides, it's really pretty and I absolutely adore it. I guess it was expensive. I have no idea how much something like this would cost, but I presume it's not spare change.

Of course, as long as I don't sleep with him, it's not an issue. It's just a very generous present from my rich boss and good friend.

If I do sleep with him... Well, I'll really have stepped into the set of *Pretty Woman. I mustn't... I mustn't...* I repeat the words to myself throughout the evening, but they have to fight with the memory of Stratton's promise ringing in my head—*I plan to take you into that bedroom and fuck you senseless*—and his phrase burns a whole lot hotter and brighter than mine.

We sit at a table for ten with some of Katoa's customers that Stratton's invited—CEOs and directors of large companies and their wives and girlfriends. I surprise myself by being able to hold my own with the conversation. The food is exquisite, and even though I try to limit myself with the Champagne and drink a glass of water between each flute, it's not long before I feel warm and fuzzy.

Stratton's his usual self, witty and entertaining, looking totally gorgeous in his sexy tux. Some of the guys take off their jackets as the evening wears on, but although he undoes the buttons when he sits down, he keeps his on. When he stands, he does the button up—he always does that, even with a normal suit. He told me once it's a gentleman's way of getting ready for action, which made me smile then and does the same now.

He's surprisingly attentive, giving me an insight into how he would be if we were a true couple. He refills my glass or offers me a bite of something from his plate while he talks to someone else, and he repeatedly asks me questions to bring me into the conversation. I would have said the attention was for Natalie's benefit, but firstly she's sitting across the hall and I can't really see her from here, and secondly I know it's not all for show because sometimes he holds my hand beneath the table where nobody can see it. I let him. I shouldn't, but I do.

I haven't really got a good look at Natalie yet, and I don't want to stare. If I do glance over, she's looking the other way, but I get the impression again that she's tiny and slight, a fact that's emphasized by the incredibly tight black dress she's wearing. I'm worried about standing anywhere near her because I know I'll feel like Princess Fiona from *Shrek*—and I am referring to the ogre version of her. Part of me's surprised that Stratton's attracted to me if he goes for tiny, skinny girls. It's clear from my figure that I've given birth, and I feel a surge of nerves at the thought of him seeing me naked with my soft tummy and stretch marks, when he's obviously used to Natalie's ironing-board figure and no doubt flat-as-a-pancake stomach. Still, I have a good pair of breasts and Stratton is a man when it comes down to it, and most men like a generous pair of boobs, so hopefully they'll distract him from any of my less attractive features.

Not that he's going to see me naked, of course. *I mustn't... I mustn't...*

MY CHRISTMAS FIANCÉ

There are silent auctions and more speeches by various people important to the NZAB, including, finally, Natalie, as president. I glance at Stratton as she takes the podium, but he doesn't look at me. He's watching her, although I can't tell what he's thinking—his expression is neutral, even guarded.

I turn my attention to her as she starts her speech. She speaks confidently and fluently, and makes the audience laugh several times. Then, when she talks about her father and what the Association has done for him, she gets emotional, and the audience reacts in kind, several women dabbing tissues to their eyes.

I glance again at Stratton, and I'm surprised to see a wry twist to his lips. He doesn't believe her emotion, and suddenly I don't either, because once that part of her speech is done she switches quickly to a request for everyone to continue to donate generously, and her tears magically vanish.

I study her with interest as she wraps up. She's slim, beautiful, accomplished, confident, sexy. She's gorgeous, and any man would be lucky to have her on his arm. And yet Stratton broke up with her. Why was that? Was it only because she pressed him too hard to have children? I think on that as she steps down and returns to her table. Presumably, she must have thought that he didn't love her enough because he refused to change his mind about having kids. Is it fair to blame him? It's not as if he doesn't have a good reason for not wanting them. My sympathies tend to lie with him, but then I have a child. I try to imagine how I'd feel if I didn't have Oscar, and the man I loved told me he didn't want kids.

But I'm guessing that's not all it is. Stratton refused to give in to her. And she doesn't look like the kind of woman who's used to being refused what she wants.

I turn my head, and to my surprise Stratton is watching me. He doesn't smile for a moment. He insisted he's not interested in getting back with her. And he's also made it very clear that he wants me. Still, his intense stare unnerves me, and I wish I could read him better.

There's a brief pause while a thirteen-piece-band takes the stage, and then the music starts and, almost immediately, people take to the dance floor. Stratton turns to talk business to one of the guys at the table, so I stand and make my way to the ladies'.

I go to the loo and touch up my makeup, then come out and cross the foyer. I stop in my tracks as I see Natalie in the doorway. She sees me and walks toward me, so she's clearly been waiting for me.

I'm tempted to run back to the ladies' and bolt myself in a cubicle, but I hold my ground and watch her approach.

I've spoken to this woman many times on the phone. I'm glad now that I've always been polite, and never told her what I really think of her pestering Stratton.

"You must be Meg," she says, although she obviously knows who I am.

"And you're Natalie." I hold out a hand, and she takes it briefly. She's slim and tiny—she must only be five-feet-four or five even in her high heels. The black dress emphasizes her doll-like figure. Everything about her is elegant and refined. Suddenly I feel like the fat girl at the prom, who thinks she looks beautiful until she sees the popular, cool girl.

"So," she says. "You and Stratton are engaged? That came out of the blue."

I glance around, wishing fervently that he was with me, but he's nowhere to be seen, and I'm going to have to deal with this on my own. *This is part of the job*, I tell myself. I'm here to play a role, and this is my big moment.

"Not really," I say. "We've been dating for a while, and neither of us saw any point in having a long, drawn out engagement."

She surveys me with her cold green eyes. I can see she's suspicious of me. Does she suspect him of hiring me to play the role? Surely not. I think it's probably more that she thinks Stratton's doing it to punish her.

There are people all around us, but I feel isolated, as if we're standing on an island surrounded by icy water. I feel as if the temperature has dropped around us. This woman is a very cool, calm customer, and suddenly I'm not surprised at all that Stratton broke up with her. He's warm-hearted, open, and honest, and Natalie's not right for him at all. It makes me feel nauseous to think of them together, to remember what Teddi said about Natalie not letting him out of bed. I don't want to think about his hands on her, his mouth on hers, him sliding inside her. It makes me shudder.

"Has he said much about me?" she asks.

"Not really." I try to act disinterested.

"I'm not surprised." She leans close, conspiratorially, as if we're best friends. "We had a very intense relationship. I wouldn't think he'd want to reveal details to his new girl in case you found it intimidating."

This woman isn't just cold and calculating, she's fucking nasty. Anger rises inside me, but I can see that she wants a scene, so I keep a lid on it. "I don't find you intimidating," I say. "In fact now I understand why he broke up with you."

Her eyes flash. She lets her gaze slip down me and then back up, taking in my gown, my figure, my makeup and hair, her lips curling as if she finds my appearance amusing. "How strange. You don't seem like his sort at all. He never went for the wallflower type."

If she thought I'd find that insulting, she's mistaken. I know perfectly well I'm not the sort of girl who'd be the belle of the ball and it doesn't bother me. It's like accusing me of having brown hair. I know what color I am beneath the blonde, and I'm not ashamed of it.

She looks at my necklace and earrings. "Nice baubles," she says, "pretty, although not as nice as the ones he gave me for my birthday. They cost ten thousand dollars."

It's so incredibly rude of her to talk about money. I try not to blanch at the amount she mentions, even though my insides twist at the thought of Stratton buying her really expensive gifts.

"How nice," I say, because I can't think of anything else.

Her gaze drops to the engagement ring on my left hand.

"It was his great-grandmother's," I tell her. "I'm so very touched he gave it to me."

"What is it, one carat?" She sneers. Somehow, I think she's more jealous of the fact that I have access to Stratton's money than that I have his great-grandmother's ring, which surprises me. Is that what this is about? His money?

I can sense that she won't be happy until she's reduced me to tears, and I refuse to let this become a slanging match. I wish I hadn't drunk so much Champagne and could think of something clever and cutting to say to end this conversation, but I can't.

I step to the side to walk around her, but to my annoyance she moves to block my path.

"I feel it's my duty to warn you, girl to girl," she says, continuing with the fallacy that she's my friend. "I'm sure he thinks that because you're older than me, you'll be as sexually experienced, so I feel as if I should give you a few pointers."

Jesus, that's the last thing I want. I try to back away, but she has a tight hold on my arm.

"I'm sure you've already discovered that he likes it rough," she says.

"Let me go."

"You should know that he likes pain. Giving and receiving. He even pushed me to my limits and shocked me a few times, but there's not much you can do when you're handcuffed to the bed."

For a moment I consider throwing up over her. "Natalie…"

"And of course, there's the anal sex. He can be a bit rough there, too, but you do get used to it. Just make sure you have plenty of lube handy."

My blood turns to ice. I stare at where she's gripping my arm, and eventually she opens her fingers and releases it. I turn away, but once more she blocks my view.

"Did he tell you he doesn't want kids?" she says.

It's her last ditch attempt to shock me, to drive a wedge into our new relationship. I'd been prepared for this, and I'd planned to tell her that it was okay because I don't want them either, but as I look down into her cold green eyes, I want to hurt this woman, and so I change my response before I can think better of it.

"Sorry," I say, "but you're mistaken there. We're already trying for a family."

I watch her eyes widen, her jaw drop. Smoothly, I step around her and walk away, and this time she doesn't try to stop me.

I walk into the ballroom and across to our table, and sink into my chair. My heart is racing, and I have to fight a wave of nausea. I should have returned to the ladies'. I can't possibly throw up over the dinner table. I fight it hard, hoping I don't hyperventilate, trying to take deep, calm breaths.

I hate her. I hate her with every bone in my body. Now I understand why Stratton went to the lengths of getting a fake fiancée to try to convince her it was over. I'd assumed she was just clingy, broken-hearted, and a bit misplaced in her belief that he's doing this to punish her. But now I understand Teddi's description of her as a psycho.

MY CHRISTMAS FIANCÉ

I can't believe that Stratton would have gotten involved with her if he knew what she was truly like. I imagine that she hid her true nature well, reeling him in with sexual favors and taking advantage of his good nature until he was in too deep. I believe that she loves him, and clearly she wants to marry him and have his children. But she also wants his money, and she's emerald with envy that she's lost it all.

I think I may have won that encounter, but I don't feel victorious. Her words ring in my head. *He likes it rough. He likes pain. Giving and receiving.* I shudder at the other things she said. I don't know the man of whom she spoke, and I don't want to know him. Natalie's right—I'm not prepared for this. Jesus. What have I got myself mixed up in?

Chapter Twenty-Three

Stratton

The guy sitting next to me has finished his business talk, and now I'm having to hear about his recent holiday to Fiji. I listen politely, mainly because I'm hoping he's going to come on board in the New Year as a major stockist of Katoa software and technology, but my mind starts wandering, and tends to happen, it wanders to Meg.

I was aware that she'd left the table for a while, presumably to visit the ladies', but when I feel her return to my side, I reach out for her hand. Not finding it, I glance at her, and I see immediately that something's wrong. She's white as the tablecloth, and her whole posture is defensive, her shoulders hunched, her hands clasped tightly beneath the table. She's staring at her Champagne glass, and she doesn't look at me.

I bring my gaze back to the man on my right and wind up the conversation, rising to prove that we're done, buttoning up my jacket. I hold my hand out to Meg. She doesn't take it, and I'm shocked to see her eyes glittering with tears.

I'm pretty sure I know what's happened. I straighten and scour the hall, finding Natalie back at her table. I hear her high-pitched laughter from across the room. She's well on the way to being drunk, and she's trying to prove she's unaffected by the encounter they've obviously just had.

I bend down to Meg as I say softly, "Come with me."

She stares at my hand, then eventually takes it and rises. I tuck it into the corner of my arm, and lead her out through the tables.

The band is playing well, and more and more people are rising to dance. The music's loud, and it's a relief to go through the doors and out into the coolness of the foyer. I don't stop there though—I don't want any eyes on us. Instead, I lead her across to the bar, which is nearly empty.

I order two glasses of a limited release, Devil's Cask Bowmore Islay malt whisky. We don't say anything while the barman pours the deep mahogany liquid over ice. He slides them to us, and I take a sip of it, breathing in rich, exotic fruits and treacle, and tasting chocolate fudge and smoky fruitcake. I'll definitely have another glass of that before the night's out.

Looking at Meg, I think I'll need it. I can't decipher her mood—I don't know if she's upset or furious. Maybe both.

I walk across to a table, and she follows and sits beside me. I give her a moment to settle. We both sip our whisky, and Meg takes a shaky breath. She still won't look at me.

The band is playing Wizzard's *I Wish It Could Be Christmas Every Day*. Irritation rises within me at the fake Christmas jollity we're all supposed to be feeling. It might be Scrooge-like, but I wish the festive season would fuck off.

"Tell me what happened," I say.

I wait for her to say *Nothing*, like women always do. Normally you have to pry information out of them, I don't know why, I suspect because it makes them feel more important, and increases the drama of the situation.

Meg doesn't though. Instead, she says, "Natalie stopped me."

I'd already guessed, but even so it makes my heart sink. "What did she say?"

"Pretty much what we expected. She thinks you're engaged to me out of some twisted attempt to make her jealous. She tried to imply that she knows you better than me."

"We talked about this," I say, bending my head to catch her eye. "You knew she was going to try to catch you at some point. I told you she's smart and astute—she knows exactly how to get under a person's skin."

"I didn't realize she was so…" Her gaze flicks to mine, then down to her glass again. "Cruel."

Natalie's hurt her feelings. Anger sears through me, taking me by surprise. It's the kind of rage I used to feel when someone made fun of Teddi if she walked into a chair or had a smudge on her nose. I tell myself it's because Meg's my PA and I asked her to act as my fiancée, so I'm partly responsible for what's happened, but even as the thought forms, I know I'm kidding myself. I'm angry because my ex has hurt the girl I'm falling for, and it makes me want to march out there and shake her until her teeth rattle.

"I tried to tell you what she's like." My voice is hoarse.

Meg frowns, and finally her gaze rises to mine. She looks genuinely puzzled. "I don't understand why you would date a woman like that for so long. You're a better man than that. Why didn't you run a mile as soon as you saw what she was really like?"

I need to be honest now, or we won't get past this. "Truthfully, she kept it hidden for a long time. She covered it well with a witty sense of humor, and I was busy. I didn't actually see her that much, and didn't think about it at all. We never had the sort of conversations you and I have had over the past few days. She rarely stayed over. We met for… you know…"

"Sex," Meg says flatly.

"Yes. Sex." I don't miss the jealousy that flickers on her expression. "And we were together socially. But we weren't the adoring couple she thinks we were. Not by a long shot." I still can't work out what's gotten to Meg. "Did she mention children?"

"Oh yes."

We'd discussed this, and she'd told me what she would say. "So you said you didn't want any more?"

For the first time, she looks embarrassed. "Ah, no. By that point she'd tipped me over the edge, and I wanted to hurt her." Her eyes flash.

I've never heard Meg say anything mean like that before. Half of me is pleased that she seems to have stood up for herself. The other half is sad that Natalie's brought her down to her level.

"So what did you say?"

She scratches her nose. "I told her we're already trying for a baby." Her wary gaze meets mine.

My lips curve up. "Yeah, I guess that would do it." Actually, Meg's a genius, and I don't know why I hadn't thought of it myself. Nothing would make Natalie understand it was over more than for me to consider having a family with another woman.

"You're not angry?" Meg whispers.

"No. I don't understand why that upset you, though."

She raises her glass and takes a big swallow of her whisky. "It wasn't that."

I remember she'd said that by that point Natalie had tipped her over the edge. "What else did she say?"

Meg gives a long sigh, tips back her head, and looks up at the ceiling. "Stupid things, Stratton, things meant to hurt me."

"Like what? Tell me."

She fingers the necklace around her neck. "I'm embarrassed to say."

"Why?"

Impatience flickers on her features. "Because I adore the gift you gave me, and I'm ashamed that she made me feel jealous."

I frown. "Jealous of what?"

"She told me about her expensive birthday gift. I felt jealous that you'd bought her something nice, and I'm embarrassed by that."

My lips curve up. "Sweetheart, what you're wearing cost ten times what I bought for Natalie, which, incidentally, I had my previous PA choose out of a catalogue. I didn't even see it until she opened it."

Meg stares at me. "Ten times?"

"Yes. Ten times. Hers was white-gold. Yours is platinum. The diamond in your pendant is three-carats, and a far-superior cut to anything I ever bought her."

Meg looks so shocked it's almost comical. "But she said hers cost ten thousand dollars."

"I know, I bought it, remember?"

"But that means that these cost..." She touches an earring. Her jaw drops.

"Glad to see you know your ten times table."

"Stratton!"

"What? I have money, big deal. I wanted to buy you something nice."

"Something... *nice*?" She looks as if I told her I bought her the moon.

"Come on," I say. "What else did she tell you?" I want to know what's gotten to her so bad.

She's still reeling from the cost of the jewelry. "Um... she said you don't normally go for wallflowers. She managed to make me feel like the fat chick at high school who goes to the ball and then realizes she doesn't actually look as beautiful as her mum's told her." She gives me an amused look. That's not what's bothered her.

Still, white-hot anger sears through me. "And?"

"She just…" For the first time, a flush appears in her cheeks. "She made me feel…" Her voice trails off.

"What, Meg? For fuck's sake, just tell me."

"She made me feel foolish." The flush darkens. "She said things about the two of you, about what you did in bed. She wanted to make me feel naïve and inadequate, and it worked. Although I have a child, I'm not that experienced in bed. The things she said made me uncomfortable because I don't like thinking about the two of you doing them together. And I'm not sure how I'd feel if you did them to me. She implied I wouldn't be able to satisfy you. That's what upset me."

We stare at each other for a long time.

"What sort of things?" I say eventually.

"Stratton…" She looks away, embarrassed and exasperated.

"I can't defend myself unless I know what she said." I slide a finger beneath her chin and lift it so she's looking at me. "You have to tell me, Meg."

"She said you like to tie your partner up."

"I don't tie a girl up and then walk off and watch TV, if that's what you're worried about."

"Stratton…"

I tip my head and observe her. "You don't like the idea of being at my mercy while I arouse you with my hands and mouth until you can't bear it anymore, and then take my pleasure from you?"

Her eyes widen. "Jesus. Don't say things like that."

I remind myself that I need to take this slowly. I don't want to scare her off. "Is that all?"

"No. She said you liked pain. Giving and receiving. That you pushed her to her limits."

"That's a lie," I say steadily. "Pain is one thing I'm not into."

She meets my gaze again. "You're just saying that."

"I'm really not. Don't you remember what a fuss I made when I had to have a flu jab?"

Her lips gradually curve up. "You were worse than Oscar."

"I was. I'm terrible. Pain most definitely does not turn me on. I don't know what made her come up with that, but it was an outright lie. What else did she say?"

"That you like it rough. Especially during…" She obviously can't bring herself to say it.

MY CHRISTMAS FIANCÉ

"During?"

"During anal sex, Stratton," she snaps, "if you're going to make me say it."

I exhale slowly. *Wow, Natalie*, I think. *You really went for it, didn't you?*

I take Meg's hand, the one with my ring. In the ballroom, the band is playing *Do They Know It's Christmas*. It feels like Christmas Eve, and tomorrow could be gloriously sunny and the best Christmas Day I've ever had, or it could be cold and rainy and flat as a possum on the road. There's the potential for something to happen between Meg and I, but it won't unless I tackle this right.

"Sweetheart," I say, "I don't know what's going to happen between us. All I can tell you is that I like you a lot, and I've enjoyed our time together over the past few days. In fact, I think I'm falling for you, which is taking me by surprise because I didn't expect it, and I'm not quite sure what to do about it."

She stares at me. "Oh."

"The thing is, I've fucked everything up, because I should have been able to make it clear to Natalie that it's over, but I could only come up with this stupid plan to have a fake fiancée, and because of that I've somehow—in my own, inimitable style—managed to make you feel like a hooker."

She gives a short laugh.

"I feel terrible about that," I tell her. "It's the last thing I would have wanted you to feel. Because I really like you, and I *really* want to take you to bed."

She looks at me for a long time. "Don't you think you'll get bored with me?"

I sip my whisky. "No. The thing is, in its basic form, sex is just mechanical. Tab A into Slot B or C."

"Or D, in your case," she says.

I give her a wry look. "What I'm trying to say is that when sex is the only thing that brings two people together, it can become dull. You have to keep finding new ways to make it interesting. It becomes all about the finish line. Do you want to know the truth? The reason I broke up with Natalie wasn't that I didn't want kids and she did. At least, that wasn't the only reason. I told her that was the reason because I didn't want to be cruel. But the reason I didn't want to stay with her was that the more I was with her, the less I liked her. It's not a nice thing to say, and I'm not proud of it, but it's the truth."

Meg thinks about that. "But you like me?" she asks eventually.

It's such a genuine, gentle question that it makes me smile. "Yes, Meg. I like you a lot."

"So my lack of experience isn't a problem?"

"Of course not. Don't you think it would be fun to try things together?"

She flushes. "I guess. I know that Natalie was trying to hurt me, and I accept it's possible she said things she knew would get to me, even if they weren't true. I suppose sex is a sore spot for me, that's all."

"Sex is like ice cream," I tell her. "There's a reason they call basic sex vanilla. A good vanilla ice cream can be fantastic, just what the doctor ordered. But sometimes it's nice to try other flavors. It'd be fun to see what flavors you like, Meg. You can have a taste of all different kinds, and if you like one, you can have a bit more. But I'd never force-feed you. And it wouldn't bother me if you liked different flavors than I did, because as long as there's ice cream around, I could eat vanilla for the rest of my life. Does that make sense?"

That makes her laugh. "Yes, it does. It's a lovely thing to say. I suppose I just worry that I won't be... enough for you."

I could drown in her blue eyes. I love the way this woman is courageous and spirited, and yet she also has a vulnerability that makes me want to pull her into my arms and protect her from the world. How can I explain to her how different she makes me feel?

"Sex is about sating a physical need," I tell her. "But making love is about sharing yourself with another person. I'm ashamed to say it, but I didn't do a lot of that with Natalie. I didn't love her, Meg. Not the way a man should love a woman. I realize that now. There was no magic between us. And it wouldn't surprise me if she admitted that, if you were to ask her. We were convenient for each other. And, I suspect, she liked my money. She wants to get married and have children because she wants the social status of a rich married wife, and she wants to prove to her social circles that she could be a young, trendy mother." I sigh and run a hand through my hair. "Jesus, I sound mean."

"No, you're just telling it like it is. If I'm honest, I think it's probably more than that for her—I think she genuinely loves you. But I have no doubt that she also enjoys the fact that you have money and status. Things like that are very important to women like her."

"But not to you?" I tip my head and study her.

Her brow furrows. "I've been thinking a lot about whether any part of the attraction I feel for you is due to you having money. I'm trying to be honest with myself."

"And?"

"Hand on my heart? I can't say it's not exciting." Her hand rises to touch the pendant where it lies on her throat. "Having a beautiful gown, lovely jewelry, a gorgeous house… It's a dream come true for someone like me. Cinderella meeting her prince." She smiles. "But even though I've tried to tell myself that I'm only interested in you for your money, the truth is that I'm not." She meets my eyes.

"So what are you interested in?" I murmur.

"You." She looks at me that way she does that gives me goose bumps. Not just with desire, but as if she really likes me.

I swallow hard. "So you don't want to go? You don't want me to call a taxi and take you to the airport?"

"No. I want you to tell me, hand on your heart, that you and Natalie are over, and that you're not interested in getting back with her."

I place my hand on my chest. "I do so solemnly swear."

Her lips curve up. "Then what I want is to go back into the ballroom and have a lovely evening. I want to dance with you and show everyone that we really are interested in each other. And then I want to go back to our room, get into bed, and make love with you. Does that sound like a good plan?"

Chapter Twenty-Four

Meg

I'm done with feeling guilty, with worrying about everything, with trying to second guess myself and Stratton and Natalie. I don't know if it's the whisky, or that I'm here dressed like a princess, or the fact that he's told me he's definitely over her, but I'm done with letting other people dictate what happens in my life. I want this man, and he appears to want me, and I'm not going to let a jealous ex spoil what promises to be a magical connection between us.

Stratton doesn't say anything, but he replies by finishing off his whisky, then standing and holding out his hand. I finish mine, wincing at the last mouthful, slip my fingers into his, and let him lead me back to the ballroom.

I don't even look at Natalie. I don't have eyes for anyone but the man in front of me. He walks confidently to the dance floor, which surprises me as I wasn't sure if he was the kind of guy who enjoyed dancing, but once we're on the wooden floor, he twirls me to face him, holds me tightly, and then we start moving to the music.

I'm in high heels, which would normally preclude me from getting too carried away when I dance, but with Stratton's arm around me I feel safe and steady, and soon I'm spinning and rocking with him, thoroughly enjoying myself. He has natural rhythm, which delights me, and once I realize that he's enjoying himself too, time flies as we dance to song after song. The band is fantastic, playing all the famous old Christmas tunes as well as new ones, anything to get the feet moving.

I know that Stratton was furious with what Natalie said to me—it was written all over his face. Half of me expected him to march over to her and have a big scene in front of everyone. But maybe he's realized that's what she wants, because he hasn't looked her way

MY CHRISTMAS FIANCÉ

once, even though I've seen her dancing with other men, presumably to try to make him jealous.

Instead, he barely takes his eyes from mine, and as the evening wears on I think he's probably as excited as I am about what's going to happen when we go back to our suite. I'm still worried that I'm too dull for him, but maybe he's right, and even knowing the whole of the Kama Sutra doesn't make up for the connection that's forming between us, making us sparkle like the fairy lights above our heads. Tonight it's brighter than ever, and I wouldn't be surprised if we're lighting up the dance floor with our energy. Half of me wants to drag him up to our room now, but equally I understand how special this time is. The anticipation of our first time is exciting, a thrill I'll never get again, and I can see why he wants to prolong it, like a kid staying up as late as he can on Christmas Eve.

He's such fun to be with. He constantly makes me laugh, and then he pulls me closer and whispers in my ear or touches his lips there, and I shiver and feel my nipples tighten in my bodice, and I glow all over.

Later, the band plays one or two slow songs, and Stratton doesn't lose the opportunity to pull me close and mold my body to his. His hand slides down to my hip, and I know he's testing again that I'm definitely not wearing any underwear.

"I can't wait to strip this dress off you," he murmurs in my ear, sending a frisson down my spine. "I want to feel you against me, skin on skin."

"It'll have to wait," I whisper back, even though he's turned my legs to jelly. "I have something special to show you first."

"Oh?" He raises an eyebrow, but I shake my head, wanting to save it for later.

The heat in his eyes could melt gold, and my sigh is almost a whimper. I can't believe I'm going to bed with this man. I really do feel like Cinderella. I just hope I don't turn into a pumpkin at midnight.

We have a few more dances, but I can see that Stratton's getting hot under the collar, and I'm not surprised when eventually he takes my hand and leads me back to our table. We both finish off our soft drinks thirstily, and then he pulls me to him and whispers in my ear, "I think it's time we adjourned, don't you?"

I nod, pressing my lips together, and he smiles and says goodnight to those sitting at the table.

"Night, Stratton." The man sitting next to me rises to shake his hand, and his wife comes over to kiss us both on the cheek.

"You make a lovely couple, dear," the older woman tells me. "He can't take his eyes off you. It's lovely to see."

I'm so warm that luckily I don't think my blush will show. "Thank you," I say, touched to think others have noticed the connection between us.

We say goodbye to everyone else and head for the elevators. Unfortunately, there are quite a few people waiting to return to their rooms, so we have to content ourselves with holding hands as the carriage rises. Stratton dips his head as if to whisper in my ear, but instead he touches his lips there, and then I feel the warm slide of his tongue beneath my lobe. I shiver, and he chuckles, slipping an arm around my waist. Jeez. If he can make me clench inside just by doing that, how the hell am I going to cope when we're naked?

We reach our floor and exit, and he leads me along the corridor to our room. Outside, he extracts the key card from the inner pocket of his jacket, then pauses and looks down at me. I look up into his blue and green eyes, catching my breath at the warmth in them.

"What?" I murmur self-consciously.

"You look so beautiful." He cups my cheek with hand, and strokes his thumb over my skin. "You were amazing tonight. I think I'm half in love with you, Miss Meg."

My lips part and my head spins, and it's nothing to do with the Champagne. "Oh."

He moves close, pinning me against the wall, and lowers his lips to mine, and we exchange a long, leisurely kiss, our tongues entwining. I manage to keep calm, even though inside I'm screaming with excitement like a toddler. Oh, I'm crazy about this man, and he's half in love with me! I can't be this lucky. Something has to go wrong, surely.

He lifts his head, and as he moves back, I see someone further along the corridor, watching us. I blink a few times to focus, and then I realize it's Natalie. I'd completely forgotten about her.

Seeing the look on my face, Stratton turns to follow my gaze, and for a brief moment we all stand there, frozen.

Natalie's clearly just watched us kiss. We didn't know she was there, so obviously what he feels for me isn't an act he's putting on for her benefit. I know we've looked good this evening, and she must have seen us dancing and being intimate together.

Stratton moves, and for a brief, panicky second, I think he's going to walk over to her, beg her to forgive him, tell her it's all a mistake, and he wants her back.

He doesn't, though. He slides the key card in and opens the door. Then, without looking back at her, keeping his gaze on me, he takes my hand and leads me in.

I glance over my shoulder. I can see in her forlorn, heartbroken expression that she finally understands she's lost him.

She does genuinely love him. For some reason, even though she's been a complete bitch to me, the thought makes me sad.

Stratton's still leading me inside, and so I pass through the door and let it close.

He takes me into the center of the room, then turns to face me. He slides a hand under my chin and lifts it, then kisses me, lightly, a brush of his lips to mine. He raises his head and looks at me for a moment. Then he says, "Are you okay?"

I nod. "She really does love you," I say. I feel guilty. Why do I feel guilty? I'm not stealing her man. Their relationship was over before I came on the scene.

He shakes his head. "I don't want to talk about her. Not anymore. In here, it's just me and you. Understand?" He gives me a warning look. If he'd been wearing glasses, he would have looked over them like a schoolteacher berating a naughty child.

I shiver. His lips curve up, and he slides an arm around me. "Understand?"

I nod. My heart's racing so fast I'm hoping I don't pass out in his arms. I can't believe he's chosen me over her. We're really here, in this hotel room, just the two of us. It's late, but we can take as long as we want to play. It's possible that he might throw me onto the bed and do me in seconds. Which sounds pretty fantastic right at this moment. But somehow, I don't think that's what he's got in mind.

He kisses me, and I close my eyes, drop my clutch bag, and lift my arms around his neck. I press up against him, and he's warm and hard and so… manly, all muscles and aftershave and short dark hair. I slide my fingers into it, scraping my nails lightly along his scalp, and am rewarded when he shudders, his hands splaying on my butt and pulling me against him. He's already hard for me. Oh… sweet Jesus, I can't wait.

I move back, breathing heavily. "Give me one minute, okay?"

He nods and runs his hand through his hair. "Any longer, though, and I'm coming in to get you."

I laugh, slip my shoes off, and run across to the bedroom. It's like I'm six years old and have just woken to find the shining pile of parcels at the bottom of my bed. They're all mine, and I can open them as fast or as slow as I want. And every one is going to contain my heart's desire.

I slip into the bathroom and close the door, let out a shaky breath, and then hurriedly strip the gown off. I bet Cinderella felt like this when she got home, I think, hanging the gown on the back of the door. I remove the nightie I'd left there when I dressed earlier. I bought this at the same time as the gown. It was a naughty, extravagant purchase considering I wasn't sure we'd end up in bed together, but I'm so glad I bought it. I slip it on, enjoying the feel of the silky material over my skin. It's a plum color with net over my breasts and a beautiful shiny material that falls in flattering folds to the top of my thighs.

Carefully, I remove the diamond jewelry and place it on the side. I can't believe it cost Stratton over a hundred thousand dollars. That's silly money. I should give it back to him, because that much money could do so many things in the world, and it's greedy and ridiculous to wear it because it looks pretty. But I don't know that I can. I loved it before I knew how much it cost, and it's the fact that he's spent more on me than he spent on Natalie that makes me want to keep it, more than the actual cost of it itself.

I wish I had the time for a shower as I'm warm from dancing, but his threat of walking in rings in my head. As quickly as I can, I freshen up, spray on a tiny bit of perfume, let my hair down, and rinse my teeth. Then I survey myself in the mirror. I'm startled by the transformation. My skin is flushed, my eyes are bright, and I look sexy and sultry. Even I'm turned on by my reflection. Hopefully Stratton will be too!

My heart in my mouth, I open the bathroom door and walk out, then stop in my tracks. I hadn't heard him come into the bedroom, and it's a shock to see him standing there, looking out of the window across the city. He's removed his jacket and shoes and socks, and he looks *hot as* standing there with bare feet but still in his shirt and bow tie, and his black trousers. He glances over as I come out, and I have the pleasure of seeing his eyes light and his lips curve with pleasure.

"Wow." He walks over to me, his gaze searing down my body before returning to my face. "You look so fucking sexy," he says, his voice little more than a growl.

"I'm glad you like it," I squeak. I'm quite a bit shorter without my heels, and he has to look down at me as he comes close. He pushes me until I feel the small bookcase that's against the wall at the back of my thighs.

He holds my face in his hands, and the look in his eyes makes me melt. *I think I'm half in love with you, Miss Meg.* The memory of his words brings tears to my eyes.

He studies my face for a moment. And then, slowly and softly, he kisses me.

Chapter Twenty-Five

Stratton

I have no idea why I'm feeling so exhilarated. Maybe it's because I saw in Natalie's eyes the final acceptance that we're over. It's made me feel as if a huge weight's been lifted, and it's only now that I realize what a burden I've been carrying around. I didn't want to hurt her, but I'm glad she saw us, because I don't think anyone would doubt how I feel about Meg right now.

She's soft in my arms, all curves and silky skin, and I mold her to me, enjoying the feel of her womanly body against mine. Her mouth is soft, too, and she tastes sweet as I slide my tongue against hers. I love how she's eager but shy, letting me lead. I hope I don't disappoint her tonight. I want to make this good for her, because she deserves it. She's the nicest person I know, kind, warm, and beautiful both inside and out. It's odd, but I feel that when I'm with her, she makes me a better person. I like who I am when I'm with her, and that's a first.

Moving back because I'm getting hot, I remove my bow tie and toss it onto the chair. I offer her my shirt cuffs, and she takes out the cufflinks. She starts unbuttoning the shirt, and I watch her pop the buttons through the holes, enjoying her admiration when she pushes the halves of the shirt aside.

"Mmm," she says, stroking her hands across my chest. She moves her hands behind my back, skating across my skin beneath the shirt, and when she scores her nails lightly down, I shudder. "Does that feel good?" she whispers, lifting up on her toes to find my mouth again. In answer, I guide her hand to my erection.

"Oh," she says, as if surprised. Her fingers close around it through my trousers. "Mmm. Wow."

I chuckle. "How come you always know the right thing to say?"

She laughs and kisses me, lifting her arms around my neck. "You make me feel so good, Stratton. I hope you know that. I'm having such a lovely time. Thank you so much for bringing me with you."

"Aw, Meg." I let the shirt drop to the floor and then wrap my arms around her. "I'm glad you came." Moving back, I lead her to the bed, where I sit and turn to lie down, then pull her on top of me. She stretches out along me, then lowers her mouth to mine, and I let her kiss me, enjoying the gentle exploration of her tongue, the way she nibbles my bottom lip with her teeth.

I smooth my hands down over her waist, her hips, her butt, not yet delving beneath the silky nightie, then back up. For the first time since I kissed her the other day, I rest my hands on her breasts. I've been wanting to do this all evening as I watched her dancing. In spite of not wearing a bra, and having had a baby, her breasts had looked shapely in the dress. The fact that they'd not been constricted by all the wire and straps that normally restrain a woman's figure have made it difficult for me to keep my hands off her.

And now I don't have to. I cup them and squeeze gently, and Meg purrs with pleasure. I love women's bodies and how they're so different to mine, and Meg's is incredibly womanly, her breasts filling my hand, plump and soft. The silky fabric of the nightie lets my fingers glide over them. I circle my thumbs over the tips, feeling them harden, and then I tug them until her mouth opens and she moans, rocking her hips against mine. The movement is rhythmic, insistent, her breathing deepening, and with some surprise I realize that—keyed up and excited about going to bed with me—Meg's not far from coming.

Holding her tightly, I twist so she's underneath me, then shift off her a bit so I'm half lying on her. She blinks and looks up at me, her eyes widening as I slide my hand up her bare thigh, beneath the silky nightie.

"Just relax," I murmur, pushing her thighs apart before cupping her mound and sliding my fingers down into her.

Meg gasps and inhales deeply, a flush spreading across her cheeks. I feel a surge of hot desire as my fingers slide through her already slippery, swollen folds, and I groan and claim her lips while I circle my middle finger over her clit. She opens her mouth and I delve my tongue inside, forgetting to be gentle, kissing her deeply. It's only twenty seconds before she's panting and her fingers are tightening in my hair.

"Stratton," she says urgently against my mouth, placing a hand on my chest as if to stop me.

"Just relax," I say again, not stopping. She comes then, her clit pulsing against my fingers, crying out with each contraction, her eyes squeezed tight shut.

I watch her, thinking how beautiful she is like this at the height of her climax. I feel a smug satisfaction at having made her come, even though it didn't exactly take a lot of skill. But she's in my arms, and it's my fingers coaxing the orgasm from her, and I enjoy every second of it, until she goes limp and her eyes finally flutter open.

"Oh." Her chest heaves. "I'm sorry."

I laugh, still touching her lightly, as I know she'll be sensitive. "For what?"

"I didn't mean to… I wanted to wait, until you were… inside me."

I prop my head on a hand, exploring her with my fingers. "Oh, you'll come while I'm inside you, don't worry. I think we'll make that orgasm number three."

She stares at me. I laugh again, stroking slowly, and then slide two fingers down inside her. Her lips part, and she inhales, looking into my eyes.

"We're just warming you up," I murmur. I press up as I stroke, and Meg's eyes turn sleepy, sultry.

"Oh my God," she whispers. "You're trying to kill me with pleasure, aren't you?"

I slow my fingers, leaning over her to kiss her. "I can think of worse ways to go."

I kiss her long and languidly, waiting until she's relaxed and her breathing has slowed. Eventually, I withdraw my fingers. Keeping my gaze fixed on hers, I suck them.

"Stratton! Jesus."

Laughing, I roll off the bed and remove my trousers, leaving just my black boxer-briefs. I take my wallet out, extract a condom, and toss it onto the bedside table. Then I climb back onto the bed.

I kiss up from her belly, over the sexy nightie to her face, kiss her lips for a while, and then press my lips down her neck to her breasts. The lace is attractive and cups them nicely, but I'm done with clothing—I want her naked. I sit back on my heels and lift her up to a sitting position, then catch the hem of the nightie in my hands and pull it over her head. Meg blushes, and I laugh as I push her onto her back and cover her body with mine.

"You have a fantastic figure," I tell her, kissing down to her breasts. I cup one and stroke my thumb across her nipple. "I especially like these."

"Well I don't think that's the kind of—oh!" She gasps as I cover it with my mouth and suck, and she sinks her hand into my hair. "Oh God." She arches her back and groans.

I swap to the other one and play with the first with my fingers, and she tightens her hand in my hair. Encouraged, I stay there for a while, teasing the sensitive skin with the tip of my tongue, grazing my teeth on it, and then sucking, gentle at first, then harder. If there's any sign of her resisting me, I'll stop, but to my delight she just moans and writhes beneath me.

I'm tempted to see whether I can make her come like this, but in the end the desire to taste her becomes too great. I kiss down her ribs, dip my tongue into her navel, plant kisses over her belly, and then shift until I lay between her thighs.

She lifts up onto her elbows and stares at me. Holding her gaze, I part her folds with my hands, bend my head, and run my tongue up the middle. With a groan, she flops back onto the bed and covers her face with her arms.

Satisfied that she's not going to object, I turn my attention to the most beautiful part of this stunning woman and delve my tongue into her folds. She's slick and warm, and I slide my tongue inside her as far as I can before coming back up to circle over her clit. Meg makes the sexiest sounds, moaning and gasping, her girlish cries filling the room. I have to fight not to rise and slide into her—every cell in my body is crying out for me to lose myself in her soft flesh and thrust us both to a blissful conclusion.

I don't, though. I arouse her as slowly as I can bear, lapping up her moisture, teasing her clit with the tip of my tongue. I can feel her body tensing around me, the muscles in her thighs and stomach starting to tighten, her breaths turning ragged, and I know her orgasm is on its way.

So I slow even more, wanting to make this good for her. Every brush of my tongue is now making her gasp. She's lost all her inhibitions and has opened wide to me, sinking a hand into my hair as she groans and pants with pleasure, and finally I take pity on her and decide to let her come.

I slide two fingers deep inside her and stroke firmly as I return my mouth to her clit and suck. I feel the climax take her the same way she must be feeling it, gradual at first, building in intensity, her soft pants turning to long moans as she starts to clench around my fingers. I guide her through it, keeping her safe as she falls, and when she's done, I take time to lick her gently and kiss her thighs before finally lifting up and lying next to her.

Meg turns her head to look at me. Her face is flushed, her mouth open, and her eyes look dazed.

"Nice?" I ask.

She swallows, and to my surprise her eyes glisten.

"Hey, was it that bad?" I joke. I pull her into my arms, and she curls up beside me, soft and warm.

"Mmm." I kiss her hair and then run my tongue around my lips. "You taste nice."

"Oh jeez."

I chuckle and lift her chin. "Here." I kiss her before she can object, delving my tongue into her mouth. She mumbles something, but she doesn't pull away, lifting her arms around my neck, and we indulge in a long, sexy kiss that's full of promise because I know what's coming next.

When I eventually lift my head, she cups my face and strokes her thumb across my cheek. "I wondered whether you were all talk," she whispers. "But you're not."

I shrug. "I do what I can."

Her blue eyes are filled with affection, simmering with desire. "What have I done to deserve you?"

"You must have been very bad in a previous life," I suggest, kissing down her neck. "Maybe you were Attila the Hun."

She giggles. "I meant that I feel you're like an angel sent to Earth." She thinks about it. "Actually no, scratch that. You're not very angelic."

"The thoughts I'm having right now are distinctly un-saintly," I agree, kissing down to her breasts and sucking her nipple again.

"Tell me about them," she says, her fingers tightening in my hair.

I tease the nipple with my tongue, then kiss back up to her mouth. "I want to make love to you," I say, somewhat fiercely, letting all the passion that's been building over the past few hours spill over us both. "I want to slide inside you and feel you all warm and tight around me. I want to watch you come again, and I want to come inside you, Jesus, I want that, more than anything in the world."

"Do it then," she says, panting. "Oh God, please." Her eyes beg me to take her.

I feel as if the world has faded away. Natalie, my work at Katoa, the people at the ball, the sadness I always feel at this time of year, everything is in shadow, and all that exists is the beautiful woman in my arms. I've forgotten to put on the air con and the room is warm—our skin is damp and we're sticking to each other, and holy fuck, that's sexy. Meg's lost her nervousness, and she's like clay I've kneaded until she's soft and pliable. Her skin's glowing, her lips are parted, her eyes are hooded with desire.

This isn't going to be enough. I've already told her I'm half in love with her, but now I can see that was a lie. I'm fully in love with her. A hundred percent. Maybe I have been since the moment she walked into my office in her sexy gray suit. I'm crazy about this girl in a way I've not been crazy about any other woman in my life. Love's come late for me, taking me by surprise with its sweetness and warmth, like a last-minute try when the All Blacks are playing Australia, or waking as a kid to find that Santa's been, even though you stayed up most of the night and never caught him.

I want to tell her I love her, but something makes me hold back. I'm not sure she's ready to hear it. That's not what tonight is about. There are things we need to discuss if we want to make a go of it, but this isn't the time. If I say I love her now, she'll think I've got carried away in the heat of the moment.

I'm sure I haven't. But I'll keep it to myself for now.

Chapter Twenty-Six

Meg

Stratton looks at me for so long that I wonder whether there's something wrong. I feel as if he's trying to decide something—not whether to sleep with me, surely?

But he gets up and takes off his underwear before leaning over to get the condom from the bedside table, so clearly he's made up his mind.

I swallow nervously. I want this—I'm desperate for him—but although the sight of him so hard and ready for me is a huge turn-on, I feel a sudden flutter of nerves. I want this to be good for him, and I don't want to do anything wrong. I wish I'd slept with more men and had more experience, because I feel like a sixteen-year-old virgin, and I'm sure I've tensed up like one.

Should I do something? Be more active? I don't want him to think I'm lying there like a dead horse just waiting for him to do everything.

He climbs back on the bed, rolls on the condom, then leans over me. I watch him guide the tip of his erection down through my folds, and then he braces his hands either side of my shoulders and pushes forward.

I gasp. He stops and looks at me curiously. I wait, expecting him to ask what's wrong, but to my surprise his lips curve up and he lowers himself down, sliding his arms beneath me.

"Hello, gorgeous," he says, and kisses me.

"Hey." It's already warm in the room, but I know I'm blushing.

He kisses me again, soft presses of his lips from one corner to the other. "Don't be nervous," he says.

"Sorry."

"And don't be sorry." He kisses my nose. "Do you want me to stop?"

"No! God, no. It's just… it's been a while. And you're super gorgeous and experienced and everything, and I'm terrified I'm going to screw this up."

He laughs. "How could you screw it up, exactly."

"Um… I don't know. But if it's possible, I'll do it."

"You won't screw it up." He touches his lips to mine. "This is going to go very, very well." He kisses me again, giving miniscule thrusts of his hips, the tip of his erection sliding up through my folds, teasing my clit.

"Mmm." My eyelids droop. That feels nice. "As long as you're not having second thoughts."

"What? Seriously?" He stops and looks at me with amusement. "After the two orgasms you've just had?"

"You looked as if you were deciding whether to go ahead, that's all. I wondered if you'd changed your mind."

He sighs. "No. I was thinking about how I feel about you, and whether to tell you." He starts the tiny thrusts again, and I can hear the slick sound of him sliding through my folds. Clearly, the noise doesn't bother him.

My body's stirring, waking up again. I lick my lips and close my eyes so I can concentrate on the sensations. "And how do you feel about me?"

"Oh… I'm crazy about you, Miss Meg." He nuzzles my ear and places kisses around it. "I was thinking about how I've not felt about any girl this way before."

I open my eyes and look into his, expecting to see amusement, that he's teasing me. But he's serious.

"Not even…"

He shakes his head, still moving his hips. "Not even."

"Oh." I feel drowsy with desire, my emotions and thoughts blending and whirling like colored oils dropped into water. "Mmm…" I want to think about his words, but they've flicked a switch inside me, turning my dial from nervousness to arousal.

He kisses over my collarbone, down to my breast, and takes my nipple in his mouth. At the moment they've softened in the warmth of the room, but as he sucks, I feel it tighten erotically on his tongue.

He murmurs his approval, thrusting a bit more, and I feel him slide half an inch inside me, the movement eased by the moisture he's coaxing from me.

"You make me feel as if it's midnight on Christmas Eve," he whispers, switching to my other nipple, which he proceeds to tease with his tongue before kissing back to my mouth. "That moment when the world's asleep and there's magic in the air. You make me feel excited, like you're a sparkly parcel at the foot of the bed." He kisses me. "I want to unwrap you. Slowly. Untie the bow, peel off the paper, and take my time to reveal what's inside."

"Oh," I say helplessly, because his words are making me melt. Or maybe it's the warmth of the room that's making me hot. His skin is damp beneath my fingers, and when he moves back he peels from me with a sexy sucking sound. Everything feels hypersensitive and aroused, from my lips to my breasts to between my legs. He's still teasing my entrance, sinking in ever so slightly, and suddenly it's not enough.

"Please," I beg. "Stratton."

He fixes his gaze on me, and at the same time he pushes his hips forward and slides inside me, right up to the hilt in one easy thrust.

"Aaahhh." He rests his forehead against mine and closes his eyes. "Jesus, that feels good."

It's the understatement of the year. I can't believe I'm here, in this room, in this bed, with this man inside me, and he's hot and hard and *holy shit* he fills me right to the top, stretching me in a way that's so erotic I nearly come on the spot.

He opens his eyes, and we stare at each other for a long moment.

I'm crazy about you, Miss Meg, he'd said. *I've not felt about any girl this way before.*

If we did have sex, I'd assumed it would be a fling, a whim we gave into while carrying out this farcical fake fiancée plan. But at the moment, looking into his eyes, it doesn't feel like a fling. He's not looking at me like he's planning to let me go anytime soon.

As if reading my thoughts, beginning to move, he murmurs, "You know this is just the first time, right?"

"I thought it was the third," I reply somewhat breathlessly.

His lips curve up, and he kisses around to my ear before nipping it with his teeth.

"Ouch." I twitch beneath him, and he groans.

"This is definitely not the last time we're going to do this." He kisses back to my mouth, and this time the kiss is hot, insistent. "In fact, I think I might keep you in my house and not let you out. I'll throw away all your clothes so you have to walk around naked all the time."

"I think Oscar might object to that," I say before thinking that how stupid I am to talk about my teenage son when my lover has just revealed a sexy fantasy.

But Stratton just laughs and plunges his tongue into my mouth, the thrust of it matching the thrust of his hips as he slides in and out of me. The sensation is sexy and erotic, teasing me toward fulfilment in a slow and agonizing fashion.

"Actually," he whispers, "you might try to escape, so perhaps I'll have to chain you to the bed. You can be my sex slave."

Earlier, the thought of being tied up had scared me, but I close my eyes, imagining being tied to his bed, naked, lying there for him to take me the way he's taking me now, whenever he wants me. "Mmm."

"You like that idea?" He lifts up, takes my hands, and pins them above my head.

"Yes," I whisper, captivated by this strong, confident, sexy guy, and melting inside at the thought that this might be the first of many times I might go to bed with him. What other delights does he know that he can teach me?

He drops a hand briefly to lift my legs higher around his waist, changing the angle of how he's plunging into me. He catches my hand again, his magical, mismatched eyes boring into me.

"Come on, Meg," he teases, "you can manage a third, surely?" He grinds against me as he thrusts, stimulating my clit. "Is that better?"

"Oh jeez," I groan as the angle of his hips forces him in further. "Are you trying to split me in two?"

He stops, pushing forward, twisting his hips to drive deeper, reminding me why it's sometimes called screwing. "You can take all of me, baby, that's right." He pauses, letting me adjust, and I close my eyes and arch my back with a moan.

I never thought that he would be so in command of me, of my arousal. I didn't know it could be like this. Instead of me limping to the finish line long after the victor has crossed, he's taking me there with him, guiding me, and I know that with him I'm never going to have to work hard to reach orgasm, because he's the one in charge of when I come. It's a revelation, and I feel dizzy with it as I open my eyes and watch him start to thrust with purpose.

His own desire is rising—I can see it in his eyes, feel it in the urgency of his hips, and excitement floods me at the thought of giving him the kind of pleasure he's already given me, twice. I can't do much, pinned by his hands, but I rock my hips to meet his thrusts and open my mouth to his kisses. I tense inside—it's close, hovering in the wings—and he must be able to feel it because he mutters, "Yes," and thrusts harder, and that's it, I lose it and clench around him. It feels magnificent coming with him inside me, and I moan against his mouth, begging and pleading him not to stop, not that it seems there's any chance of that.

He rides out my orgasm until the tension releases me and I collapse back, and only then does he give in to his climax. I watch with delight and rising emotion as his hands tighten on mine, his body stiffens and his muscles turn to rock, and his face creases in a fierce frown. He stills, swelling inside me and giving seven or eight jerks of his hips, exclaiming with pleasure. Tears prick my eyes because it's such a beautiful sight, and I never thought I'd have this with any man, let alone my gorgeous boss, who I've dreamed of every night for months.

He remains rigid for a long time, as if he doesn't want to let go of that final moment of ecstasy. And then his body relaxes and his breaths come in gasps as he lowers gently down onto me and covers my mouth with his.

We exchange a long, heartfelt kiss, and I sigh against his lips, bathing in the beautiful afterglow of bliss.

When he lifts his head, his eyes are sleepy and there's a look of contentment on his face, like the tomcat who got the cream, drank it all, and then had a roll in catnip.

"Mmm," he says, and licks his lips. "Nice."

Not exactly Shakespeare, but it does kind of sum it up.

He withdraws and disposes of the condom, and I wonder whether he'll roll over and start snoring, but he props up the pillows behind him, lies back, and pulls me into his arms.

I curl up, my head on his shoulder, and look out the window at the summer night sky.

"So many stars," he says. "Are you interested in astronomy?"

"I love looking at the stars," I reply. "My dad used to take me out at night. We had a very basic telescope, and we used to look out for major events, comets, things like that."

He kisses my hair. "I should have guessed," he says sleepily.

I yawn. "Guessed what?"

He just shakes his head. "We have a lot to learn about each other. I like that."

I snuggle against him. He's warm, and my skin peels from his as I lift up to look at him. He studies me with hooded eyes. "What?"

Sliding a finger under his chin, I tip it up, and then I lean forward and touch my tongue to the hollow of his throat where it glistens in the moonlight. It tastes salty, giving me a buzz of satisfaction that it was me who made him hot and sweaty like this.

He eyes me wryly when I move back. "Are you trying to get me going again? Because I might need a few minutes."

"Minutes?" I laugh and settle back next to him. "I've just had three orgasms. That's enough to last most women a fortnight."

He snorts. "Most women don't go to bed with me."

It's an arrogant statement, but I can see he doesn't mean it like that. He means that he's happy to take the time to pleasure his girl, and luckily, that girl is me.

I close my eyes, then remember that I haven't checked my phone. I very much doubt that Oscar's called me, but I decide to get it just in case.

"I'll be back in a minute," I say, and slip out of bed. "Just want to check my phone." Grabbing his shirt, I tug it on and wink at him, then go out into the living room.

I'd dropped my bag on the floor, and I retrieve it and take out my phone, going over to the window as I swipe the screen. There's one message, but it's not from Oscar. I don't recognize the number. I retrieve the message and listen.

"Meg?" the caller begins.

My heart shudders to a stop. It's Bruce.

"I'm sorry about the other day." His voice is low and husky. "I just want to see you, that's all. I've got so much to say. Can we meet? Just to talk. I've been working hard, Meg, to put things right. I'm off the booze. I'm seeing a counsellor twice a week. And I have a new hand!" He laughs. "It's hard to get used to, but I'm persevering. I'm really trying. I've missed you so much. And my boy. It was wonderful to see you the other day. You're obviously doing well for yourself and that's great, I'm really pleased. But I'd love to see you and Oscar properly. Every boy needs his dad. Call me back when you get this and let me know how you are."

I hang up. I'm shivering, even though it's warm and humid in the room. For a moment, I think I might be sick.

"Meg?"

My head whips around as Stratton comes out of the bedroom. He's put on his boxer-briefs, but the rest of him is gloriously naked. He takes one look at my face and comes over.

"What's up? Did Oscar call? Is he okay?"

"It wasn't him." I stare at the screen, conscious that my shoulders are hunched and my other arm is wrapped defensively around my waist. "It was Bruce."

Stratton goes still. "What did he say?"

"Not much. Mainly that he wants to see me." My head's spinning. "He says he's changed, that he's stopped drinking, he's seeing a counsellor. He wants to see Oscar." I press the back of the hand holding the phone to my mouth. "Oh God. Why won't he leave me alone?"

"Shhh." Stratton pulls me into his arms. "Come on. I'm here, and he's four hundred miles away in Auckland. It's okay. We'll deal with this together. You helped me with Natalie, and I'm going to help you with Bruce, okay?"

I shake in his arms, but deep in my stomach I feel the slow burn of rage begin. I hate the way Bruce makes me feel. A small part of me wants to run again, but the other, much larger part plants her feet, puts her hands on her hips, and snarls, *Bring it on!*

I'm not going to let him scare me away from my new home. And I'm not going to let him make me feel guilty for finding someone else.

I press my face into Stratton's neck, comforted by the warmth of his arms. I don't have to do this alone anymore. Together, we'll find a way to put our pasts behind us and finally move on to something new, something brighter. It's terrible the way people can chain us to the past and refuse to let us grow.

Every boy needs his dad. The phrase makes me grit my teeth. Suddenly he's interested in his son? Where was he when Oscar was being bullied at school? When he had to go to hospital to have some teeth removed? Even if Bruce was on leave, he'd had no time for the quiet boy who wasn't interested in playing sport or hunting or fishing.

I wouldn't refuse to let Oscar see him, and I'll discuss this with him, but I'm already certain what he'll say—that he doesn't want his father in his life.

"Come on. Back to bed." Stratton turns, his arm still around me, and guides me to the bedroom.

I climb onto the bed beside him, and he turns me so I'm facing away and pulls me into his arms, his chest against my back. He's so calm and steady—he's like the polar opposite of my ex. I don't have that worried feeling deep inside with him, that constant fear that I'm going to say the wrong thing and upset him.

This is how it should be, I think as I force myself to close my eyes.

I shouldn't have checked my phone. Bruce's call has tarnished the beauty of the evening. Tears leak out of my eyes, and from the way Stratton kisses my hair, I think he knows I'm crying, but he doesn't say anything.

I don't think I'll be able to sleep, but, exhausted from the lovemaking and the sudden stress, and finding comfort in Stratton's embrace, I eventually relax, and everything fades to black.

Chapter Twenty-Seven

Stratton

"Any other business?" Meg asks, typing the header on her laptop.

I shake my head, and Rich and Teddi do the same. The meeting's late today because Meg and I didn't get back from Wellington until eleven. It's now Thursday, two days before Christmas Eve, and we all have a lot to do before we wind up for Christmas.

"Okay." Meg folds her laptop down, tucks it under her arm, and collects her coffee cup. "Have a great day, everyone." She smiles at us all. Her eyes meet mine for a second before she lowers them and leaves the room.

I watch her walk out, enjoying the sexy wiggle of her hips in the tight black skirt she's wearing today, and my lips curve in a smile.

I've been with my share of women over the years. When Rich and I were in our late teens, it was more difficult to pull—we were computer geeks, for a start, which most women don't find a turn on, and we were working hard at setting up Katoa, while I was engrossed in developing prototypes of various controllers, and Rich was working on *Dark Robot*. When the company took off in our early twenties, we made the most of the meteoric increase in our finances and lived the lifestyle of wealthy playboys, going to parties and nightclubs and discovering how much easier it is to pull when you have money and you're generous with it. At the time, it felt as if I'd won the lottery, literally and figuratively. As I've grown older, though, I find myself much more cynical toward those people who I'm sure are only interested in me because of my money, but that's a whole other issue.

The point is that even though I dated Natalie for five years, she was hardly my first. I like women. I like how they look, how they feel, how they smell, and I like having sex with them, too. Hand on my heart, I can say I've never had bad sex. Apart from Natalie and a couple of other short-term relationships that lasted a few months, most of it was casual, so I've had lots of morning-afters with different women. I'm used to waking up and being impatient to get rid of the girl—in the nicest possible way—and get on with my day.

The first thing that struck me when I opened my eyes this morning was that I could have lain there all day with Meg in my arms. Before I woke her, I spent a while watching her sleep, something I can honestly say I've never done with a woman before. But I found myself fascinated by her slow, gentle breaths, the light flush on her cheeks, the way her long lashes curled at the ends. I discovered that she had a mole on her cheekbone, and a chickenpox scar near her nose that I hadn't noticed before. She had one arm over the duvet cover, and where she lay on her side facing me, I could see the curve of her breasts, tantalizingly plump and itching to have a tongue run over them.

I wonder when I'll stop comparing her to Natalie. I suppose it's normal to look for differences and similarities to your ex when you're in a new relationship, but thinking about my ex in bed makes me feel disloyal to Meg. I let myself do it, though, firstly because I'm sure she's doing the same with me and Bruce, and secondly because every time I compare her to Natalie, I find in Meg's favor, and I like the glow that gives me, as if I've done something right for once in my life.

Natalie is all angles—from her tip-tilted nose and arched eyebrows, to the defined Cupid's bow of her lips and her pointed chin, to her narrow, rather bony shoulders, and even her hipbones that jut out above her almost-hollow stomach. I used to find that heroin-chic look sexy, but this morning, when I looked at Meg, I had no idea why. Everything about Meg is soft and curved, from the gentle arc of her eyebrows, to her full lips, her generous, hourglass figure, even her hair, which is all bounce and curls compared to Natalie's methodically straightened strands. She's so womanly, and eventually I couldn't bear it any longer, so I moved beneath the covers to kiss down her soft body.

After the phone call from her ex the night before, I half expected her to push me away and say she couldn't sleep with me again—why, I wasn't sure, maybe because she felt guilty, or was too upset to think about sex.

That didn't turn out to be the case. She was far from reluctant to let me go down on her, and I spent a pleasant ten minutes or so teasing her to an orgasm with my tongue before rising to pull her on top of me so I could slide inside her. I can still see her now in my mind's eye, silhouetted against the rising sun, sitting astride me and slowly rocking her hips, her hair tumbling over her shoulders. Her full breasts filled my palms, and I had the fun of playing with them to my heart's content while she rode us both to a climax.

Sex with her has been great. But I'm conscious that, compared to when I've been with other women, the moments before and after lovemaking with Meg have been very different. I like her. I like being with her. Maybe it's because we were friends first, which hasn't really happened to me before. Or maybe it's that we have more in common. All I know is that as she walks out of the room, I feel suddenly bereft, and I have to fight an instinct to get up and scurry after her like a lovesick fifteen-year-old.

I'm conscious that the room has gone quiet, and I glance at Teddi and Rich to see Teddi's head tipped to one side and Rich watching me with an arched eyebrow.

"What?" I ask.

"Told you," Teddi said.

Rich grins and sings, "Stratton and Meg, sitting in a tree, K-I-S-S-I—"

"Fuck off," I say mildly, and start gathering up my things while Rich laughs.

"What are you doing for Christmas?" Teddi wants to know. "Are you bringing her up to the bay?"

"Haven't decided yet."

"You haven't decided? Or you've made up your mind, but you haven't bothered asking Meg and Mum because you assume they'll fall in with your plans?"

I think about it. "The second option."

"Stratton…"

"Meg'll come," I say confidently, although I'm not a hundred percent sure, "and Mum won't mind."

"It's incredibly rude to invite a girl they've never met to stay in their house over Christmas. What about the food? Mum will already have planned for the right numbers."

"Mum will cook as if she's feeding the five thousand, like she always does. And she'll like Meg." I am sure of that. I can't imagine anyone—save Natalie—disliking Meg.

"Are you going to tell her the real story or the literal fake one?" Teddi wants to know.

I glare at my sister and deign to answer.

"Stop glaring at me," she says. How she always knows my facial expression, I'll never know. "You're only cross because I'm addressing the issues you're trying to ignore."

I glower, but she probably has a point. "I'm going to talk to Meg about it later, and I'll ring Mum tonight."

I haven't decided yet whether to tell my parents about the fake fiancée thing. I know they'll disapprove, because on the surface it's a stupid idea, and yet I hope they'll understand when I tell them it seems to have worked.

Part of me wishes I was staying in Auckland rather than returning home this year, but I haven't been to the bay for a few months, and I miss my parents. For the last five Christmases, I've been with Natalie, and there's no way she would have spent the festive season in the back of beyond, so it's been a long time since I've had a family Christmas. I may be thirty-four, but there's still something nice about going back to your childhood home.

Plus, deep down, I want my mum and dad to meet Meg. The cynical part of me is smirking at that.

"I've not seen you like this before," Teddi says softly, with no irony at using the word 'seen'. She's never been sensitive to words that refer to vision. "What's so special about this girl?"

"I thought you liked Meg," I say.

"I do. I think she's great. But she's very different to Natalie."

"Maybe that's what he likes," Rich says. I give a short laugh.

Teddi's genuinely curious though. "Come on. Tell me."

"I don't know." I feel irritable at having to explain myself. "She's... capable."

"Capable." Teddi somehow manages to make it sound as if I'm being sexist. "You mean she knows how to change a plug?"

"I'm sure she does, but no, I'm not being misogynistic. It never ceases to amaze me how inept most people are. She reversed into a parking space the other day that would have made me think twice."

"That doesn't sound sexist at all," Teddi says.

"I'm not being sexist! Most people can't reverse into a thirty-foot parking space without taking at least three goes at it."

"Women are worse," Rich admits. He winks at me. He's winding Teddi up.

My lips curve up. "I wouldn't have said that out loud, but he's right."

"I'm not going to bite," Teddi says. "But I am interested in your choice of words to describe her."

I'm rapidly losing patience with this conversation. "I don't know what you want me to say. She has great breasts and a nice arse in her tight skirts. Is that better?"

"Thank you for that, but you're avoiding the issue, and stop getting angry with me because you can't express yourself. I'm interested in what makes her special, that's all. I know you like her, Strat—your voice changes when you talk to her and about her. Is it because she's so different to Natalie? Is this just a rebound thing?"

Her face is earnest. I know she's been worried about me since my relationship with Natalie imploded. I also know that she likes Meg—the two of them have gone shopping sometimes, and no doubt she's worried that I'm only playing with Meg because I'm looking for an escape after the nuclear devastation that Natalie left behind.

"I like her," I say softly. "I've liked her from the beginning. Yes, it's possible part of it is that she's so different to Natalie. But that doesn't mean it's shallow or rebound." I want to explain to them how I'm feeling. How can I put it into words, and why am I so bad at this? "She's nice—a nice person, I mean. She's kind. She's funny, and she makes me laugh, without being cruel like Natalie. When I say she's capable, I mean that she's strong—she's not helpless. She was trapped in a loveless relationship that turned violent, but she didn't stay and become a victim—she took her life into her own hands and reinvented herself, which must have taken a huge amount of courage, especially with a child in tow. She got herself a new job and a new place to live, and she's tried hard to make it work. That impresses me. In spite of everything that's happened to her, she's managed to keep her sense of humor and her innocence."

"Innocence?" Teddi queries.

"Yeah." I decide to switch to language I'm more familiar with. "You know in *Dark Robot* when you're in the Vaults of Laramond, and you go through that bit that's entirely in the dark, and there are spiders dropping from the ceiling and pools of poison seeping out through the cracks in the floor, and the Spider Queen is after you? You don't think you'll ever get to the other side, and then suddenly Salvadora the Paladin appears and stays with you to guide you across." I shrug. "That's Meg."

Rich grins. "That's possibly the nerdiest analogy I've ever heard, but yeah, I get it."

"Is Natalie the Spider Queen?" Teddi wants to know.

"Mock all you want," I mumble. "But that's how Meg makes me feel."

"Jeez," she says softly. "You've got it bad."

"Tell me something I don't know."

"Now I know why you want Mum to meet her."

"I didn't realize you felt like that," Rich says. He gives me a look that tells me he's been worried about me, too. "If you really like her... Don't screw it up."

"I'll do my best," I say, and it's not entirely an ironic statement.

"I mean with the fake engagement thing," Rich clarifies. "If you're really interested in her, you need to sort it out now."

I scratch at a mark on the cover of my iPad and mumble something.

"He's right," Teddi says. "And Stratton... have you talked about children with her?"

I give a long, heartfelt sigh. "It's complicated."

"So that's a no, then."

I don't say anything.

"She's thirty... what?" Rich asks. "Two? Three?"

"Three," I confirm.

"And she already has a teenager. She probably doesn't want any more kids."

"You can't assume that," Teddi warns. "Maybe she's always wanted a large family but her partner didn't, or she didn't want them with him. And it doesn't meant she won't want more with the man she marries. It's the most natural thing to want your partner's child. You're going to have to raise it with her before you get in too deep."

Too late, I think somewhat glumly, but I just say, "Yeah." I check the time on the iPad—I need to get to work. "Okay, lecture done? Time to move on."

We rise from the table, and Teddi leaves the room with Bella by her side in the direction of her office, while Rich heads off to the hub.

I walk along, pausing at the doorway to Meg's office, which is right next to mine. I lean against the doorjamb and watch her where she's filing something in the cabinets near the windows. Today, all the girls in the office are wearing Christmas earrings. Meg's are in the shape of Christmas trees with tiny red bulbs that are flashing. It makes me smile. Natalie would have died rather than be seen with cheap, tacky jewelry, but it's typical of Meg to join in with the others for a bit of fun.

She carefully wrapped her diamonds in a piece of velvet and hid them in her underwear this morning. Before she put them away, I saw her kiss the pendant, and it made me smile.

I know I need to talk to her and sort this out, but part of me is afraid of broaching the subject in case I screw it up. I'm afraid she'll tell me she wants children, and that it's something she's not prepared to give up.

I think of how it felt this morning to be inside her, to watch her come and know I was the one to give her pleasure. I've only had a glimpse of the fun the two of us could have together, and I want more.

Meg bends over to put something in a box. I stare at her butt, then roll my eyes, push off the doorjamb, and walk back to my office.

Chapter Twenty-Eight

Meg

"What are we doing for Christmas Day?"

It's an innocent enough question, and Oscar deserves an answer—the trouble is that I don't have one.

We're sitting at the dining table, looking out at the gorgeous garden and talking, sharing a huge pizza and half a ton of chicken wings like any ordinary family. Except that Stratton's my boss, we're pretending we're engaged, and we're also sleeping together. Nothing complicated about that at all.

It's ridiculous that we haven't discussed Christmas yet, but I suppose both Stratton and I have been playing this by ear, waiting to see where our feet take us. I wish Oscar had asked me when we were alone, but it's not his fault and he didn't mean to make me feel awkward.

I don't look at Stratton. "Not sure yet, sweetie. Nan and Grandad would still love to see us."

Oscar pulls a face. "Can't we stay here?" He looks hopefully at Stratton, who's tucking into a cheese-stuffed crust, watching us. Well, watching me. I glance at him, and I can see by the look in his eyes that he's thinking about sex. Again. The man's insatiable. Holy guacamole, that turns me on.

I lower my gaze and clear my throat. "Stratton's probably busy, love. We'll talk about this later."

Stratton picks up his beer bottle and takes a long swig. "We can talk about it now," he says. "I think I should spend the day with my fiancée, don't you?" He looks at Oscar, who nods eagerly.

"If Mum's your fiancée, does that make me your stepson?" he asks curiously.

"Oscar!" My face heats.

"Fake stepson," Oscar corrects.

Stratton laughs, but his gaze when it rests on me is cautious. "I guess it does." He takes another few spicy chicken wings and puts them on his plate, picks one up, then puts it down again. "Actually, I'd planned to go back to the bay for Christmas, and I was wondering if you'd like to come with me."

I stare at him. "To your parents' house?"

"Yeah. Teddi will be there too. They're having a party on Christmas Eve. We haven't all been together on the day for years, and Mum's looking forward to a family Christmas."

"If it's a family Christmas, she won't want me and Oscar there."

Stratton starts eating the chicken. "You don't know my mother. She loves big Christmases. She'll be thrilled to have you."

I sincerely doubt that, but I appreciate that he's trying to make me feel better. I suppose he feels guilty about leaving us behind considering what's been happening.

"Have you mentioned it to her yet?" I ask.

"Not yet."

"So she won't have planned for larger numbers?"

"What is it with women and worrying about food? Mum always does too much. Dad will be relieved he won't have to eat turkey sandwiches for a fortnight."

I pick up on the phrase *What is it with women?* "So Teddi's not sure about us coming either?"

He gives me a wry look and sits back.

"I don't want to intrude," I say softly. "I can't imagine what your mother is going to think of me when she knows what's going on." I watch him look down at his beer bottle and turn it in his fingers, and a thought comes to me. "You haven't told them about our arrangement, have you?" My hearts sinks. What a fucking mess. "Stratton, we can't just turn up on their doorstep and announce we're engaged. And what are they going to think if you tell them it's a fake engagement?"

"I'm working on that."

"That means that you can't make up your mind what to say to them." I speak calmly, but my stomach's in a knot. I can't imagine how this can possibly work out without his parents thinking I'm after his money.

He doesn't look bothered, though. "My parents are great. They'll understand when I tell them what's been going on. They'll like you. Both of you." He smiles.

It registers then what he said about it having been a long time since they've all been together for Christmas. "What did they think of Natalie?"

He sighs. "They never said in so many words, but they didn't like her, and she didn't like them. Dad's an Art teacher and Mum teaches History, and they talk about politics and social issues and bicker about which subject is most important. They read all the time and they don't own a TV. They know nothing about which celebrity is getting married and Mum has no interest in designer labels—she still buys all her clothes from the local bargain store, in spite of the fact that I've tried to take her shopping in Auckland. And Natalie wasn't very good at hiding her snobbishness. She looked down her nose at Mum's friends and neighbors because of their lifestyle, and Mum didn't like that. She's big on manners, and thought Natalie quite rude at times."

"What did they say when you broke up?"

"They would never have cheered or anything, but I think they were relieved. Mum's been worried about me. You know what mothers are like." He gives my son a glance, and Oscar nods and rolls his eyes as he picks up another piece of pizza. "She'll be relieved I've found myself a nice girl." Stratton's eyes come back to mine, and he smirks as he swigs his beer.

I know he's thinking about this morning, in bed. We had sex with me on top, and he let me dictate the pace. I rather enjoyed taking charge, and when he rolled me over at the end, he murmured in my ear, *You seem like such a nice girl on the surface, but deep down you have a wicked streak, don't you?* It made me shiver. I hadn't realized I had a wicked streak until he showed it to me.

"They don't have a TV?" Oscar looks alarmed.

"I know. Crazy, eh? But they have lots of other stuff. They have a games room with a snooker table and a dartboard. They've got a huge pool. And… something I think you'd like… Dad has a studio with hundreds of art books and easels and a gazillion different color paints and brushes. I'm sure he'd be happy to let you explore that at your leisure."

Oscar's jaw drops. I glare at Stratton, who gives me a look as if to say *What?*

"Talk to your mother first," I tell him. "And be honest with me. If she's disapproving at all, I want you to tell me. I don't want to go if there's going to be an atmosphere."

"Mum's far too polite to show any disapproval," he says.

"That's hardly the point," I return, somewhat sharply, which is unusual for me. Doesn't he understand that I like him? And that it's important to me that his family likes me? Jesus, I've screwed this up big time. Why did I ever agree to pretend to be his fiancée?

"What's going on?" Oscar asks, obviously picking up on my tone.

Normally, I'd be open with him and tell him what was bothering me, but I can't with Stratton there. My gaze switches from my son to Stratton, and I can't think what to say. I feel terrible that I've put Stratton in the position of having to deal with my son. He doesn't want kids. He must think Oscar's a real nuisance. And not everyone believes in discussing everything in front of children. Maybe he's wondering why I haven't told Oscar to go to his room so we can talk.

He doesn't look angry or irritated, though. His brow flickers with concern, and when it's obvious that I'm not going to explain, he leans forward on the table, his arms folded, and addresses Oscar.

"You understand why we're pretending we're engaged?" Stratton asks.

Oscar nods. "Because you're trying to prove to Natalie that you don't want her anymore. And so you can look after Mum if Dad shows up."

My throat tightens. I wish with all my heart that Oscar didn't have to think about things like that. I hate that he doesn't want to see his father, because I know that—albeit unwittingly, and arguably with reason—I've influenced how he feels about him. It's not my fault that his father is the way he is, but Bruce is still his dad, and in spite of what Bruce did to me, I will always feel guilty for taking Oscar away.

Stratton's attention is focused on Oscar now, almost as if I'm not in the room, but when he starts talking, I know he wants me to hear what he's saying. "I liked your mum the day she walked into my office, and over the last four months I've only grown to like her more. I never said anything because I thought she was married, and I'd only just broken up with Natalie, so I felt I had to get that sorted before I started dating anyone else. And then all of a sudden, things changed."

"Mum sent that email," Oscar says, adding, "I still don't know what it said."

"That's private," Stratton tells him.

"The whole of your office building got the email," Oscar points out.

Stratton's lips curve up. "That's irrelevant. The point is, at that moment I knew she liked me too. And then your dad turned up. So we made an on-the-spot decision to pretend to be engaged. It would have been fine if we were just pretending to like each other, but in retrospect it wasn't the wisest thing to have done, because it's made things more complicated."

"Why?"

"Because we really do like each other."

I catch my breath. Although we've slept together, it's the first time either of us has put it into words.

Oscar frowns. "So why don't you just date like ordinary people?"

"There are other things to think about," Stratton advises.

"Like what?"

"Like you." He smiles.

"I don't mind," Oscar says.

"That's kind of you to say so, but we have to think about what's best for you, too."

Oscar pushes his plate away, and I know he's irritated because he thinks we're treating him like a child. But the fact that Stratton is considering what's best for my son touches me to the core. I rest my elbow on the table and put my chin in my hand, covering my mouth.

Oscar stares at me suspiciously. "Are you going to cry?"

"No," I squeak.

"She's going to cry," Oscar tells him.

"Girls do that," Stratton says. "You'd better get used to it."

I glare at them both, but they're not looking at me so it goes unnoticed.

"Will we live here while you two are dating?" Oscar asks.

Gathering my wits, I reach out and put a hand on his arm. I can't have him pushing things in front of Stratton. "That's enough, sweetie. It's a big step for a couple to move in together, a decision that's not normally made until they've been dating for at least a few months."

"You're living together now," Oscar points out.

"It's not the same thing."

"Why?" he demands, and I know what's behind this. It must be cool to boast to your mates that the guy you're staying with has a 105-inch TV screen in his playroom. He's worried he's going to have to go back to our dingy apartment, because I can't afford a new console or a new phone or the latest games.

Then I see the look on his face as he glances at Stratton, and I feel terrible. I'm being incredibly unfair, because my son's not a bad kid, and there's more to it than that. I'm sure the money must play a part, but he genuinely likes Stratton—he has since I started work at Katoa. He admires him, because Stratton's built his whole business around gaming—the one thing Oscar loves—and yet he's also altruistic. He wants to help Teddi and other disabled people to enjoy the things able people enjoy, and that's no small goal in Oscar's eyes.

Because his own father hasn't set a very good example, Oscar is clinging to the notion of being around Stratton, maybe even seeing him as a replacement for Bruce, and I have to be very careful here because if things don't work out between Stratton and me, I'm not the only one who's going to get hurt.

And now Oscar wants to know why sleeping with Stratton is different to being engaged, and I'm getting exasperated and embarrassed, because Stratton appears to be finding this funny rather than annoying. "Because we're only pretending to be together," I point out.

"So what's the difference?" Oscar asks. "The two of you are having sex, aren't you?"

I cover my face with my hands. Stratton bursts out laughing.

"For God's sake," Oscar says, "I do know about this stuff. I am thirteen."

I lower my hands, aware my face is scarlet. "Please, please stop torturing me."

"Can't you just share a room?" Oscar complains. "What's the difference between doing that and being engaged anyway?"

"Do you know why people get engaged?" I ask.

"To get presents?"

MY CHRISTMAS FIANCÉ

I grit my teeth. "It's a promise to marry the other person. It's a serious commitment, Oscar, and it's not to be taken lightly."

"Says the woman who's wearing a fake ring." Oscar's tone is snarky, and normally I'd tell him off for that, but I'm too flustered.

"It's not a fake ring," Stratton says. "It's a real ring."

"Which she's wearing for a fake engagement." For some reason, Oscar's getting upset. "It's hypo… hypo…"

"Potamus?" Stratton suggests, and Oscar glares at him.

"Yes, it's hypocritical," I snap at Oscar, and now I'm upset too. "Do you think I don't know that? Do you think I don't realize what a stupid idea this was?" I slide the beautiful ring off and put it on the table, conscious that Stratton has leaned back in his chair and is watching me with his head tipped to one side. "There. Now we're not pretending to be engaged. Everybody's happy." I stand and shove my chair away, walk off to my room, and close the door behind me.

Chapter Twenty-Nine

Stratton

We hear the door shut, and Oscar and I exchange a glance.

"I've upset her," he says, his face forlorn. "I hate upsetting her."

"I'm sure she'll be fine," I reply. "Let's give her a few minutes to cool off, and then I'll go and talk to her."

He picks moodily at a piece of pizza crust. "I don't get what's going on, that's all."

"The first thing you have to understand is that adults make mistakes." I have a swig of beer. "Being wise is about learning not to make those mistakes more than once, but you still have to make them the first time to learn. Your mum and I screwed up by pretending to be engaged. I shouldn't have suggested it to her. I thought it would solve our problems, and it may well do that, but even though I liked her, I thought we'd be able to keep our distance and just stay friends, but we..." My voice trails off as I become conscious that I'm talking to her teenage son.

But he just shrugs. "You hooked up in Wellington," he says.

I don't see any point in lying. "Uh, yeah..."

He scratches at a mark on the plate in front of him. "I'm glad. She likes you a lot. She's had a hard time, and she deserves to be happy."

"I'm sorry you've both had it tough," I say softly.

"She cried a lot," he says. "At first. When we were living in the apartment in Christchurch, after I'd gone to bed. She thought I couldn't hear her, but I could. She was calm whenever dad called around, but after he left she always cried."

I clench my teeth hard enough to make my jaw hurt. "I'm sorry, Oscar."

"I hate that he did that to her. Pushing her, breaking a rib, was bad enough, but making her cry was worse somehow. You don't do that to someone you love, do you?"

I happen to agree with him, but equally I don't want to take the stand that everything his father's ever done is evil, because I'm hardly an angel, as Oscar will no doubt discover.

"No relationship is perfect, and it's okay if a couple don't always agree with each other. It's healthy to argue sometimes because it can clear the air, like having a storm, and it can help to make sure that you don't take each other for granted."

Oscar thinks about that. "But what Dad did, not listening to her when she said she didn't want to see him anymore, and what Natalie's been doing to you, that's not right is it?"

"No. That's not right. It can be hard to lose someone, but you have to respect the other person's wishes if they want to end it. I suppose some people think that if they love the other person enough, they can convince them to stay, but it doesn't work like that."

"I like how Mum is with you," he says. "She laughs a lot. She comes home every day and tells me what funny things you've said to her, and that you've taken her to lunch, or that you've bought her something nice to put on her desk. She glows when she talks about you."

"That's nice." It makes me smile.

"She hasn't cried since she started working with you," Oscar says. "You're not going to make her cry, are you?"

I meet his gaze, and for a brief moment I see the man inside the boy, the young man who feels he has to take the place of his father and look after her. He's warning me, and I understand why he feels the need to.

"No," I promise, although my stomach rumbles with unease, "I won't make her cry."

I look at the ring lying on the table, pick it up, and put it in my pocket. "I'm going to ring my folks. Do you want to go in the playroom? I got the new *Andromeda Space Station* game yesterday."

His eyes light up. "Can I?"

"Of course."

"My mates will be so jealous." He rises hurriedly.

"Plate?" I suggest.

"Sorry." He picks up his plate and glass and takes them to the kitchen, then scurries off.

Smiling, I take the rest of the crockery out and stack it in the dishwasher. Then I pick up my phone and walk out onto the deck.

It's a balmy evening, the sun that's low over the horizon still throwing out a decent amount of heat, but even so I know it'll be a few degrees warmer up in the Bay of Islands. I dial my parents' number and press the phone to my ear.

"Hello?"

"Hey, Mum."

"Stratton..." She sounds wary. "I was just talking to your father about you."

"Uh-oh."

"Is this a call to say you're not coming on Saturday?"

"No, nothing like that."

"Oh, thank God." She blows out a relieved breath. "I was certain you were going to cancel."

"Aw. Don't you trust me?"

"I don't trust Natalie," she says, then stops as if she's bitten her tongue. "Oops. I mean... You haven't gotten back with her, have you?"

I smile wryly. "No, don't worry."

"Ah, don't make me feel bad. I was sorry that you broke up. You'd been with her a long time, and I know it was hard."

"Well, I think that's done and dusted," I tell her.

"I'm pleased and sorry at the same time. I hope it leads to better things for you."

"The thing is..." I still haven't made up my mind how much to tell her. How should I phrase this? "I wondered if I could invite someone to come up with me over Christmas?"

"Rich?"

"No, Rich would never come." Rich always goes away for the week after Christmas, and, I suspect, spends it in an alcoholic stupor somewhere. I don't like it, but it's his decision, and I never pressure him to join me.

"So... Is it anyone I know?" she asks.

"Actually it's two people. If it's too awkward, just say—Teddi said it was unfair of me to give you so little notice for food and bedding and stuff."

"I always do too much, you know that. So come on, who is it?"

"His name's Oscar. He's thirteen. He's only been in Auckland four months."

"A teenager? Oh. I didn't expect you to say that. Who's the other person?"

"His mother."

"Ah... I see. What's her name?"

I sigh. "Meg."

"Meg... As in Meg your P.A.?"

"Yeah."

"Why didn't you just say so? Of course they can come."

"The thing is..."

"How many bedrooms do I need to get ready?" Her voice is full of smiles.

"It's complicated," I admit.

"Love always is, sweetheart."

"Oh we're not... that is, I'm not sure..." I give in and huff another sigh.

My mother chuckles. Then she says, "Wait, isn't she married?"

"No... that's the complicated bit." One of the many. "She's from Christchurch."

"Yes, I remember you saying. And her husband was in the army."

"Turns out they weren't married, and he's a nasty piece of work. An alcoholic who turned abusive."

"Oh no."

"Yeah. She left him and didn't tell him where she was going, but he's followed her up here. She's staying at my place at the moment because I was worried for her safety."

"Has she told the police?"

"No, she didn't want them involved, although she might have to call them if the guy won't leave her alone."

In the background, I hear my father's voice, and then my mother telling him what's going on.

Eventually, she comes back to the phone. "He wants to know if she's pretty."

I laugh. "Tell him yes. She's gorgeous."

"Stratton says she's gorgeous." I hear Dad's voice again. "Your father says 'That's my boy.' So... you still haven't answered my question."

"What was it again?"

"How many bedrooms do I need to prepare?"

I sigh. "Mine and one for Oscar."

"Right. Stratton, I have to ask, do you know what you're doing?"

I think about the fake engagement and my great-grandmother's ring in my pocket. "Almost certainly not."

"All right. Well, you're a big boy now. I'm sure you don't need me telling you to be careful. See you Saturday. Eight-ish?"

"Yeah. I'm planning to leave by five latest."

"Drive carefully. Love you."

"Love you too." I hang up.

I go back inside and into the kitchen, and take out a bottle of an expensive Pinot Noir from the wine rack by the fridge. As I pour two glasses, I debate whether I should have mentioned the fake engagement. They would have thought I was an idiot, but I think they would have understood. Or maybe they wouldn't. At least this way I don't have to explain it.

I'll worry about it later.

Vaguely aware that decision is probably going to come back and bite me in the ass, I walk through the house, pause outside the playroom to check that Oscar's okay, then carry on down to Meg's room. I place a glass on the floor and knock on her door.

"Come in," she says listlessly.

I turn the handle, pick up the glass, and go in.

She's lying on the bed, but she sits up when she sees it's me and moves back against the pillows. I offer her a glass, and she takes it with a wry smile.

I climb onto the bed and sit beside her. I haven't sat on this bed before, and with some surprise I realize it has a lovely view to the east across Hobson Bay. The setting sun has coated the bed in buttery yellow, making Meg's skin glow as if she's been gold plated.

I sip my wine and glance across at her. "You okay?"

She shrugs. "Is Oscar all right?"

"He's fine. Worried about you."

"I'm sorry I went off on one in there."

"It's okay."

"It's not really. I suppose he forced me to confront what we'd done, and I realized how stupid we've been."

It's my turn to shrug. "Maybe we have, maybe we haven't. The reason I suggested it was to get Natalie off my back, and I think it's worked. And hopefully it'll do the same with Bruce. If it does, then it was worth it."

"And what about us?" She turns her large blue eyes up to me. "Has it made things more difficult for us?"

"I don't see why."

"But… what do we do if we decide that after Christmas we want to keep seeing each other?"

My gaze drops to her mouth, and now I'm thinking about kissing her. "I suggest we keep seeing each other."

"Stratton…"

"As far as everyone thinks, we're engaged. I suggest we don't say anything to the contrary, unless there's something to say."

She studies her glass, then takes another sip.

I put my hand into my pocket, pull out the ring, and offer it to her.

She looks at it for a long moment. "I shouldn't," she whispers. "We're not really engaged."

"I want you to wear it."

"Why?"

"I don't know."

"That's not a good enough answer, Stratton."

I sigh. "Because it makes me feel that I'm keeping you safe." I hold the ring out, and when she uncurls her fingers I place it on her palm. "Because I like other men thinking you're unavailable. Because it's like I've branded you as mine."

Her gaze rises and she studies me. "That sounds a bit possessive."

"It is possessive. I've not felt this way before. I wouldn't have let Natalie within a hundred yards of this ring. But with you…" I lift my arm around her shoulders and pull her closer to me, then kiss her forehead. "I feel differently than I've ever felt before."

She swallows and looks at my mouth. "In what way?"

I brush my nose against hers. "You know I'm not any good at this."

"Have a try," she says. "I want to know how you feel."

I think about it. "Protective. Affectionate. Warm. I never believed in love at first sight before, but I don't know how else to explain what I'm feeling. I don't want to be apart from you. I think about you constantly. I want to have sex with you all the time."

Her lips curve up. "I think that's your default setting, isn't it?"

I can't think how to tell her about the hunger I have inside for her. "Yes, I like sex, I've always liked sex, but this is different. Before it was a physical urge I had to satisfy. But with you, I want to feel you against me, I want to be inside you, I want to watch you come again and again. I want to see that heat that appears in your eyes when you look at me, as if you're thinking about my mouth on yours, about me sliding inside you, filling you up. I can't stop thinking about it."

And thinking about it now has made my erection spring to life, and I put my wine glass on the table, and take hers and place it next to mine. I note that she's slipped the ring on her finger, and I feel a swell of smugness.

"We can't," she whispers. "Oscar."

"He's up to level four," I murmur back as I nuzzle her ear. "He won't be getting out of that chair any time soon."

I slide my hands beneath her T-shirt and kiss her, delving my tongue into her mouth, relieved when she lifts her arms around me. My blood's up, thundering through my veins, and I want her, now. I want to wipe away her sadness, her worry, her guilt, and her fear, and make her look at me when she comes, so I can see the pleasure in her eyes and know she's thinking only of me.

Chapter Thirty

Meg

I don't know what this man does to me. I feel as if he's cast some kind of spell, because one kiss, or one stare from his mismatched eyes, or one touch of his hands, and all my willpower vanishes. His mouth slants across mine, and he moves his hands up my back to undo my bra, and I'm shivering like a teenager, a moan escaping my lips when his hands finally rest on my breasts.

There's a noise outside—probably Oscar yelling because he's reached a new level—but it makes me twitch. Stratton moves back, rolls off the bed, goes over to the door, and locks it. Then he comes back to the bed and pulls me into his arms.

"Is that better?" he murmurs.

"Yes." I still feel unnerved, though, and I'm conscious that I'm stiff with tension. "I'm sorry. I just worry that he'll walk in."

"It's okay." He kisses my cheek. "I don't want to make you feel uncomfortable doing anything you don't want to do."

"I do want to." My body aches for him. "I've never done this before, that's all. Been with a guy other than his father, I mean. I worry what Oscar will think of me." My face flushes.

Stratton slides his hand up my top and pushes the loose bra up so he can cup my breast. His lips brush my cheek, and my nipple tightens in his fingers. "He told me he's pleased we're together."

"Did he?" They've been talking about me?

"Yes. He knows you've been unhappy and he likes that you seem happy now."

"I want to do the right thing, that's all. He's had such a tough time, and I know it's not my fault, but I don't want to make things worse. I haven't always done right by him."

Stratton removes his warm hand from my breast and rests it on my hip. I miss it immediately, and have to stop myself arching my back to push toward him.

"What do you mean?" he asks.

"I didn't marry his father," I point out. "As Maggie, I did so much wrong. I got pregnant, which was so, so stupid. Then I refused to marry Bruce. I thought I was doing what was best for Oscar, but now I'm not so sure. If I'd married Bruce, if I'd been more supportive, maybe things wouldn't have gone so badly."

For the first time, I wonder whether Bruce felt the same way Natalie does—that I didn't love him enough to marry him. I've never considered that before, and it makes me feel ashamed.

"Hey." Stratton slips a hand beneath my chin and lifts my gaze to meet his. "You've not done anything wrong. Shit happens, Meg. You did your best, and now you're here. Or do you wish you weren't?"

"No! No, that's not what I mean at all. It's just… as a parent, you want to set a good example to your children, and I haven't done great so far. And now I'm with you… I don't want Oscar to think his mother's a loose woman, sleeping with the first guy she meets."

"Is that all I am? The first port in a storm?"

"No. Of course not."

"Well, then." He returns his hand to my hip, brushing down with his thumb and making my stomach quiver. "I don't think sleeping with one other guy makes you a loose woman. Oscar is your son, Meg, and I wouldn't presume to tell you how to bring him up, but I don't think that showing him you're now in a relationship that's loving and affectionate, in which you're having good, healthy sex, is a bad thing."

"Are we?" I whisper. "In a relationship, I mean?" I haven't known what to call it.

"We are, if you want to be." He bends his head and kisses me. "I've spoken to my parents, and you and Oscar are very welcome to come and stay for Christmas."

"Oh." I move back when he tries to kiss me. "What did you tell them?"

"Almost everything."

"Almost?"

"I didn't mention the fake engagement bit. But I told Mum we're together, and that it's complicated because of your past. They're looking forward to meeting you."

He told them we're together. He said we're in a relationship, if I want to be. It dawns on me that even though we went about it in a mixed-up, somewhat idiotic way, and even though we're both still reeling from our pasts, we're actually dating.

He lifts my hand and shows me the ring. "Let's start again and forget all the fake engagement nonsense. This is a partnership ring, and I'd like you to wear it. It means we're in a relationship, and it's a promise to be honest and open with each other. Does that make sense?"

I nod, feeling happier than I have for some time. "You want more than sex?"

His lips curve up. "I hope that sex is still up for grabs. But yes, I want more than sex. I want you, Meg. All of you. And Oscar. I know you come as a package and that's fine by me—he's a great kid."

If this turns out to be something, we'll need to talk about the future—about his role with Oscar, about where we live, and whether I continue to work for him—but for now knowing that he wants more than just sex is enough to make me glow.

He kisses around to my ear and murmurs, "Turn over."

My heart racing, I do as he says, facing away from him, and I let him pull me back against him. He slides his hand beneath my T-shirt and up to cup my breast. "I want to make you happy," he says softly, and tugs gently at my nipple. "I'm crazy about you, Miss Meg."

I close my eyes and give myself over to his skillful fingers. "Mmm…"

He kisses up my neck to my ear and sucks the lobe into his mouth. He grazes his teeth on it while he plays with my nipples, and I lean back against him and turn to offer him my mouth so he can kiss me.

I raise my hand to his cheek, and open my eyes a crack to see the ring there glinting in the late evening light. A partnership ring. It symbolizes the connection between us that is still in the process of forming. We have a long way to go, but Stratton's telling me that I'm his girl, and it feels like a great start.

His tongue slides against mine while he continues stroking my breasts and teasing my nipples with his fingers. I can feel his erection pressing against my butt, and suddenly, desperately, I want him inside me.

I roll away from him, unbutton my jeans and kick them off, tear off my T-shirt, and chuck my bra and underwear on top of the pile. Naked now, I move back to him, and I shudder as his hands brush over my skin as if he wants to touch every inch of me. He moves one hand down over my belly and between my thighs, then slips his fingers into me.

He groans. "You're always ready for me, Meg." He strokes me, his fingers sliding easily through my folds. "Jesus, you're so fucking sexy."

God, this man's so naughty, but it turns me on, and I give my body over to him and let him tease me with his expert fingers until I'm moaning and my breaths are coming in gasps. He moves back and I let out a long sigh of frustration, but I stop as soon as I see him unbuttoning his fly. He doesn't undress, though, and there's something sexy about him being clothed and me being naked.

He drags a pillow down and tucks it under my belly, then pushes me onto my front so my hips are slightly raised. My heart bangs against my ribs. Bruce liked me on all fours, but we never did it much like this. Stratton seems determined to show me as many different ways of having sex as he can, and as my gaze falls on my left hand where it clutches the pillow and I see the ring again, I know what he's doing. It's like he's factory resetting a computer, wiping its memory so he can start again from scratch. He wants to erase Bruce from my mind, and install himself there, overriding my previous memories. And I'm happy to let him do it. I only want Stratton inside me, from here to eternity.

A rustle from his wallet, and then he's pushing up my knee, leaning over, and pressing the tip of his erection into my folds. He braces his hands on either side of my shoulders and bends to nuzzle my ear.

"Ready, sweetheart?"

"Yes," I whisper.

He pushes forward, harder and faster than I expected, and slides into me up to the hilt.

"Aaahhh." I bury my face in the pillow, dizzy at the sensation of being stretched and filled to the brim, but he winds his hand in my hair and pulls it gently back.

"Feel me," he demands, kissing down my neck and sucking where my pulse is beating frantically. "Feel me inside you, Meg. Get used to it. Because I'm going to spending a lot of time doing this." He pulls back and thrusts firmly, making me gasp. The angle lets him sink in deeper, and as he lowers down onto his elbows and slides his arms underneath me, I feel completely wrapped, like a Christmas parcel.

"Relax," he murmurs, slowing his thrusts and kissing my neck. "You smell so good." He nuzzles my hair. "Everything about you is soft and sensual and sexy. I've been thinking about doing this to you all day. Do you mind?"

"No," I say, breathless with desire and disbelief that this gorgeous man wants me. What have I done to deserve him?

He slides one hand down over my belly and between my legs. His fingers part to feel where he's moving inside me, and then he brings them up to stroke my clit. "It's all right," he whispers. "I've got you. Just let go."

It's a strange thing to say, and it tells me that he can feel my tension. I want to please this man, to do everything right, to show him that I'm enjoying it, but it's as if I'm trying too hard. He's moving slowly, and his fingers are skilled and sure. He'll take us both to the edge—I don't have to do anything. I don't have to try to feel pleasure. I just need to let him take me there.

I close my eyes and rest my cheek on the pillow and relax. Stratton murmurs his approval, his fingers moving faster, and I widen my thighs and tilt my hips up to give him better access.

"Yes," he whispers in my ear, "that's it, sweetheart. Just let it happen."

His body is warm against mine, his strong arms holding me tightly. I've never felt like this, so secure in a man's arms, so much a part of him. I'm just being romantic, I tell myself, like a schoolgirl, but I don't care if I am because it feels so good to give myself over to him.

I can feel my orgasm approaching, the muscles deep inside me beginning to tense, and Stratton must be able to sense it too because he lifts his hand to slide it back under my shoulder, and he says, "Slowly." He pulls almost out of me, then pushes forward with agonizing slowness, and I feel every inch of him moving inside me, sliding through my sensitive skin.

"How does that feel?" he asks. "Tell me, Meg."

"Mmm, it feels good," I whisper.

"Fast or slow? Tell me."

"Slow."

So he does it again, pulling back, pushing forward, kissing my neck, my ear, my hair, and my lips when I turn to look over my shoulder at him.

"Like that?" he asks.

"Yes…" I try to stifle a moan, but he shakes his head.

"Let me hear you."

I let it escape, a soft sigh of longing, of pleasure.

"Tell me what you're feeling," he whispers.

I flush. I'm not used to talking during sex, or trying to explain myself. Oddly, it feels more intimate and personal than the actual act. "I feel… safe," I say without thinking. What a stupid thing to say.

But he kisses down my neck and tightens his arms. "You'll always be safe with me."

Tears prick my eyes, even as muscles deep inside me tense again.

"Tell me," he says.

"I can feel it… oh… it's like a train in the distance, speeding toward me…"

"Let it come." He keeps up the slow, sexy thrust of his hips. He cups a breast and plays with the nipple. "Come on, beautiful. Give yourself to me."

So I do. I let the train slam into me, and I bury my face in the pillow and muffle my cries with it as I clench around him, the exquisite pleasure only serving to increase the tears that were already threatening to overflow.

He stops as I come, holding me tightly, and it's only when the contractions release me that he begins to move again. This time he lifts up onto his hands and thrusts with purpose, and I realize how good his self-control is, because within about twenty seconds he stiffens as his climax hits. I murmur my approval at the feel of him taking his pleasure from me, pulsing inside me, his deep groan in my ear. I love this sharing of our bodies, and at that moment I know that I'm in love with this man, and I never, ever want to let him go.

Chapter Thirty-One

Stratton

"Typical man," Teddi says, "leaving the shopping until the last minute."

"We're not exactly your normal couple." I open the door and let Bella lead her into the jewelers.

Normally, we don't work on Saturday, but most of us had stuff we wanted to get done before the summer break, and half the office turned up when we offered to pay double. Not that the majority of them are doing much work, but I guess that was to be expected.

It's lunchtime now, and Teddi and I have popped out to buy Meg a present.

"Don't you want to get her some fake jewelry to match the fake engagement?" Her tone is sarcastic, somewhat cutting, which is unusual for her. Maybe it was a mistake asking her to come with me. I never forget about Will, but I suppose he's not on my mind twenty-four seven like he must be with Teddi.

I remember the look on her face when Rich said that Meg was thirty-three and probably wouldn't want any more children—Teddi turned the big three-oh not that long ago, and although she protested at the time that she didn't care, I think it's had more of an impact than she realized. She's afraid to love again, but she wants children, and her body clock's ticking. Nothing's been easy for her. I soften, even though her words have made me bristle.

"The engagement might be fake," I tell her. "The relationship's not. I like her, Teddi. And it's Christmas Eve. They've had a tough time, and they're coming to stay with us. I want it to go well. Are you going to help me? Because if not, it might be better if we stay here in Auckland."

She bumps me with her shoulder. "Of course I'll help. I'm sorry. I'm a bit grouchy. Don't mind me."

I kiss her forehead and lead her over to the counter. "It's okay. Come on, help me choose something nice for Meg." I smile at the assistant, who's waiting patiently to help us. "I'm looking for something special for my fiancée."

"Yes, sir." Her gaze skims down my suit, no doubt spots the cut and the cloth, the expensive watch on my wrist. It's an exclusive shop, quiet even on Christmas Eve, and I don't think there's anything in here that costs less than a thousand dollars. She leads me over to the cabinet to her left that glitters with diamonds. "Might I suggest we start here?"

I know I've already bought Meg some nice jewelry, but I want to get her something else for Christmas. Teddi's happy to handle the five-thousand-dollar-plus jewels, her fingers gently exploring the shapes and weight of the pendants, and we spend a pleasant thirty minutes or so poring over necklaces and bracelets until we decide on a necklace in the shape of a pohutukawa flower because she loves the trees, the red petals formed by tiny rubies surrounded by diamonds.

I feel an unusual burst of happiness as I pay and the assistant giftwraps my purchase. I used to buy Natalie jewelry, and she was always appreciative of my gifts, but I feel different getting something for Meg. Natalie would wear her jewelry to show and impress other people. Meg will wear it because it means something special to her. I can imagine her fingering it when she thinks I'm not looking, the way she does the pendant I bought her, and my great-grandmother's ring. A secret smile touches her lips when she does so, and I know she's thinking about me.

I picture her the way she was last night, lying beneath me, her face buried in the pillow as she came. She was soft and hot and wet and tight, and I had to fight with every ounce of willpower I possessed not to come until she was ready. We're definitely doing it like that again. Although next time I think maybe we'll do it standing up…

"Stratton!"

I blink, and Teddi gives a snort. "Stop daydreaming about having sex with Meg. We don't have all day, you know. It's already one o'clock."

I give the shop assistant a wry look and pocket my receipt, then take Teddi's arm and lead her out of the shop. "I wish you wouldn't be quite so frank in front of other people," I scold her as we walk along the street back to the car, Bella trotting by her side. "Not everyone's as open-minded as you."

"Sorry, was there someone there?"

I open my mouth to reply sarcastically, but someone says, "Stratton," and I turn to see Natalie standing a few feet away.

"Shit," Teddi says, obviously recognizing her voice.

I stare at my ex. My first reaction is fear—I'm expecting her to make a scene, or to say something, anything, to put me on edge.

Then my vision clears, and I look properly at her. She's pale, and, for maybe the first time since I've known her, she isn't wearing makeup. She's shoved her hands deep in her pockets and her shoulders are hunched. Her hair is tied back in a ponytail—very un-Natalie.

"I'll go back to the car," Teddi says, holding her hand out for the keys.

"Okay." I let them drop into her palm, knowing she'll find the car, which isn't far away, by pressing the unlock button and listening for the beep. I watch her walk away, then I turn back to Natalie.

It's a hot day and the sun's streaming down on us—automatically we move under the canopy of the nearest shop. It's a baker's, and the window's full of small fruitcakes in the shape of Christmas trees, gingerbread Rudolphs, and mince pies. The shop next door is playing Dean Martin's *Let it Snow*. I'm used to Christmas Down Under now, but it occurs to me how anyone from the northern hemisphere would find it odd celebrating the festive season in summer.

"I just want to say I'm sorry," Natalie whispers.

I'm not quite sure what she's sorry for, so I just say, "Okay."

"I couldn't bear the thought of losing you." For once her eyes are tearless, and she's not accompanying her words by crying. I study her warily, wondering if this is a new ploy.

"Don't look at me like that," she pleads.

"Like what?"

"Worried. I'm not going to make a scene."

"It wouldn't be the first time," I point out.

"I know. I've never had anyone dump me before. And I've always gotten what I wanted eventually. I figured if I tried hard enough, I'd be able to convince you to come back to me. But I can't, can I?"

I shake my head, and I can see acceptance on her face.

"Okay," she says. "It's okay. I just thought… we were so good together. In bed, I mean. Weren't we?"

Scenes flicker through my mind of memorable moments with her, and I wait for regret to filter through me, but I surprise myself by feeling nothing except a dull sense of sadness. "Sex isn't everything, Natalie. It was about the only thing that was good between us, and it's not enough."

"No." She looks down and sees the package in my hand. "Is that for Meg?"

"Yes."

"She's a lucky woman."

"I'm the lucky one."

"Are you really going to marry her?"

"Yes," I say, and at that moment I know it's true.

"I hope you'll be happy together."

I'm not sure she means it, but at least she's trying.

"You'll meet someone else," I tell her gently. "You're too beautiful to be on your own for long, and I know he'll be better for you than I am."

"No one will be better for me than you, Stratton," she says without a hint of guile. With some astonishment I think that she really did love me, and perhaps I truly have broken her heart. For that I'm sorry. I wish I could have done things differently, but relationships end, and it's how we deal with those endings that matters.

She turns away. "Merry Christmas, Stratton."

"Merry Christmas." I watch her walk away, and then I return to the car.

Teddi and Bella are already in. I get in the driver's seat, close the door, and blow out a long breath.

"All right?" Teddi asks.

"Yeah," I say, and for the first time I mean it.

*

I return to the office in high spirits. It's Christmas Eve, and Meg and Oscar are coming with me to the bay. I'm excited about that, about them meeting my parents, and about having a few days with them as if we're a real family. I'm looking forward to giving Meg my present, and the one I've already bought Oscar is packed in my bag.

MY CHRISTMAS FIANCÉ

I have a few things to do before the end of the day, and I go into my office with the intention of cracking on with work. I have a meeting in about ten minutes with a businessman from Dunedin who's flown up for Christmas and thought he'd call in while he was here, and I want to wind up my emails and make sure all my correspondence is up to date. But it's difficult to concentrate.

I lean back in my chair and sip my coffee, thinking about Natalie. I feel so relieved that she's finally accepted we're over. I hadn't realized how worried I was that she was going to try to get revenge for seeing me with Meg the night of the ball. I feel some sadness as I remember the haunted look on her face, and her protest that she doesn't think she'll find someone as good as me. She's wrong, of course. When you're comfortable in a relationship, it's scary to think about starting again, and we try to convince ourselves that it's better to stay as we are. But we weren't right for each other. She needs someone more pliable, who'll pander to her every whim and treat her like a princess. And she'll find him, because she's beautiful and elegant and for some reason some men like being treated like shit.

I don't want to think about her anymore. I put my memories of her into a box and tie a bow around it, then place it in the dusty attic of my mind. We're done.

I really should do some work. I flick through my emails, but I can't concentrate. The office girls have been out for lunch and they're a little raucous, playing Christmas music loudly down the hall. Part of me is tempted to join in the party. But I have to work.

I shuffle some papers and think about Meg on top of me, her mouth on mine. I'm feeling horny, and in spite of the fact that we had sex last night and this morning, I want her again. What the hell's wrong with me? I don't want to scare her off by coming on too strong. Not that she seems to mind at the moment. It was she who woke me up at first light by disappearing under the bedclothes to explore the morning glory I just happened to have at that moment. I gaze off into the distance as I think about how it had felt when she'd taken me in her mouth, pleasuring me while I was still in that hazy state between waking and sleeping where I wasn't quite sure if it was a dream. She'd taken me deep when I came, and, to my shock, she'd swallowed, one of the few things Natalie had disliked doing, leaving me almost tearful with stupid, inexplicable joy. Sated and content, I'd then pulled her up into my arms and stroked her with my fingers until she'd come. Then I'd sucked my fingers, and she'd blushed. Even now, it makes me smile.

I shift in the chair. *Concentrate, Stratton.*

It's Christmas, though, and I don't want to work. I stare longingly at a bottle of whisky that one of my business associates bought me. I can't drink because I'm driving later, but I decide to have a mince pie with my coffee. While I munch on that, I unwrap the present Rich has left for me on my desk. It's a model of my favorite female warrior character from *World of Warcraft*, with her name and title, Braced, The Proven Defender, beneath it. I laugh and put it in prime place next to my laptop. I love it. Maybe I'll get one of Meg's character so they can stand side by side.

I roll my eyes at myself. I'm definitely going soft.

I need to concentrate. But I picture Meg beneath me, imagine plunging into her soft, yielding body, filling the air with her cries as she comes. I want to fuck her right now. I have so many things I want to do to her, with her.

And now I have a hard on. Jesus. I'm never going to get any work done. Part of me considers locking my door and taking myself in hand. I don't want that, though. I want Meg.

As if I've conjured her up, the door opens and the light of my life comes in. I stand and walk over to meet her, and she slides her arms around my waist and lays her cheek on my shoulder.

"You're so wonderful," she says. "Thank you."

Happiness sweeps through me at the thought of a future with her, bright and sparkling as the tinsel around the door. I can feel her breasts pressed against my chest and her hair smells of exotic flowers, stirring my blood. It's hot, and she's wearing a bright red summer dress today that's smart and yet Christmassy but also sexy. The skirt's above her knees and the material's soft and flowing over her hips. I know she's got red underwear on beneath it.

I lean around her, close my door, and lock it.

Meg looks up at me in surprise. "What are you doing?"

Kissing her neck, I walk her back until she meets my desk and press her up against it. "I want you."

"Now?"

"Yes."

"Here?"

"Right here."

"Stratton! You have a meeting in five minutes."

"I can make you come in three."

She laughs and pushes at my chest. "No you can't. I can't give myself an orgasm in three minutes."

"Wanna bet?" Lust courses through me, and I hold her gaze, trying to tell her with my eyes how much I want her.

Her lips part. She looks into my eyes for a long moment, and then her lips curve up.

"Go on then," she whispers.

Chapter Thirty-Two

Meg

I thought Stratton was joking, but I'm beginning to understand that he doesn't joke about sex.

He crushes his mouth to mine and sweeps his tongue inside, and while he does that he's tugging the spaghetti straps of my dress off my shoulders along with the straps of my bra. Without further ado, he hooks the lace of both bra cups beneath my breasts, leaving me exposed, and lowers his mouth to my left nipple.

He sucks, relatively hard, and I tip my head back and gasp, unable to catch my breath. He swaps to my other nipple, starting to play with the wet, sensitive skin of the first one with his fingers, and by the time he comes back to my mouth, both nipples are shining and hard like wet pebbles.

He unzips his fly, but doesn't release the erection that's straining the elastic of his boxers. I see why when he pushes up my dress and moves my knees apart. He thrusts his thick, hard length against my mound, right against my clit through my underwear, and within seconds it feels as if he's accessed all of my erogenous zones and turned them up to eleven.

I don't know if it's his skilled hands and mouth, that I'm practically naked on his desk with the hot sun pouring over me, or just the fact that this man wants me so badly, but within moments I'm so turned on that I know he was right and it's not going to be long before I come.

He lifts his head and I open dazed eyes to see him extracting a condom from his wallet. In seconds he's torn off the wrapper, pushed down his boxers, and rolled the condom on, and then he pushes aside my underwear and he's inside me, balls deep, and I almost come right there and then.

I hang on, embarrassed that I don't think it's even been two minutes, but Stratton's not in the mood for waiting. He sweeps aside the folders and laptop on his desk, pushes me back onto my elbows, wraps my legs high around his waist, and leans over me, thrusting hard, grinding against my clit.

I bite my lip as I drop my head back, dizzy at the speed of my arousal.

"Ah, Meg, you're so fucking sexy," he tells me, lowering his mouth to my breast, and I want to tell him the same because he looks so gorgeous in his suit—he hasn't even removed his jacket, and I feel like I'm being fucked by James Bond.

But I can't say anything because pleasure's building inside me, and when he switches his mouth to my other nipple and sucks, my climax hits. I clench around him, and he pushes up so he can thrust hard, coming within a few pushes of his hips. We lock together, and I force my eyes open to see his burning into me, victorious, and yet there's something gentle in there too, real, warm affection that gives me tingles to the roots of my hair.

I glance to my right and see the new statue of his warrior. "Hello, Braced," I say. "Wow, that's a cool model."

He kisses my nose. "Jesus, I love you."

He then looks slightly astonished. The words obviously slipped out without thinking. My heart leaps, but I decide to play it down.

"God help me." I roll my eyes. "Three minutes. I'm so embarrassed."

"Two minutes forty-two seconds, if we're counting." He grins. "Told you."

I thump his arm, hot, flustered, cross that he's so smug, and incredibly happy too at his words. "Get off me. You have a meeting."

"Merry Christmas." He kisses me, holding it until I go limp and stop resisting, and then he withdraws.

He disposes of the condom, zips his trousers, then helps me rearrange my clothing. I examine my reflection in the mirror by his door. I look just-fucked. My lipstick's gone, my hair's all over the place, my cheeks are red, and my eyes are glazed.

"Aren't you going to apologize?" I say, a bit irritably.

"Nope." He nuzzles my neck. "That was nice."

He slips a hand under my dress and slides his fingers beneath the elastic of my underwear. "Ah, Jesus, Meg." He strokes my wet, swollen folds. "You're so fucking hot."

"Will you stop!" I groan and push his arm away. "Meeting! Now!"

He sighs and releases me, and I walk out of the office and back to mine without glancing over my shoulder, because I know if I do I'll turn right around and go back to him.

When I'm finally at my seat, I lean my elbows on the table and cover my face with my hands. I feel as if I'm going a little mad. My body's hot and throbbing, and yet I know if he came in here and locked the door, I'd let him do me all over again.

I lower my hands and blow out a long breath, then smile as my gaze falls on the flowers on my desk. He's such a sweetie. There are a dozen beautiful red roses, and the card says "Mine, forever." The other office girls are so jealous. The word Forever makes me shiver. He's just said he loves me. Even if it slipped out, it was still a wonderful thing to hear.

"Hey."

I look up to see Rich leaning against the door.

"Hi!" I stand, so fast I almost fall over, suddenly afraid I've forgotten to straighten my clothing and my boobs are still out.

He raises an eyebrow. "You okay? You look..."

I blush scarlet and press my hands to my face. "I was just... we were just... Oh jeez." I'm glad I've never had to undergo torture. I couldn't lie to save my life.

He laughs. "Oh. I see."

"Rich..."

"I just wanted to say goodbye. I'm leaving now."

Immediately, I forget my embarrassment and walk around the desk to give him a hug. "Oh Rich, I wish you were coming with us."

"I'm not very good company at this time of year." He hugs me back. "I hope you all have a great time, though. Stratton's a new man when you're around."

I pull back and look up at him. He's Stratton's best friend, and they've known each other a long time. I also know he was wary of our fake engagement. "I hope you don't think badly of me, Rich."

"Of course not. I worry about him, that's all. Natalie screwed him up. I was just concerned that you were using him to get back at your ex."

"Well the idea for both of us was to use the fake engagement to help end our relationships," I remind him. "But I think deep down we both knew there was more to it than that, even before we got involved. I've liked him from the start."

"Are you going to keep working here?"

I hesitate. I've yet to have that conversation with Stratton. We haven't discussed anything about a future yet, but there's time for that, I figure. "I don't know yet. I'll see how Christmas goes."

"All right. Well have a great time, and I'll see you in the New Year."

"Yeah, stay safe."

I watch him walk away, feeling a touch of sadness. I can't imagine what it must be like to lose a sibling, let alone a twin.

My phone rings, and it's the receptionist to say that Stratton's appointment has arrived. I quickly apply some lipstick and smooth down my hair, then show the guy to Stratton's office. I offer the visitor some coffee. Stratton smirks at me as I ask him if he wants anything.

"Coffee?" I prompt him with a glare.

"Please. And any mince pies going? I'm hungry." His eyes glitter.

I walk out with a pounding heart. This man is going to sex me to death and I don't think there's anything I can do about it

Mind you, what a way to go.

*

I spend the rest of the day shifting bits of paper from one side of my desk to the other and scolding the junior secretaries who are doing a conga around the office, and then finally it's five o'clock and it's time to leave. My flowers are still in the cellophane they came in with their bases wrapped in a damp cloth, so I pick them up with my bag and head out to Stratton's office.

He's ready, and once Teddi and Bella join us, we head to the elevator and go down to the car park.

"Are we picking Oscar up from Alyssa's?" Teddi asks.

"Yeah." Stratton presses the button on his keyring, and the car's indicator lights flash. He pops the boot and lifts her bag into it while she gets into the back with Bella, who'll have to sit between her and Oscar all the way up to the bay. Oscar will love that.

I hand Stratton my bag, then turn as someone calls my name.

My heart shudders to a stop. Bruce is standing by one of the large concrete posts. He's obviously been waiting for me. He doesn't look pleased to see that I'm with other people.

Stratton puts my bag beside his and straightens, closes the boot, sees me staring, and turns.

Bruce walks toward us and holds up a hand as Stratton moves in front of me. "I just want to talk."

"No," Stratton says flatly. "Fuck off."

I'd have laughed if I wasn't panicking so much. "What do you want?" I ask, taking a step back until I feel the car behind me.

Bruce stops and looks at the flowers in my arms. "I'm glad you liked them. You always did like roses."

I feel as if I've swallowed a whole glass of iced water. I stare at Stratton, horrified. "I thought you sent them."

"That's why you said thank you when you walked into my room." He closes his eyes briefly. "I thought you'd bought them for the office."

I turn my gaze to the flowers and feel as if I'm going to vomit over them. Resisting the urge to throw them as far away as I can, I put them on top of the car boot. Stratton glares at them, and with a sweep of his arm he knocks them onto the ground where petals spill across the concrete like drops of blood.

Mine, forever, Bruce had written.

"Let's go," Stratton says, but I pull away from his hand.

I face Bruce. "You've got to stop." I'm shaking now, but I need to end this, otherwise it's going to cast a permanent shadow over whatever I have with Stratton. "It's over. You need to let me go."

"I'll never let you go." His expression is determined. "I've done things in the past, things I'm ashamed of. I didn't treat you as well as I should have. But that's all changed. *I've* changed, for you, Maggie."

"I'm not Maggie anymore." But my voice sounds weak, even to me. "How did you find me?"

"I tracked Oscar down at his school and it was fairly easy after that." He fixes me with his dark eyes, and I feel a buzz in my head, a faint fear at the memory of how he'd control me with that gaze. "I don't mind what you call yourself—Maggie, Meg… But you're mine, and I want you back."

Stratton hasn't said anything, but he hasn't moved, either. I'm very conscious of him standing next to me. He's thrown his jacket in the boot, removed his tie, and rolled up his shirt sleeves. I can smell his aftershave from here. I can still feel his mouth on my breast, him moving inside me. He wants me in a way that Bruce never did—not to control me, or to mold me into the kind of person he wants me to be, but because he likes me.

My hand slips into his by our sides, and his fingers tighten on mine. That gives me the strength to lift my chin and reply.

"I'm not coming back. Ever."

"Don't be like that. I've traveled across the country to find you. I've rebuilt my life. I've worked hard to be a better man, Maggie, all for you." He looks suddenly earnest. "And for Oscar."

For the first time, anger flickers in my belly. "Don't bring Oscar into this. You never cared about Oscar."

"Oscar's my son."

"Are you sure?" I look him in the eye. "Are you a hundred percent sure?"

I never slept with anyone else when I was with him, but I see the doubt appear in his eyes. "You're just saying that," he snaps. "Trying to put me off."

"The point is that it *would* make a difference to how you feel about him," I bite back. "You're only using him now to get to me. You don't really care about him and you never have."

"Of course it would make a difference! No man's going to give two fucks about a kid that's not his."

I glance at Stratton, and his lips curve up in one corner. I think of the easy banter he has with Oscar, the way Oscar looks up to him. He's closer to Stratton after four months than he is to his father after thirteen years.

"Enough of this," Stratton says. He lifts our hands and turns them to show Bruce the ring. "That's my ring on her finger. We're getting married."

"You can't," Bruce says, appalled.

"You lost her, man. You treated her badly and you fucked up. It's your loss. Come on, Meg, we're going."

Bruce moves forward and catches my arm. "Don't go."

Stratton whips around and pushes him back. "Don't touch her." He moves close to the other man, pinning him against the car next to us.

Bruce knocks his arm away. "Fuck off. You take her, then, but you're not having my boy. Oscar's mine, and I have a right to see him."

I feel slightly faint, but when I look at Stratton's face, I'm shocked by his furious expression. I've never seen him angry like this.

"Now you listen to me," he snaps. "Meg's kept the police out of it so far for Oscar's sake, but I'm inches away from calling them and telling them you've threatened her."

"I haven't threatened her!"

"Your word against mine, you fucking moron. Who do you think they're going to believe?"

I watch Bruce glance around and spot the expensive cars. He must have done some research after he saw me in the foyer when Stratton pinned him to the wall—he must know who Stratton is, how rich he is.

"I won't stop Oscar seeing you if he wants to," I tell Bruce, not bothering to add that Oscar doesn't want to be within a light year of him, and I can't see that changing anytime soon. "But until then, I want you to keep away from us or Stratton's right—I'll go to the police and I'll get a protection order against you. And I'll get it. Don't forget that you hit me."

"Your word against mine," he says.

If there was any affection remaining inside me for what we had together, that sentence kills it. I push Stratton aside and stand in front of Bruce. I'm not scared anymore. I'm so angry I want to spit in his face, but I content myself with channeling my fury through an icy stare.

"Did you really think I'd come back to you?" I can hear the curiosity in my voice. "After what you did to me? After how you treated me? It wasn't just when you struck me. You strangled the life out of my feelings for you day by day, with every harsh look, every scornful word. Love's not about saying it. It's about showing it. And you never, ever, made me feel that you loved me."

Bruce looks as if I've punched him in the stomach. "You don't understand what I've been through." He gulps in air as if he's drowning. "Losing my arm. Coming out of the army. I'm a soldier. I couldn't bear it."

"I know. And I'm sorry for what happened to you. You look like you're turning yourself around, and that's great. I hope you go on to have a really happy life and meet someone else you love. But that person's not me, Bruce. You're hanging on to an illusion. And you need to move on."

He looks at the flowers on the ground. "You always liked roses," he says dully.

Without another word, he turns around and walks away.

Chapter Thirty-Three

Stratton

At just after eight thirty, I pull up outside my parents' house in Paihia and turn off the engine.

Relief fills me that we're finally here. I only stopped once so Oscar could visit the Gents' and the rest of us could pick up a coffee before we set off again. It's a beautiful drive through hills and valleys with flat-topped volcanoes in the distance and palms lining the roads once we enter the Northland, but it's a long way and we're all glad the journey's over.

I can't quite read Meg's mood. When we picked up Oscar, she told him briefly what had happened, promising to talk more about it later. Then, almost purposefully I'm sure, she moved the conversation on, and after that it hasn't been mentioned again. She's been chatty and bright, but I'm sure it must have affected her. She's been fine with me, just a tad distant, and I'm not sure if that's because she's angry that I interfered, or if she has mixed feelings about Bruce leaving. I find it difficult to believe it's the latter, but I know from my experience with Natalie that emotions are rarely black or white.

Part of me wishes there wasn't a party tonight. I'm not sure I'm in the mood to be sociable. I want to get Meg on her own, pull her into my arms, and make love to her, because I'll know then how she feels about me. But that will have to wait until later.

"Are you sure about this?" I murmur to her as we get our bags from the car. "If you'd rather, I can always take us to a hotel somewhere."

Even as I say it, I realize it's doubtful there will be any room at the inn this late in the day, but luckily she gives me a warm smile and says, "Of course not. I'm looking forward to meeting your parents."

Suddenly nervous, I lead her across the lawn and around the back of the house. I look over my shoulder and see Oscar offer Teddi his arm. Normally, she would have said no, but I'm touched when she acquiesces and takes it.

The house is low and long, brick built, which is fairly unusual for the Northland, and painted white. Palms fill the front garden and line the large lawn of the back garden, and a huge deck runs the length of the house and continues down to a gorgeous pool.

There are people everywhere, and it takes us a while to find my parents. I see people I haven't seen for years—other teachers, some of whom taught me; extended family—aunts, uncles, cousins and their children; neighbors and their families; kids and dogs that don't seem to belong to anyone but who appear to be having a great time.

I introduce Meg to everyone as my girlfriend. I know she's never going to remember all the names, but she nods and smiles and looks as if she's enjoying herself. I can barely take my eyes off her. She's like a tropical flower with her bright blonde hair, her red dress, and her exotic scent, and she fits the evening perfectly.

Christmas songs and carols echo across the lawn, mingling with the yells and shrieks of kids splashing in the swimming pool, and those playing ball games on the grass. The air is filled with the scent of the lavender and jasmine growing around the deck, as well as the mouthwatering smells from the barbecue, and I realize I haven't eaten since lunchtime. There's a small Christmas tree in the center of the lawn and another by the poolside, and there's tinsel all around the deck and a huge picture of Santa stuck on the window. It's a typical Kiwi Christmas party, and I feel a strange pang of nostalgia, as well as a sense of wellbeing at the notion of coming home.

"Stratton!"

I turn as my mother calls me, and bend to greet her when she flings her arms around my neck. Jenny Parker is short and slender, with graying hair cut in a neat bob not unlike her daughter's, and an attractive smile that everyone says she handed to me.

"Oh, I've missed you," she breathes in my ear, hugging me tightly.

"Me, too." I kiss the top of her head. "Are you shrinking?"

"Cheeky." She pulls back, wiping her eyes, and wallops my arm. "You're never too old to put over my knee, you know."

I glance at Meg as my mother hugs Teddi, and I bend to murmur in her ear. "I could say the same thing to you."

"Stratton!" She glances around, blushing, then looks back at me. "You're such a naughty boy."

"You don't know the half of it." Seeing my mother pull back from Teddi, I hold out my hand to Meg. She slides hers into it shyly, and I bring her forward. "Mum, this is Meg. Meg, this is my mother, Jenny."

"Hello, Meg." Mum holds out her arms and envelops Meg in an embrace. "It's so lovely to meet you at last. I've heard so much about you."

"Likewise," Meg says, blushing again as she moves back. "This is Oscar, by the way, my son."

"Hello, Oscar." Knowing that teenage boys aren't keen on hugging older women they don't know, she holds out a hand.

Oscar shakes it solemnly. "Pleased to meet you."

"What lovely manners. I like you already." She beckons to someone behind me, then says, "I have someone I'd like you to meet. This is Greg, he's the son of a good friend of mine." Greg Parsons comes over—he's a year older than Oscar, with the lanky limbs of a growing teen and a shock of dark hair.

He nods at Oscar. "Hey."

"Greg, I wondered if you could get Oscar something to eat because I'm sure he's starving, and then show him the games room?"

"Yeah, sure." Greg indicates with his head for Oscar to follow, and Oscar—trying to look as if he goes to parties all the time—strides after him as nonchalantly as he can.

Mum takes Teddi's hand and holds her other out to Meg. "Come on, girls. Let's get you a glass of wine, and then I want you to tell me everything. I'm starved for gossip here." She leads them away. Meg gives me a brief look over her shoulder, but she's gone before I can protest.

"Kidnapped, eh?" Dad appears by my side with a glass of red wine and hands it to me.

"Yeah, sorry. I wanted you to meet Meg."

"Did Mum like her?"

"I think so."

"Then I'll like her. Come on. I need your help with the kingfish on the barby."

*

MY CHRISTMAS FIANCÉ

The evening passes quickly, filled with barbecued kingfish and snapper pulled fresh from the sea that day, prawn kebabs, salads, mince pies, and sherry trifle, with cheesy Christmas songs in the background. Later, as some of the families with kids leave and the gathering shrinks in size, we listen to carols as the sun goes down, and Mum lights citronella candles all around the deck to keep away the insects.

Unfortunately, I don't get to see a lot of Meg. Teddi takes her in hand and introduces her to some of her oldest friends, a couple of whom are pregnant, and soon they're gathered on a circle of chairs by the poolside knee deep in conversation. When I do call by, I overhear talk about how long you should breastfeed and something called transition and the best cream for stretch marks, and when they see me listening someone makes a comment about putting in an extra stitch and Meg blushes, so I wryly turn and walk the other way, conscious of their laughter following me back to the house.

I search out Oscar instead, desperate for some manly talk. I find him sitting on the edge of the deck, drinking a Coke Zero with Greg. My parents' house is high atop a hill overlooking the bay, and they're watching the sea, lit by the rising moon. As I approach, I hear them talking about who's the best healer to take into a dungeon, and I smile.

Greg excuses himself to go and get a drink, so I sit beside Oscar, beer in hand, and take a swig. "How's it going?" I ask him.

"Yeah all right. Your parents' house is cool."

"You like the games room?"

"Yeah, and the pool too. It's not as big as yours, but it's still nice." He scratches his nose. "Do you mind if I ask you a question?"

"Sure."

"Did you buy this place for them?" He hesitates. "I hope that's not a rude thing to ask. Mum says that people don't like talking about money."

"I'll talk about anything you want, Oscar. Yes, Teddi and I gave Mum and Dad some money to help them buy this place. They weren't keen at first, because it's not easy to accept money from your children, but we talked them into it. What's the point in having money if you can't spend it on your friends and family?"

Oscar nods sagely. Then he says, "Are you really a billionaire?"

"Something like that. The company's done pretty well. You stop counting after the first few million." I laugh at the look on his face. "I didn't mean that to sound as flippant as it came out. I appreciate having money. We didn't have a lot when I grew up, and I had to wait for birthdays and Christmas for new toys and games."

"Mum says that makes you appreciate them more when you do get them."

"That's true," I say so I don't disagree with his mother in front of him, although I haven't found that to be the case—I get great delight in buying whatever I want throughout the year.

"Are you going to stay with Mum?" The question is so sudden, it makes me blink with surprise.

I take a swig of beer. I do need to speak to Meg first, but it's Christmas Eve and I'm here with Oscar, and it seems like the time to be honest with each other.

"Ah, I hope so. We need to have a talk, me and your mum. Sort a few things out."

"Would I live with you?"

"Things like that. I need to ask her what she wants first."

He looks at the can in his hands. "Will you send me away? To live with Dad?"

I stare at him in shock. "Of course not. Unless you want to go."

"I don't." He speaks fiercely. "But I thought you might want to be with mum on your own. I thought I might be in the way."

My stomach knots at the thought that Oscar has been worrying about this. "Hey." I put my arm around his shoulders. "Who would I play *Dark Robot* with if you went away? You're my gaming partner."

He gives a short laugh. "I guess."

"Oscar, I'm well aware that you and your mum come as a package. You're part of why I'm attracted to her, don't you get that?"

He frowns. "What do you mean?"

"Well, I don't have kids. And it's been nice having another guy around. Look, I don't want you to think I'm trying to replace your dad, because I'm not. Whatever you think of him at the moment, he's still your dad."

"You don't want me to call you dad, then?" Oscar asks.

I study him for a moment. His eyes are hopeful. Emotion rolls over me, unexpected and fierce enough to make me catch my breath. All boys need a role model when they're growing up, and it doesn't sound as if Bruce has been much good. Meg's told me that all his teachers at school are women. There's been no adult male in his life for some time, and the thought that he might look up to me is both startling and oddly touching.

I want to make him all sorts of promises, but I need to speak to Meg first.

"I don't mind if you do," I tell him, "but let me check with your mum. Once I've done that, we'll talk again, okay?"

"Yeah."

I ruffle his hair. "All right. What are you doing now?"

"I'm going to play snooker with Greg and a few of his mates."

"Okay. Catch you in a bit."

I rise and walk across the deck, smiling to see my parents dancing on the lawn to Wham's *Last Christmas*.

"Look at you, you old romantic couple." I toast them with my beer.

"Stratton!" Mum beckons me toward her. "Come here. We want to talk to you."

"I was going to see Meg."

"Just quickly." She takes my hand and pulls me to the swing seat that overlooks the lawn. I sit in the middle between them as if I was ten years old all over again.

"Meg seems like a lovely girl," Mum says.

"She has nice legs," Dad comments.

"George!"

"Well she does. My boy knows how to pick 'em."

I chuckle. "Thanks, Dad."

"I saw that she's wearing my grandma's ring," Mum says. "Something you need to tell us?"

Shit. I'd forgotten about the ring.

I lean forward, my elbows on my knees, dangling the bottle of beer from my fingers. "It's a long story."

"You see us going anywhere?"

It's Christmas Eve and I don't want to lie to two of the most special people in my life, so I take a deep breath and tell them. About Natalie. About wanting a partner for the ball. About my bright idea for a fake engagement. About Bruce turning up. And about me suggesting that Meg play the role of fiancée.

"So it's just pretend?" My mother sounds surprisingly disappointed.

I meet her gaze and purse my lips. "Well..."

"Oh..." She says softly.

"I've sort of screwed up," I say. "I wanted Natalie off my back, and I liked Meg and wanted to protect her from her ex. And somehow I fell for her along the way. Actually, that's a lie. I fell for her the moment I met her. I wanted her—I've wanted her for months, and I talked her into this, and now I'm not sure what to do."

"How does Meg feel about it?" Dad asks.

"That's what I was just going to talk to her about."

"Do you think she wants a relationship?" Mum wants to know.

"Yes, I do. But there are things we need to sort out."

"Like..."

"Where we live, for a start."

"She doesn't like your house?" Mum asks.

"She loves the house. It's not as simple as that. There's Oscar to think about."

"How does he feel about you being with his mum?"

"He seems cool about it. He just asked me if he can call me Dad."

"Aw, Stratton." Mum presses her fingers to her lips, and my father pats my knee approvingly. They appear to like the idea of me having a stepson, and that surprises me.

I sigh and place the empty beer bottle on the ground in front of me. "None of that is a problem, not really. I need to talk to her about whether she wants any more children."

"Ah." Mum rests her hand on my back. It's a delicate subject. She decided to risk having children, and Teddi inherited the mutated gene. It makes her sad, but she understands my decision not to have kids. "Has she mentioned wanting more?"

"No." But I remember that she said to Natalie that we were already trying for a family. It was because she wanted to hurt Natalie and get her off our backs, but even so I can't help but wonder if there was a hint of longing behind it. I wouldn't blame her if there was. I understand that broodiness is a chemical, physical thing that can't necessarily be controlled.

"Oscar's thirteen," Mum says. "That's quite an age gap if she were to have a baby now."

"True, but it's not uncommon. I can't just assume." I sink my hands into my hair. "I've done this the wrong way around. We've not even dated, not properly, but I'm sleeping with her, and I'm in love with her. In many ways, it's far too soon to talk about marriage and whether she wants children, but we're f…" I remember I'm sitting next to my mother. "…fricking engaged, publicly anyway, and I'm scared. Scared of falling for her too far and then discovering we're poles apart on this."

"You're in love with her?" Mum asks.

"Yeah."

"Well, hallelujah! Thirty-four years old and at last you've fallen in love."

I give her a wry look. "You don't think I was in love with Natalie?"

"Were you?"

"Probably not," I concede. "That's why I feel so annoyed now that I fucked up." She raises an eyebrow, and I wince. "Sorry. I really like Meg, and I want this to work, but it feels wrong to start talking about forever. What if we have a big long discussion about the future, and we get serious too soon, and it doesn't work out? I could screw it all up, Meg, Oscar, everything."

"Or it could all work out beautifully," Mum says. "It's just as likely."

"I suppose," I say doubtfully.

"You know I proposed to your mother two days after I met her," Dad announces.

I stare at him. "Two days?"

"Yep."

That shocks me. "How could you be sure she was the one?"

Dad shrugs. "I just knew."

I want to press him and demand an explanation of how he knew, but he's looking at Mum with adoration on his face, and I know he's about as skilled as me at explaining himself, so I don't bother.

My mother smiles. "Go and talk to her. Be open and honest. Tell her how you feel. Everything will be all right. It's Christmas Eve, for crying out loud. Miracles happen on Christmas Eve."

I figure it'll have to be a big fucking miracle to stop me screwing up, but I smile and lean over to kiss her cheek. "All right. Thanks for the chat."

"Go get her, tiger."

I stand and walk down the steps of the deck toward the pool. It's a clear, warm night. In the distance, someone's letting off fireworks, and new, multi-colored stars join the white ones already sparkling in the sky. The air smells clean, scouring out the smell and dust of the city from my lungs. In the bush, a morepork hoots, and far off in the distance a kiwi gives its mournful cry. I've missed the sounds of the country, and the ever-present whoosh of the sea. It's good to be back.

Meg's still sitting by the pool with Teddi and the other women. She's had a few glasses of wine, and she looks relaxed and happy. She glances up as I approach, and I have the pleasure of seeing a smile spread across her face.

"Hey, Stratton." Genie, an old friend of Teddi's, winks at me. "Are you about to steal away the new member of our gang?"

"I certainly am. I think you've had enough time to corrupt her with your wicked ways."

"Ha!" Genie pokes her tongue out at me.

"I'll have to have a word with Niall," I tell her as Meg rises. Niall is Genie's husband, and she's pregnant, her hand resting on her bump. "Clearly he's not doing a very good job at keeping you in line."

"I'd like to see him try," she scoffs.

I chuckle and hold my hand out to Meg. "Fancy a walk?"

She slips her hand into mine.

"You'll have trouble controlling that one," Genie calls out as we walk away. "He's not been broken in yet."

"It's okay, I like them wild," Meg calls back, making them all laugh.

I pull her to me and move my arm around her waist. "*Now* you tell me," I whisper in her ear. She smells of sherry trifle and wine and the exotic, sensual smell that's all hers. My heart starts to race at the thought that later she'll be lying naked next to me, warm and soft in my arms, her sweet mouth on mine.

If everything goes according to plan, that is. I'm tempted not to have the conversation, not now, poised on the edge of Christmas. If it doesn't go well, it'll spoil everything, and I'm terrified of ruining it. I don't want to lose her or Oscar. How can I make sure I don't screw this up?

MY CHRISTMAS FIANCÉ

Chapter Thirty-Four

Meg

It's been a strange evening, not at all what I expected. I thought that we would show our faces, and that Stratton would be distant and reserved, making excuses after an acceptable amount of time so he could escape from the large crowd of people.

Instead, he's been completely the opposite. He spent ages introducing me to everyone, and he seems to know the name of every person here. He's completely at home, relaxed and comfortable with his family and friends.

I don't know why I didn't expect him to be like that. Maybe it's because since I started at Katoa he's not socialized much, but now I can see why Rich and Teddi have been worried about him. Watching him with customers and at the Solstice Ball has shown me that he's good with people, but I thought it was a show, a mask he wore to enable him to carry out his business. Now, though, I see how wrong I was. He's a family man at heart. And that must make the decision not to have children even more difficult for him.

I've had an enjoyable evening, and I've got on really well with Teddi and her friends, but it's nice to be alone with Stratton again, and we fall into a companionable silence as we walk away from the others, following a line of solar lights down to where the river runs past the Parkers' property.

"Have you got insect repellent on?" he asks.

"Yes, tons of it."

"Good." He leads the way to the water's edge, where there's a bench overlooking the water. Colored solar lights are strung along the willow overhanging the river. It feels like Santa's grotto, and I half expect to see elves running around frantically, gathering together last-minute presents and checking their lists twice.

We sit, and he puts his arm around me and kisses the top of my head.

"Thank you for bringing me." I lean against him and cuddle up. I've had a few glasses of wine, and, feeling a streak of naughtiness, I undo a couple of his shirt buttons and slide my hand against his warm skin.

"Mmm." He studies me for a moment, then lowers his lips to mine. We exchange a long, lingering kiss that give me goose bumps and leaves me sighing with pleasure. Part of me hopes he'll pull me onto his lap, maybe slide his hand up my top, but he doesn't.

When he eventually lifts his head, he rests his lips on my hair for a moment.

"You okay?" I ask. "You seem… pensive. Is it nice to be home?"

"Yeah, it's good to be back. Nice to see everyone."

"You're more family oriented than I thought you'd be," I admit. "I can see now why Rich and Teddi have been worried about you. You're obviously quite sociable, and yet you've been very withdrawn since I started at Katoa."

"I didn't feel I was good company when I broke up with Natalie. I didn't want to see her, and I didn't want to talk about what happened. It was easier to stay at home."

"I'm sorry it's been hard for you." I kiss his shoulder.

"We've both had it tough. You probably more than me. I have nothing but admiration for what you did—moving across the country, starting all over again. That takes some guts."

"I suppose." I bend and pick up a pebble, and toss it into the river. "I always think of it as running away, as something cowardly."

"I think we both know that once you've done everything you can to convince someone the relationship is over, drastic measures need to be employed," he says wryly. He sighs then, a long, heartfelt sigh of resignation. "I want to talk to you about something, but it's late on Christmas Eve, and I can't make my mind up whether I should wait for a few days."

The river trickles over the rocks, and there's a morepork right nearby, hooting away. Stratton's hair has silver highlights, and his eyes shine like white discs. I've enjoyed being here with him tonight, watching him interact with his friends and family. Occasionally, we've exchanged a private glance, a secret smile, and I've known that, like me, he was thinking about the moment tonight when we'll slide into bed together and make love.

What does he want to talk to me about? The pessimist in me wonders whether he wants to bring this to an end. Is he saying he's had enough? He's just sat here and kissed me, though, and I'm not getting that vibe from him. He just seems… sad.

"Talk to me," I say. "Cards on the table, remember?"

He nods, somewhat solemnly. "You're right. Well, first, I want to apologize."

I hadn't expected that. "For what?"

"For the whole fake fiancée debacle. It was a stupid idea, and I shouldn't have suggested it to you."

I smile. "It worked didn't it?"

"Yeah. But that's not the point. Part of me suggested it because I wanted to get close to you. I wanted to get you into bed."

"Well, duh." I smile, amused that it's Stratton turn to be naive. "You think I didn't know that?"

He casts me a wry glance. "I guess you expected it. But it's complicated where we go from here."

"Spit it out, Stratton. What's up? Do you want to call it a day?" My heart thuds painfully, but I make myself stay calm. "Come on, we're both grownups. I can't say I wouldn't be devastated, but I'm not going to do a Natalie on you. I've had a terrific time, and I don't regret any of it."

He looks at me with alarm. "No, I don't want to end it. Quite the opposite."

"Oh." Relief washes over me.

His expression turns hesitant. "Unless you want to…"

"No."

We study each other for a moment. It sinks into me that we're saying we definitely want to stay together, and that fills me with a rising joy that makes me want to throw my arms around his neck.

I wait though, because something isn't right.

"We'd have to talk about where you live," he says, "and about Oscar. He's worried I might not want him around."

My jaw drops. "What?" That's the first I've heard of it.

"Don't worry," Stratton says, "I put him straight. I told him that I know he's part of the package, and I'm more than happy for him to live with us, if that's what you want. I wanted to talk to you first. I told him that I don't want to replace his dad. But I hope we can be good friends, and that he'll come to me for help and advice if he needs it."

I swallow hard, determined not to burst into tears. "That was very kind of you."

"I like him, Meg." He puts his arm around me and kisses my nose. "He's a part of you, and he's a great kid. I'm not anti-children." He looks pained. And then it hits me what he's been worried about.

"You want to discuss having kids," I say softly.

He looks away, across the river, and I know I've guessed right.

"My stomach's in a knot," he says. "I keep thinking about what Natalie said, how if I'd loved her enough I'd have done what she wanted. I keep asking myself if that's true. Was the problem that I didn't love her enough? I don't know. I do know that I didn't feel about her the same way I feel about you. I'm in love with you, Meg." He gives a helpless smile, still looking at the river. "I'm certain of it. I've never felt this way before about anyone. I know it's early days—we're not even dating properly yet, and it seems ridiculous to pin each other down about the future. But I can't help but wonder how I would feel if you tell me you want more children. I want to give you everything. But I don't know if I can do that."

Finally, he turns his gaze to me. His eyes are scared. His chest rises and falls quickly. He doesn't want to lose me.

I lift a hand to cup his face. "Sweetheart… It's okay. I don't want more children."

He goes still. "How do I know you're not just saying that?"

Natalie must have told him the same thing at the beginning to hook him, and she only admitted her true feelings once she'd reeled him in.

Everything's going to rest on how I handle the next five minutes. I look deep into his eyes so he can see I'm not lying.

"Because I already have a son. I'm thirty-three. I know that's not old to have a baby nowadays, and I admit there have been times when Oscar was young when I felt broody and thought about having another child. But it never happened, and he's thirteen now, and I really don't want to go back to nappies and sleepless nights again. If you told me that you desperately wanted a child of your own, I'd consider it because I think it's sad if you want kids and can't have them. I do sympathize with Natalie's predicament. But equally, I don't think you should be forced into having children if you really don't want them."

He's looking at me as if he can't bring himself to believe me. "Do you mean that?"

"Yes, I do. Children are a blessing and God's gift and arguably your life's not complete without them, blah blah, but equally they're hard work, they're a huge tie, they're a constant worry, and that's before you take into account the main reason you don't want to get someone pregnant. Stratton, I completely understand why you're worried about passing on the mutated gene. I think your comment about blaming yourself if the baby had it is a bit harsh, but I've tried to put myself in your shoes and think about how I'd feel if it was the other way around, and I do understand. And I'm happy with that. I'm not going to suddenly announce six months or a year or five years down the line that I want a baby."

I mean it. I can't say that the thought of having a baby with Stratton doesn't send a little frisson down my back, but that's all it is, a shiver of excitement at the notion of being intimate enough with him to consider that kind of tie. It's the idea that's exciting more than the notion of having an actual baby.

"You can't say that, Meg. You don't know how you're going to feel in five years' time."

"True, but then neither do you. There might be medical advancements that mean it's possible to make sure the baby wouldn't have the gene. All either of us can say is how we feel right now. Unfortunately, love doesn't come with a guarantee. We've both been burned, and it's understandable if either of us were to say we don't want to take that risk again. But here we are, having this conversation because we're both attracted to each other. It's human instinct to love, to want to share ourselves with someone. All you can do is try on people until we find one that fits, and hope you don't outgrow each other as the years go by."

It's sounds quite cynical and unromantic as I say it, but neither Stratton nor I are teenagers, and we've both been through enough over the past few years to make us prefer honesty above everything else.

He's looking at me now, his lips curved up a little, admiration in his eyes. He reaches out a hand, and when I slip mine into it, he holds them up and interlaces our fingers.

MY CHRISTMAS FIANCÉ

"So you're sure about taking on Oscar?" It's a horrible thing to have to ask, but as much as I'm crazy about this guy, Oscar comes first in my life. I've made sacrifices for him before, and I'd make them again, even if it broke my heart.

"Of course." His lips twist, and his thumb brushes mine. "He asked whether he should call me Dad."

I press my fingers to my lips as emotion washes over me. *Oh, Oscar.* "What did you say?"

"I said I wouldn't mind, but I'd check with you first. I surprised myself by kind of liking the idea of being a stepdad. But I want to do this right, Meg. Bruce might be a shit, but he is Oscar's father, and I don't want to get in the way of that."

"He's not interested in Oscar, whatever he says," I tell Stratton as calmly as I can. "He never has been."

"Yeah, I get that. I just want both you and Oscar to know that whatever happens between us, even though I'd flatten the guy if he hurt either of you, I wouldn't stand in the way if Oscar decided he wanted to see him." He brings my fingers to his lips and kisses them.

"I don't think he will, but I appreciate that."

"And as far as our relationship, mine and Oscar's... I have no problem with being a father figure. I'd be happy to treat him as my own, if that was what you both wanted. Maybe even adopt him eventually." He smiles.

It's more than I could ever have hoped for. I had friends back in Christchurch who'd remarried, and whose new partners paid no interest at all in the kids by their previous marriages, so I know this is rare and special. "You want us to move in with you?" I clarify.

"I'd like that. There's plenty of room in the house for Oscar and his friends if they come over, but we can discuss moving somewhere else if you'd rather."

"No, I love the house." I can't believe this is really happening. "So what do you think we should do about the fake engagement?" I look at his great-grandmother's ring where it sparkles in the moonlight. We're supposed to go back to work after Christmas and say we've broken it off. "What should we tell people?"

"We could make it not fake," he suggests.

I look up at him. "What do you mean?"

He studies me, and then, to my shock, he slips off the seat and onto one knee. "Marry me, Meg."

My jaw drops. "Stratton!" My head's spinning. "We've only been together a week."

"My father proposed to my mother two days after they met."

"Oh! Well. I… um…"

"I know it's not the same as dating, but we've been together all day every day for over four months. I've wanted you since the day you walked into my office. I've watched you, dreamed about you, even though I thought you were married. I love that you're calm and capable and strong. I love your husky laugh and how you look at me over the top of your glasses when you're telling me off. I love that you're kind and warm to everyone you meet."

"I have bad points," I whisper, almost in tears.

"I know. You're grouchy until you've had your morning coffee. You're a bit OCD and like everything lined up and squared off. I adjust the pictures on my wall so you'll come in and straighten them."

I give a short laugh. "I didn't know that."

"You don't like spicy food and complain even if there's a bit of pepper in a sandwich. You like your boobs but think your bum's too big. It's not, by the way. You don't like ginger but you love cinnamon. You can't sing to save your life."

"That's true." A tear trickles down my cheek at the loving look in his eyes. "I didn't realize you knew me so well."

"When you drink chamomile tea it's because you have a migraine. When that happens, I tell the girls in reception to divert calls straight to me for a few hours."

"I didn't know that!"

"You love the color orange and the taste of citrus fruit, but not grapefruit." He rises and sits beside me, pulling me into his arms. "You're devoted to your son and you're a fantastic mother. You're a superb PA and a good friend to Teddi. You're great in bed. And when you eat chocolate, you give the same sexy sigh that you do before you come."

"Stratton!" I wipe away my tears, my face growing hot.

"I know you," he whispers, his lips grazing my cheek. "I'm in love with you, and I want to be with you. I want to provide for you and Oscar—I want to give you both some stability after what you've been through. We can wait for a while if you want—there's no rush. But when you're ready, I promise you now that I'll want to marry you. So let's stay engaged. I like having a fiancée. And I like it that other men can see you're taken." He lifts my chin so he can kiss me. "You belong to me," he whispers. "You're mine, Miss Meg, and at this moment I can't see myself ever wanting to change that."

I open my mouth and let him kiss me deeply, our tongues entwining, as I slip my hand into his hair and hold him tightly.

When he eventually lifts his head, I give a little nod. "Okay."

He wraps his arms around me and rests his lips on my hair. "Merry Christmas, Meg."

I feel so happy I think I might explode. Not only does Stratton like me, not only does he like my son, but he loves me, he wants to marry me, and he wants to stay with me.

I look up at the stars. A shape passes briefly across the moon, and it's probably a bird, but I think it might be Santa, out delivering presents. I send him a silent thank you for granting my wish. Miracles do happen, I think.

"Merry Christmas, Stratton."

"I love you."

"I love you too."

Epilogue

Stratton

"We should have a party on Valentine's Day," Meg says.

It's the first of February, and after a week or so of summer rain, the weather's turned scorching hot and humid again. It's late evening, and the three of us are sitting on the deck, drinking Meg's homemade iced lemonade, watching the sun set.

"Don't you want to go out for a romantic dinner or something?" Oscar asks. "I can stay on my own now so you don't have to worry about finding me a babysitter." He turned fourteen last week. He's wearing the watch we bought him, and the new phone I gave him for Christmas is resting on the table next to him.

I raise my eyebrows at Meg. Her suggestion has surprised me. I've already booked an expensive restaurant in town, and I thought she'd enjoy the whole Valentine experience.

She shrugs. "We could, that would be nice. But it feels kind of hypocritical. All these years I've hated Valentine's Day. It's a day when everyone who has someone is smug, and everyone else feels miserable. If you're in a relationship, the guy has to put on a grand performance that has to be better than whatever he did last year. I'm sure most guys hate it. Love shouldn't be about showing it all on one day of the year anyway."

I smile at her. "That's fair enough. So what sort of party?"

"It could still have a Valentine theme, but it could just be a general party like the one your parents had on Christmas Eve. We could invite all our friends, and then those who don't have partners, like Alyssa, won't feel left out. We know a lot of single people, including Rich and Teddi. They might even meet someone on the night."

I have my suspicions that Rich has already met someone but is keeping it under his hat, but I decide not to say anything in front of Oscar. I don't keep secrets from Meg, but Rich is a very private person, and I wouldn't want Oscar to blurt something out in front of him.

"Can I invite some friends?" Oscar asks.

"Of course. If Stratton thinks it's a good idea."

I know what Meg's trying to do—drag me back into the real world after my self-imposed isolation last year. The two of us have been tied up in one another since Christmas, but she told me the other night that we should spend more time with our friends and family, and she's right.

"Sounds great," I tell them. "We can get a company in to organize it so it's not too much work for you."

"Ooh," she says, "really? I thought I'd have to do all the cooking."

"Of course not. We'll get them to draw up a few menus."

"I'll decorate the house, though," she says. "I'd enjoy that."

"Whatever you want, my love." I lean over and kiss her, and her mouth curves up under mine. We haven't had sex for a few days because she had her period and suffers from cramps, but I can tell she's feeling better today. From the look in her eye, she's ready for some loving, and my heart begins to race.

"Get a room you two," Oscar says mildly.

I laugh and finish off my drink, then cuff him lightly around the head, messing up his hair. "Bedtime for you, junior."

He pokes his tongue out at me, and I grab him around the neck. We wrestle for a minute before Meg scolds us both and we break apart.

"I can't tell who's the fourteen-year-old sometimes," she says. Oscar laughs and walks off.

"Night," he calls back, and we wish him goodnight before he disappears into his room.

I pull Meg to me and nuzzle her ear. "Want me to prove how much of a man I am?"

"I was hoping you'd say that," she replies breathlessly. "Come on."

She takes my hands and leads me to our room, and I've only just closed the door when she starts pulling off her thin summer dress.

"I've been thinking about this all day," she murmurs, slipping off her panties and undoing her bra. Now she's naked, and I pin her up against the sliding glass door and crush my lips to hers. She's soft and warm, and I have a hard-on in seconds. When she takes my hand and guides it between her legs, I find that she's ready for me, too, so clearly she was telling the truth when she said she's been thinking about having sex.

"I love you," I mumble as she pulls me back to the chest of drawers. The words keep spilling out of me, like beads from a bag that's been overfilled, tumbling from my lips uncontrollably.

She laughs and rests on the chest of drawers. "I love you, too." She pulls my lips down to hers, and I kiss her hungrily, delving my tongue into her mouth, tasting the mint choc chip ice cream she had a while ago, and the sweet lemonade.

"Are you sure you don't want me to take you out for Valentine's Day?" I murmur, kissing around to her ear. I suck the lobe and dip my tongue into the shell of it, feeling her nipples tighten in my palms as I do. "I want to make it special for you. I want to show everyone how important you are to me."

"You show me every day," she says, lifting her arms around my neck. "Love shouldn't be for show. Everyone can see we're crazy about each other anyway."

"That's true." We decided that Meg would carry on working at Katoa for a while, and we'd see how it worked out. I love having her nearby, and being able to see her whenever I want. We do our best to stay professional in the workplace, but I think sometimes we make Rich and Teddi envious when they catch us having a sneaky kiss by the coffee machine or a cuddle in my office.

"You can still get me a present," she says impishly.

I nuzzle her ear. "I thought I might give you a pearl necklace."

She laughs. "You're so rude."

"I meant it! A real one. Natural pearls. Very expensive."

"No, you didn't."

"No, I didn't." I nibble her earlobe again, turned on at the thought. "Jeez, you make me hot."

She sighs. "I just don't want anyone to feel sad on Valentine's Day." She tightens her arms around me for a moment. "I've felt sad for the last fifteen years and I know how it feels, so I don't want to go around shoving what we have in the faces of those are still single."

I don't have to ask to know that Bruce wasn't the romantic type. I doubt he was even aware when it was Valentine's Day, and no doubt he was often away and wouldn't have bothered to arrange anything for her.

"All right," I say softly, running my hands down her back. "We'll make it one hell of a party."

"I wish everyone could have what we have," she whispers. "Rich and Teddi."

"I have a sneaky feeling that Rich has met someone," I admit.

She looks up at me in surprise. "Oh? Why?"

"Dunno. There's just something about him. He usually comes back from the Christmas break listless and hung over, flat, you know? But this year he's been different, and I caught him on the phone yesterday, smiling."

She laughs. "How did you interpret that as him having met someone? He smiles a lot."

"It was a different smile." I can't explain what I mean. I just know that smile—it's intimate, meant for only one person.

"I hope you're right. Maybe he'll bring her to the party."

"Maybe." I don't want to talk about Rich or Teddi or anyone else at the moment. I want to concentrate on Meg and her soft body. "Come here. Enough talk."

I lift her, carry her over to the bed, and lower her onto the mattress. I quickly divest myself of my clothing, then start kissing down her body.

"It's so hot," she complains. "Can you switch the fan on?"

"No." I kiss between her breasts, then run my tongue underneath one. "I want you all hot and sweaty."

"Stratton! Gross."

"It's not gross. It's a turn-on, and it's your job to keep me happy, so you'd better let me do whatever I want." I lace my tongue across her stomach, and she wriggles.

"Whatever you want?" she asks. "Don't I get a say in this?"

"Nope." I kiss over her hip and across her stretchmarks. She smacks my arm—she hates me doing that. I chuckle, kiss down her thigh, then part her legs and plunge my tongue into her folds.

"Oh! Ohhh... what's got into you?"

"You." I lick right up her center and swirl my tongue over her clit. "I'm obsessed by you. I can't get enough of you. I think you've cast a spell on me." Mmm, I've missed this. Three days is far too long to go without sex with Meg.

"Ahhh... You'd better behave or I won't give you *my* Valentine's present."

"Oh?" I lift up and move over her to look into her eyes. Over the past month, we've explored each other in the most intimate ways a couple can. I know she's been wary of some things, so I've taken it slow, introducing the occasional different position, a sex toy, even tied her up one night, which she discovered was much more fun than she thought it would be.

"Mmm." She lifts her arms over her head, stretching out beneath me. "Let's just say it has particular meaning for us. Something I've wanted to do to you since I met you." She giggles.

I think back to the email where she admitted how she daydreamed about coating me in melted chocolate and then licking it off. The thought of Meg doing that to me, and then me doing it to her—painting her nipples with chocolate and taking a long, long time to lick it all off—makes me groan.

"Please stop," I beg her, "I'm so fucking hard I could use my erection as a battering ram."

She laughs and kisses me. "Come on then." She wraps her legs around my hips.

"Already?" Normally I try to give her at least one orgasm before I slide inside her.

"Now," she whispers.

We stopped using condoms when she moved in with me. It was a big moment for me when she suggested it, saying she was on the pill and we didn't have to use them, and I knew I trusted her enough to agree.

I don't have to be told twice. I move back so I'm sitting on my heels, push up her knees, and then straighten her legs.

"What are you…"

Ignoring her, I cross her ankles and hold them with one hand, then with the other I stroke down her calves, the back of her knees, and the backs of her thighs, before moving my fingers to the plump flesh that's glistening ready for me. Gently, I slide my fingers down through her folds and inside her.

She moans, and I feel her clench around my fingers. "Slowly," I scold, moving them in and out of her.

"It feels so good," she whispers, closing her eyes.

Smiling, I tease her for a while, then when I can't stand it any longer I guide the tip of my erection there. It feels amazing skin-on-skin, and I stroke the tip up and down through her folds a few times before pressing it against her opening. Because I know she likes it like this, I push forward slowly until I've filled her up.

Her cheeks flush, her eyelids flutter, and her lips part with a long sigh of pleasure. "Oh, that feels fantastic," she whispers.

I move inside her, sighing myself at how tight she feels in this position, and I kiss her feet while I make love to her, sliding my tongue between her toes and along the sensitive skin of her instep. It's not long before her breaths turned ragged and her sighs turns to moans, so I uncross her ankles and let her wrap her legs around me, and then I drop forward so I can kiss her. We're both really hot now, and my skin slides against hers, which is so fucking sexy it makes me groan.

"What do you do to me?" she murmurs, opening her mouth to my searching tongue.

"Love you," I tell her. "Want you. Need you." My body's taking over, and I forsake gentleness for urgency as I begin to thrust harder, grinding against her while I do so. "I love you, Meg."

"I… oh… love you too…"

I lift up and let my hips pump as hard and fast as they want, filling the air with the slick sound of me sliding through her swollen, wet folds, and it's less than a minute before her orgasm hits. She tightens around me in short, strong pulses, and she gasps against my lips, crying out my name, which fills me with such pleasure I want to yell my triumph to the world.

I don't, though. I tell her I love her again and thrust until I climax, and then I shudder, and there's nothing else in the world except the sensation of pulsing inside her.

"Ahhh…" I collapse as all the tension flows out of me. "Holy fuck." I bury my face in her neck and bathe in the bliss as long as I can.

"Oh dear God," she says, "I'm so hot. You're squishing me."

"Don't care."

"Jesus. Stratton, I'm melting."

I sigh, lift off her, and collapse onto the bed beside her. She reaches up and flicks on the switch, and the large fan above our heads starts turning, sending cool air wafting over us.

"Mmm." She stretches out again, her arms above her head. "I feel all loose and floppy, like a piece of steak that's been beaten with a mallet."

I mumble something, closing my eyes and enjoying the breeze on my skin.

"You're so sexy. You're just the right amount of rough and *grrr*. You're like a tiger," she tells me, rolling onto her side and lifting onto one elbow.

I'm so tired—the after-sex hormones have taken me over—but I open one eye and study her. "*Rawr*."

"That was more like a tomcat."

"If the cap fits," I mumble.

She chuckles, leans over, and presses her lips to mine. "Can we really do this forever and ever?"

"I might need some occasional downtime," I murmur against her mouth. She tastes sweet, and she smells like the jasmine growing in the garden.

"Stratton... I mean it. I can't believe that you're really mine."

This time I open my eyes and look into her baby blue ones. "I'm yours," I say. "For as long as you want me."

"Does forever sound okay?"

"Forever sounds pretty damn great," I tell her happily.

Then I fall asleep.

More from Serenity Woods

In the Love Comes Later series:

My Christmas Fiancé
My New Year Fling
My Valentine Seduction

If you'd like to try some more of Serenity's romances, why not sign up for her newsletter and receive her free Starter Library?

http://www.serenitywoodsromance.com/newsletter.html

SERENITY WOODS

About the Author

USA Today bestselling author Serenity Woods lives in the subtropical Northland of New Zealand with her wonderful husband and gorgeous teenage son. She writes hot and sultry contemporary romances, and she would much rather immerse herself in reading or writing romance than do the dusting and ironing, which is why it's not a great idea to pop round if you have any allergies.

Website: http://www.serenitywoodsromance.com
Facebook: http://www.facebook.com/serenitywoodsromance
Twitter: https://twitter.com/Serenity_Woods